Spectre

A Revelations standalone novel

Written by: R. E. Graham

Novels in the Revelations SciFi Universe
available on Amazon

"Rise of the Inquisitor"

Kingdom of Sand – Book 1
"Judgment Day"

Kingdom of Sand – Book 2
"Rain of Fire"

Kingdom of Sand – Book 3
"The Skull King"

Revelations: Spectre

First Edition: October 2019

ISBN-13: 978-0-9980312-5-5
ISBN-10: 0-9980312-5-9

This book is dedicated to Jesus Christ, for without Him, I wouldn't even be on this path of being an author in the first place…

Acknowledgments

I want to take a quick moment to thank a couple of people that have specifically helped to make this book you have in your hands possible. Without a doubt, my most significant support has been my fantastic wife, Erin. She has put up with a lot from my creativity in this project and has been more than happy to help in any way she can. She truly is a companion that any man would be incredibly blessed and fortunate to have alongside through life. The next person would be my friend, Jerry. Even when he had crazy things going on in his life, he still found time to read early drafts of my first stories, help with online discussions on our Facebook page, and more. He is a true friend and has contributed to motivate me to continue when I have been discouraged.

"There are men who are much more dangerous than others. That makes the most hardened men quake in fear. Spectre is one of those particular men. He is a man of intense determination and is incredibly lethal. I feel for whatever poor bastard gets caught in his crosshairs..."
- Taravis Dole 396 ANE

Chapter 1

Cycle: 397 Month: 6 Rotation: 17
Corre Republic Space
Prefecture: Expansive
Planet: Benedictus
Location: Downtown Avalon

The overmodulated beats of hypnotic music rattled the windows of the Sweet Willy's club. A line of guests waited alongside the front of the building and disappeared around the corner. Several large muscle-bound men stood watch at the front door while one of them allowed select individuals access to the exclusive joint.

A gentle rain had already moved through earlier that evening, which left the stonecrete sidewalks covered with a slightly moist sheen from the surrounding lights. Upon a nearby building, a bright blue light grew then faded just before a lone figure appeared out from the shadows. While the people continued to wait their turn to hopefully gain entrance, the armored man's helmet scanned the civilians and staff down below. The crowd turned their heads to watch as a long black hover limousine pulled up and came to a stop. A professionally dressed man stepped out from the front passenger seat and walked to the back-right side of the vehicle to open the door.

While no one looking on said a word, many of them knew Frankie Corbo Junior. While his father,

Frank Sr., was widely known throughout Avalon, Frankie had made a name for himself on the streets and back alleys. He was dressed head to toe in his absolute best black suit. A beautiful slim blonde woman stepped out after him and began to slide her arm through his when Frankie instead reached back and flung his arm over her shoulder. He abruptly pulled her close to him and stood there for a half-second, silently boasting his power and success over all the other envious men. His cheesy grin spread across his slimy face as he nodded to one of the nearby male onlookers.

Several other men exited the prestigious vehicle and formed up behind their group leader. Each of them was scanned by the observer from up high. Their hidden pistols and other weapons they carried became illuminated in red on the helmet's Heads Up Display. The man up above remained silent as his target strode confidently into the club. One of the bouncers waved his hand over the panel mounted onto the wall, and the thick door slid open silently for the new arrivals. Many of the men watched in awe as Frankie passed them while several of the women became jealous of the blonde.

Once inside, Frankie released the woman. She began to bob her head to the beat of the intensely loud music while her fiancé walked boldly toward the rear of the building. Any of the other attendees to the club that was in the way spotted the sharply dressed man and moved aside.

Men like Frankie and his father were respected, or rather feared, by anyone in the know. While some considered them dangerous, others loved them due to the protection they offered from rival gangs in the capital. Either way, Sweet Willy's was in the Corbo's district. Here, Frankie was like a prince.

Another bouncer stood guard in front of a hallway with strands of beads hanging from above. He spotted the approaching entourage, and he used his left arm to move the beads out of the way.

"Mr. Corbo," the large man said with his deep voice.

Frankie didn't even bother acknowledging the other man. He strode right on passed, and the others followed him one by one.

A metal door on the left slid open, and a thin well-dressed weasely looking fellow stepped into the hallway. The glow from the lights situated above added a glimmer to his glasses, which only helped to accentuate his toothy smile.

"Frankie, a pleasure as always," he said smoothly.

As with everyone else at the club, the younger Corbo didn't say a word as he entered the room. He didn't need to be cordial. That was for chumps and poor people.

The skinny man waited patiently as the other guests that recently arrived all went inside. An upbeat melody filled the room, marking a change in atmosphere from the main area right outside.

Many of the lights illuminated the private room in a purplish glow that seemed more surreal. Four long couches were positioned around a small stage with a dance pole anchored in place at the center of it. Off to the right of the room sat a wooden bar with a wide variety of alcohol arranged behind the bartender.

Several scantily dressed female staff members, each with a different hair color but same uniform, stood together in a line to the left. They each bowed their heads as the high-ranking man placed his hands in his thigh pockets. He looked about the room as the door slid shut.

"Is it to your liking?" the thin man asked nervously.

Frankie glanced around the room once again then stared for a long moment at the assembled women. He then sneered and snapped his fingers.

"Change the song. Make it… festive."

The event organizer nodded to the DJ, who quickly searched through his library of songs to find a suitable choice. He worked his magic on his electronic controls so that the previous beat faded out as the next one began to play. The colors in the lights changed to more of a red hue and Frankie tapped his foot to the melody.

"That's more like it. Now, let's party!" Corbo shouted excitedly.

The men in his group cheered, and the blonde fiancé winked and blew a kiss at Frankie.

As the women staffers began distributing drinks to the guests, Frankie reached back and smacked the redhead's bottom so hard it made her jump slightly. Thankfully she successfully saved her tray from spilling and sending the remaining drinks she carried from flying across the room.

Corbo winked at the woman who smiled anxiously while she backed up. One of the men poked his elbow into his friend's shoulder, and they shared a laugh at their boss' promiscuity.

It wasn't long before many of the guests were throwing drinks back and began using narcotics. Frankie sat on one of the couches with two of the female workers beside him. He took a fistful of an orange powder in a bowl, held it up to his mouth, and inhaled as deeply as he could. The drug immediately began to alter his mind. His hand lowered slowly while he relaxed his head on the brunette's shoulder. She caressed his hair as the intensely pleasurable sensation rushed through his body.

The fiancé seemed entirely oblivious by her future husband's behavior while she flirted with the bartender.

A soft knock came at the door. The event organizer barely was able to hear the noise over the loud volume of the music. He rushed to the entrance and swiped his hand over the control panel.

The metal door slid open, but no one was there. With his eyebrow now arched, the skinny man stuck out his head. A strong hand hefted him up by his collar and threw him down the hallway beside the incapacitated bouncer guarding the beaded entrance. He screamed in terror but none of the guests inside noticed what happened. Only the bartender spotted the door left open and had a strange feeling that something was up. He finished pouring another round for one of the men then ducked beneath the bar counter, pretending to be looking for something in case he was wrong.

An armored shape stepped into the doorway, and one of the armed men noticed the dark gray figure. His eyes grew wide as his brain recognized the terrifying sight of the bounty hunter. The head-to-toe armor was exquisitely designed and was clearly power armor. Still, it appeared lighter and less bulky than other designs in various militaries. Small blue lights emanated from across the advanced suit, giving it an even more impressive appearance.

"Spectre!" he shouted as he dropped the glass in his hand and reached for his weapon.

Everyone else in the room spun toward the door in surprise to see the famous hitman. The bounty hunter raised his arm, and an elegant laser pistol formed in his right hand out of a neon blue mist of particles. A bright blue bolt fired out and pierced through the first man's temple, killing him instantly. The body of the dead man began to crumble to the ground just as his own drink smashed against the floor.

Several of the other thugs reached for their own pistols. Spectre strode in the room calmly, firing bolt after bolt. Each laser methodically killing one man after another.

One of the female staffers ducked down and darted out the doorway while the bounty hunter dispatched another two of the men. Frankie grabbed the brunette as she began to flee and used her as a human shield.

Spectre saw his target attempting to get away and didn't hesitate to fire his weapon. Frankie barely avoided the bolt, but the woman wasn't so lucky. Her body went limp, and the thug leader dove to the ground.

Before the bounty hunter could finish the job, he was hit in the chest by a short barrage of explosive bullets from one of the last men's artificial arms. The impact pushed him back several steps, but he managed to stay upright.

His attacker's eyes grew incredibly wide that the shot didn't kill Spectre outright. He aimed his arm weapon to fire again. Frankie didn't hesitate and used the moment to spring up to his feet and burst for the door.

Under his armored helmet, Spectre's eyes burned angrily. He discarded the pistol in his hand, and it vaporized into a puff of blue specs. The thug fired his weapon but missed. A sword appeared in the bounty hunter's grip, and he sliced the augmented limb off at the elbow.

The man screamed out as the hitman slashed him several times with the bladed weapon across the chest, blood spraying out of the wounds. Spectre happened to turn his head in time to see his target slip through the opened door on some broken glass. Frankie bashed his shoulder hard into the hall but forced his feet to get moving.

Spectre released his sword and sprinted out of the room, pursuing his bounty. Music blared through the hovering speakers while Frankie pushed his way through the crowd of dancers. Lights in the room flickered and transformed colors with the flow of music.

"Get the frag out of my way!" Corbo shouted.

Several of the dancers made way for him and he rapidly skittered toward the main door.

Spectre spotted the escaping man and launched himself up and over most of the crowd, landing in a crouch. The sight of an armored man hopping through the club got the attention of every guard and bouncer inside. Bullets and laser bolts began firing in his direction from multiple attackers. As the sound of weapons fire broke above the volume of the music, the crowd dispersed in fear.

The bounty hunter rolled to his left behind a granite pillar, providing himself with some cover. A slick rifle formed in Spectre's arms as he raised them to a lowered position. The thick post began to break away from the guards' onslaught. With his window to kill Frankie closing, the armored man stood up and fired a burst of blue laser bolts into one bouncer who got too close. One shot blasted his left knee, while the next two lanced through his lower torso. He slumped to the ground, his pistol scattering across the floor.

Spectre dealt with several other guards as they each tried getting a killing shot against him. Patrons continued running in every which way, attempting to escape the madness.

14

This is taking too long…

The bounty hunter's HUD displayed his target's heartbeat through the wall as he ran further away from the club. Holding onto his rifle, Spectre ran for the door.

One unlucky bouncer that had guarded the front door happened to be stepping inside as the hunter reached the entrance. Spectre used his left arm to block the laser pistol up as it fired. A red bolt burned into the ceiling as he jammed his own rifle into the man's chest and fired.

Meanwhile, a large puddle down an alley behind the club reflected the lights of a neighboring business. A splash of water shot up the fearful man's pant leg as Frankie ran for his life. His body still felt rather numb from all of the drugs, but his heart pounded inside like crazy.

He pulled out his communicator, but his hand fumbled, and he dropped it in a mound of bagged garbage that was piled up beside a full dumpster.

"Poosh!" he exclaimed as he turned back down the alley.

The thug hadn't seen the bounty hunter, but he wasn't about to stop running until he put some serious distance between himself and the club. His mind continued to race as panic set in.

He exited the alley he was on and darted across the busy street. A yellow-striped hovercar honked aggressively as it slammed on its brakes, nearly avoiding splattering the terrified thug into a chunky paste.

Another vehicle honked from the other lane, but Frankie continued on his way. He started to trip as he entered the next alley and was barely able to keep himself from falling. The sound of something loud landed behind him, and his enthusiasm to run multiplied. Before he knew it, an intense pain shot up from his left leg, and he tumbled to the wet ground.

He rolled hard and scuffed himself up badly.

"Aaaaah!" Frankie screamed out as he tried to move his injured leg.

He managed to roll himself over onto his back and looked up to see the bounty hunter stepping toward him. His helmet made him appear more like a machine than a man.

"No, no, no, nooo…"

Spectre came to a halt and just stared at his target.

Frankie held up his hand. "Look, I can pay you whatever you…"

The thug died instantly as a bolt burned through his head and exited the other side.

Breathing heavily, the bounty hunter felt a bit of disgruntled joy from within.

He glanced at the clock counting down in the corner of his HUD. "00:39."

That was close, but it's finally done. Now I can leave all of this behind me.

Spectre took a quick picture of the deceased Corbo with a communicator of his own, then headed off into the night. Just before he reached the end of the alley, a bright light again showed then faded. Now in street clothes, the bounty hunter blended into the crowd.

Chapter 2

Cycle: 412 Month: 8 Rotation: 13
Turon Commonwealth Space
Planet: Antioch
Location: Braeville

A gentle breeze caressed a cluster of bright orange flowers in a small garden. They swayed pleasantly from side to side, dancing in place.

Several children shouted in joy as they played a game in the front yard of a cozy little white house. The youngest child, a little girl with her hair braided tightly, dodged to the right, barely avoiding her older brother from catching her.

"Ha, ha. You missed me!" Aiyla Adama blared out happily.

"Oh yeah?" Kev replied sarcastically before he thrust his arm out and tagged his sister.

The little girl's bottom lip stuck out. "Aaaaw…"

"Quit your pouting," Izzie Adama teased. "You wanted to play. Now you're it."

A brown wheeled truck up the street turned left and approached the lone house.

Aiyla spotted the vehicle, and her sour look transformed into pure glee. "Daddy's home!"

The other two children stopped in their tracks and turned to confirm the sighting. Their father had left several hours ago to tend to some matters in town.

Even though his family had lived in the small home for a number of cycles, Gideon Adama still felt a sense of peace wash over him every time he saw it. After a rough life, this was as close to paradise as he could imagine.

As the truck slowly pulled up the long driveway, loose gravel crunched beneath the tires. The father waved to his youngest daughter as she swung her hand back and forth enthusiastically.

Izzie and Kev stepped up to the truck to happily greet their father.

"Hey, Dad," the son said neutrally.

Gideon exited the truck and slammed the door shut. "Hey, guys. You having fun?"

"Well, we were. Aiyla doesn't quite get the game yet," Izzie said plainly.

"I do too!" the youngest daughter shouted as she rushed up. "Kev's just a bully."

Gideon walked around the front of the truck and stopped within arm's reach of his children. He leaned down and looked at his daughter in her eyes.

"Is your brother really a bully?"

Aiyla rocked on her heels as she thought. "Well, he tagged me."

The father allowed a hearty laugh to ring out from within. He gently placed his hand on his daughter's small curly-haired head, but her face displayed she wasn't sure what was going on.

"Where's your mother?" Gideon asked his two older children.

"Momma's inside cooking," Kev said confidently.

"Alright, well, you all have fun."

The father made his way up to the front porch while his kids went back to playing. Each step of his boots on the wooden walkway echoed beneath the raised porch. The door creaked when it first opened, then became silent as it swung the rest of the way.

"Joan. I'm home," Gideon said as he stopped at a stand near the door and began removing items from his pockets.

Not hearing his wife's response was odd for the husband. "Joan?"

"Oh, hey. I'm in the kitchen," his wife called out from deeper in the home.

Gideon stretched his long back and flexed his shoulders. He smoothed out his short dark beard with his right hand as he headed for the kitchen. The aroma of something delicious wafted through the air.

"Smells great," he said energetically.

"Oh, thanks," Joan Adama replied without turning around.

The husband walked up behind his wife and wrapped his arms around her slender waist. She twisted to look up into his eyes and gave him a tired smile.

"What's the matter?" he asked sadly.

"Oh, nothing. I'm just worn out."

Gideon's eyebrow raised. "It's only twelve-twenty."

Joan shrugged her shoulders. "I don't know. Maybe I didn't sleep good."

"Do you need help with anything?"

The wife shook her head and gave her husband another small smile. "No. I'm good, but thank you."

Gideon leaned in and gave her a tender kiss on the lips, then released her. He stepped over to the counter across from him and leaned up against it.

"I saw Matty Williams while I was out."

"Oh?" Joan asked as she turned back to finishing her meal.

"Yeah, he said he could bring the lumber down for that big job by the end of the week."

"That's good."

Joan stirred the food in a pot on the stove with a plastic spoon.

Gideon studied his wife for a few moments without saying anything else. She finally realized the silence that had fallen in the kitchen and looked back at him.

"What's up?" she asked.

"You just seem… off."

The wife turned back to the pot and placed the lid on top. "Sorry. I'm just out of it. Food's done, though. Could you get the kids?"

Gideon uncrossed his arms and pushed himself off the counter. "Sure thing."

Lunch had been, for the most part, very ordinary, much like many other meals the family had shared together. Gideon continued observing his wife and knew that something was wrong. It was extremely out of character for Joan to be so quiet. Normally she was boisterous and energetic. It was one of the things that greatly attracted him to her when they first met.

The husband gathered up the dishes while the children ran off to play some other game together. Joan, however, remained in her seat. Her left hand rubbed her forehead as she looked down at the wooden table.

When Gideon was finished cleaning up after lunch, he returned and found his wife was still where he had left her. Joan's face looked pale, and her eyes heavy.

"I don't feel so good..." she said weakly.

The husband's heart beat faster as he began to worry. "Uh... I'll call Mrs. Landry to watch the kids. Be right back!"

Gideon disappeared around the corner and phoned their neighbor up the road. "Hello, Mrs. Landry. I apologize for the short notice, but can you come over and keep an eye on the kids? Joan is sick. I need to take her to the doctor."

Joan's complexion continued to worsen in the short amount of time that it took for their neighbor to arrive from up the road. Aiyla was excited to see Mrs. Landry, but Izzie and Kev noticed their mother's appearance.

"Dad, is Mom, okay?" Kev asked.

"I'm okay, Hunny," the mother said meekly.

"I'll call you as soon as I know something," Gideon said to their neighbor as he leaned down to help his wife up from her chair.

Mrs. Landry waved away his concern. "Don't worry about anything. You take care of her. Everything will be fine here."

The husband helped his wife outside and opened the door of the truck. Joan struggled, but she was able to climb up into the cab of the vehicle.

Gideon threw the door shut with a *whump* and jogged to the other side.

"Why are you in such a hurry?" the wife asked softly. "I'm fine. Just a little under the weather… or something."

Gideon pressed the "On" button built into the dashboard of the old truck. Its engine roared to life, and the vehicle rumbled beneath the passengers.

"I'm not taking any chances."

Joan laid her head back on the headrest and stared out the window. She knew Gideon was much too stubborn once he made up his mind. Besides, getting checked on wouldn't be so bad.

The truck reversed down the driveway. Mrs. Landy held the youngest child in her arms, and the pair waved to the parents as they drove away.

Towering trees and other plants lined the two-lane highway on either side. A massive red semi-truck drove by in the alternate lane with a *whoosh*.

Gideon glanced over at his wife and tried to keep himself calm.

Her condition is getting worse. Could this be something really bad? What if it is the same thing Dan had?

The man shook his head to clear his internal thoughts. A long time ago, his brother had become ill with a very rare disease that overtook him in a short amount of time. He hadn't personally seen anything like this since then. Still, it wouldn't benefit him to worry too much without a physician's diagnosis.

Much of the ride was quiet, but every now and then Joan would wheeze when she breathed. She would then cough and would be fine again for several minutes. Gideon pressed the accelerator a little harder, bringing the truck's speed up over the local speed limit.

An elderly man was being brought into the emergency room of Braeville General Hospital when the truck pulled up. The husband thankfully found a parking spot near to the door. Joan again breathed heavily as she brought her right arm across her stomach to unfasten her seat belt.

"Here, let me help you," Gideon said as he reached over and disconnected the safety harness for her.

He flung open his door and ran around to the other side to assist his wife. Joan slowly made it out of the vehicle and put her weight on her husband as he helped her inside.

A woman with her hair in a tightly made bun peeked up above the tall counter.

"How can I help you?" she asked, smiling.

"It's my wife… she's sick."

The receptionist saw Joan's face, and her own turned much more somber. "Please check-in at the terminal."

Gideon guided his wife over to the console to his right.

"Welcome to Braeville General. If you have a chip, please scan your hand. Otherwise, please enter your information using the keyboard below," the computer said with its synthetic male voice as the pair approached.

Joan reached out her right hand slowly until she reached the red glowing light shining below the scanner. The console made a *ding* sound, and her medical records were being brought up in the system.

"Welcome, Mrs. Adama. Please have a seat. A nurse will be with you shortly."

Gideon began to turn his wife around when the door off to the left leading into a hall in the hospital opened.

"Joan Adama," the heavyset female nurse called out.

"That was fast," Gideon remarked under his breath.

He raised his left arm, and the nurse stepped toward the Adama's.

"Would you like a wheelchair?" she asked Joan.

"Yes, please," her husband answered as he held her up.

The nurse briskly walked back down the hall and returned a moment later with a thin silver wheelchair. A long pole attached to the back of it raised up above so that it wouldn't fit outside the main door. Joan grunted as she lowered herself down onto the seat and gripped the armrests. The nurse breathed heavily as she bent over carefully and lowered the flaps for the patient's feet.

Gideon's face was covered with concern for his wife. She happened to notice and glanced up at him.

"You look like crap," Joan joked.

The husband didn't feel right being playful back, and instead just awkwardly smiled.

"Alright, Hun, let's take you back to your room," the nurse said as she walked around the wheelchair and gripped the handles.

Gideon noticed the look on the receptionist's face. He noted her own concern. Both of the doors closed behind the trio as they walked inside. They passed by an additional desk with several other nurses and personnel going about their duties.

The smell of the hospital was very reminiscent of every other one Gideon had ever been to.

It doesn't matter what planet I'm on, they all smell the same...

The nurse went through the routine medical procedures of the Turon Commonwealth, which greatly resembled that of other nations. She recorded the patient's weight, blood pressure, and the like before she helped her back to her seat.

After walking for a minute or so further into the building, the nurse wheeled Joan down a second hall and made a left. The door to the sterilized room was open. Gideon spotted the number on the door and committed it to memory.

Room two-oh-four.

The heavyset woman pushed Joan inside then turned the wheelchair around to face the entrance.

Gideon stepped aside, allowing the nurse to exit the room.

"The doctor will be with you in a moment."

"Ugh…" Joan moaned.

"What's wrong?" the husband asked as he took a seat in the chair left for patients.

"Nothing… I just feel like garbage."

Gideon rested his head in his right hand as he placed his elbow on the arm of his chair. "Hopefully, all it is, is that you have a bug or something."

The wife slumped in her wheelchair. "Yeah. Hopefully."

Several more minutes slowly ticked by before a quiet knock came at the door. A short man with a white lab coat stepped inside. He held an electronic tablet under his arm and wore a broad smile on his face.

"Hello, Mrs. Adama," he said as he took a seat on a wheeled stool. "I'm Doctor Gallus. What seems to be the trouble?"

"Well… I'm not feeling too good," she answered.

The doctor glanced at Gideon from above his glasses.

"About two weeks ago, she was sick. Nothing serious. Just mild symptoms."

"Mhmm," the physician said as he began typing on the tablet, making notes on her record.

The husband continued. "We didn't pay much attention to it because it just seemed like a regular bug or something."

"Why bring her in today then?"

Joan sniffled. The noise was sharp sounding despite the room being small.

"I went out to run some errands this morning. She seemed alright when I left. But when I came home, she seemed off," Gideon said as he observed his wife with concern on his face. "After we had lunch, her condition worsened, so we came straight here."

"I see," the Doctor said.

He set the tablet down on the counter beside him and scooched his stool over to the patient. The husband had noticed that the other man was already wearing gloves when he entered the room, which didn't make him feel super confident that they were exactly sterile.

"Hey, Doc."

The physician's hands froze in place as they reached up to Joan. "Hmm?"

"I don't want to question you or nothing. But, would you mind changing your gloves?" Gideon asked politely.

With an obvious disdain, the Doctor wheeled the stool backward and removed his gloves. He set the discarded pair next to the tablet and pulled a new disposable pair from a box hanging in a frame mounted to the wall. The Doctor didn't say a word, but he was obviously annoyed for being caught breaking protocol.

He returned to the patient and began the examination. "Okay, Mrs. Adama, can you stick out your tongue for me?"

Joan complied.

The Doctor then pulled an instrument out of his pocket and checked both of her ears. After placing the other tool back into its home, he retrieved a small light and shined it into her eyes one at a time.

Something caught his attention. "Hmm."

Gideon noticed the subtle sound. "What is it?"

"Well… I don't know."

Around both of Joan's pupils, her eyes had begun to yellow. Dark bags had formed nearby, and she physically appeared very weak.

"I want to run a test. It shouldn't take long for us to get the results."

"What sorta test?" the woman asked, interested in what could be wrong with her.

"Just a simple blood test. It will help give us an idea of what might be going on."

Joan moaned at the idea. The Doctor again glanced at her husband for clarification of what was happening.

"She hates needles," Gideon said plainly.

"Oh, so do I!" the Physician said emphatically.

He stood up and went to the cabinet above the counter behind him. A white box with a bunch of words on it fell onto the bar, and its contents rattled from the impact.

"Dangit," the Doctor snarled at himself.

He picked the box back up, removed a small gray cylinder from it, then returned it to the cabinet.

"This does all the work for me. I press it against your skin, you feel a slight prick, and it gets the sample in a second. As easy as it gets."

Joan pursed her lips but knew she still had to go through with it. She turned her head to face away from the Doctor as he sat back on the stool. He let out a sigh of relief as he got situated.

The Doctor then rolled up her right sleeve and cleaned the location with a sterile pad. He set the cylinder up to her arm and pressed a small button on the bottom of it. There was an audible *click*, and it instantly drew blood.

"Youch!" the woman blurted out.

After removing the small device, the Doctor again rubbed the area with the pad and held it for a moment so the bleeding would stop.

"See, that wasn't so bad."

"Yeah, but you didn't get pricked…"

Gideon chuckled a little to himself at his wife's comment.

The Doctor looked to both of them then stood up. "I'll be back as soon as I know the results."

"Thanks, Doc," the husband said with a nod.

The two sat quietly as they waited for the return of the physician. Gideon absent-mindedly toyed with the bracelet he wore on his left wrist. The black sphere-shaped beads lined the entire strand except for the lone white one at the center of it.

After a while, it felt like a small eternity passed as the pair waited patiently. Every now and then, they could hear muffled voices from the rooms to either side of theirs or in the hallway as medical personnel passed by.

Joan had been wheezing for the last several minutes. It seemed that keeping her eyes open was becoming more difficult. She also was more lethargic than even when they arrived.

Gideon leaned forward in his chair. "How do you feel?"

"Exhausted."

"Alright. Well, I'm going to go see where the Doctor is."

Joan said nothing as her husband stood up and waved his hand over the door panel. He walked down the hallway but saw none of the staff. Gideon became frustrated and decided to walk back to the desk they passed on the way to their room.

An older woman with gray hair noticed his approach and sat up straighter.

The man pointed his thumb over his shoulder. "Hi, I'm looking for Doctor Gallus. He took a blood sample from my wife, and it has been a while. She's in room two-oh-four."

Before the nurse could respond, she noticed the Doctor storm down the hall from one of the other walkways. She gestured with her head in his direction.

"Seems he is heading back toward your wife's room."

The husband twisted around and saw the physician moving quickly away from the desk. He stopped for a moment in front of his wife's door then went inside.

Uh oh...

Gideon returned to his wife's room and went inside. Doctor Gallus' own countenance had changed from the last time the couple had seen him.

"Ah, Mr. Adama. I'm glad you're here. As I was just starting to tell your wife, I have the results back."

The Doctor held up a cluster of pages printed out from the analysis.

"And?" Gideon asked.

Everything about this had him on edge. None of this was looking good, and he was starting to get worried.

Gallus turned to face his patient. "I... I'm sorry to bring you bad news. According to your blood sample, you have Yokum's Disease."

The husband's head became dizzy, and he put out his arm to steady himself.

Joan looked absolutely devastated. "Ho... how could I have Yokum's?"

The Doctor held back a shrug. "I can give you something for your symptoms, but this is very serious."

"How serious?" the husband inquired.

Gallus looked up to the taller man in the room. "There is no known treatment in Turon."

"Wha... what do you mean?" Gideon's blood started to boil. It wasn't that he was mad at the Doctor, but more at the situation.

"The best I can suggest is if you can secure travel to the Corre Republic, do it quickly. I know that they have the means to treat this disease, but unfortunately, we cannot here."

"What are my options?" Joan asked, her voice barely above a whisper.

"You are in the later stages of the disease. The initial symptoms mimic a lot of minor sicknesses, and that can make it hard for it to be discovered early on. At this rate, your body is going to shut down in the next month or so. Yokum's is very rare, but it moves very rapidly once it gains a foothold in the body. Your options are going to the Corre Republic and get treatment. The closest world that would probably be able to help you would be Benedictus. Or, I… can make arrangements for you to be… comfortable."

Gideon clenched his jaw as he looked down at his wife. Her eyes began to swell as she understood her prognosis.

"Um… Doc… could you give us a minute?" the husband asked.

"Of course," he said.

A painful silence fell on the room as the two Adamas listened to the door open then shut.

"I… I'm not ready to die," Joan whispered as a tear ran down her cheek. "What about Aiyla, she's so little. I want to see her grow up…"

Gideon quickly moved across the room, squatted down, and cupped her left hand in both of his.

"The Doc said that there is a treatment in the Republic."

"But it's on Benedictus… of all places. You know what might happen if you return there…" the wife began to say before Gideon cut her off.

"I'll deal with whatever I have to. What's important is getting you cared for. I can get a shuttle to leave in the morning."

Joan held back, crying as her emotions swirled around in her head. She reluctantly nodded her head. "Okay."

"I love you, Joan." Gideon gently pressed his forehead against hers.

"I love you too," she replied.

Her struggle against her tears failed. The two held each other as they both were terrified and nervous about what would happen over the next few weeks.

Chapter 3

Cycle: 412 Month: 8 Rotation: 13
Turon Commonwealth Space
Planet: Antioch
Location: Braeville

The Adama's brown truck pulled up the driveway to their home and came to a stop. Gideon quickly hopped out and moved around to the other side to assist his wife down from her seat. A cool breeze greeted them both and caused the big tree in the front yard to gently sway.

"Ooooh…" she moaned in pain.

"Doc said the pain medicine should be kicking in soon. It will at least make you feel a little better."

"Not a moment too soon," the wife mumbled.

Mrs. Landry had spotted the vehicle and opened the door in time to greet the homeowners.

From the front door, Gideon could see that all three of his children were sitting at the table, eating dinner. He tried to keep his face neutral to not alarm Izzie, the oldest sibling, but she saw her mother's pale complexion.

"Momma?" she asked hesitantly.

Mrs. Landry realized the seriousness of her neighbor's appearance and rushed up to aid Joan inside.

The wife was helped to their tan-colored sofa. She eased herself down while all of her children stared at the back of her head. They knew something was up, but Gideon would have to address that afterward.

"Could I speak with you outside?" the husband asked his neighbor.

"Sure," she said as she looked up and made eye contact.

"Kids, your mother isn't feeling so good. Keep eating your dinner, and I'll be back in a minute," Gideon said as he followed Mrs. Landry back out the front door.

"Mommy, are you okay?" Aiyla asked with her sweet little voice.

Once the door was shut, Gideon allowed himself to show how he was feeling.

"What did the Doctor say?"

I need to keep myself focused. There is still a chance she'll be okay. I can't get lost in my own head!

"He said that... uh... she has Yokum's Disease."

Mrs. Landry held a hand up to her mouth. While rare, she understood that Yokum's was a very unpleasant way to die. "They say that is incurable..." she said as her voice trailed off.

Gideon shook his head. "Not quite. We were told that there is a treatment available in the Corre Republic."

"How are you going to get there, though?"

The husband took a deep breath. Inside he fought a mix of pain for the condition of his wife and another on returning to the Republic after all this time.

"I used to do some work there. Actually, it's where we met before we moved to the Commonwealth."

"Oh? I never knew that."

"The Doctor said that she may have a good chance if we can get to Benedictus soon."

Mrs. Landry steeled herself. "I know that neither of you has any family in the area. You just let me know if I can be of any help. That is quite a trip you'd have to take with the little ones."

"Well, come to mention it... I was wondering if you'd be able to watch the kids for a couple of weeks?"

Without a moment of hesitation, the neighbor smiled kindly. "I'd be more than happy to. I raised my own little batch of kiddos in the past."

"Thank you, Mrs. Landry. I can't tell you how much this is a help to us."

"Stop it, you. Go get your arrangements made. I'll help out wherever I can."

A strange shout came from inside. The two quickly returned inside and found that Joan had fallen. She was not moving.

"Is Momma alright?" Aiyla asked, with her eyes already swelling with tears.

The husband knelt down and checked his wife's neck for a pulse.

Oh, thank the Creator...

"Yes, she's okay." He leaned down further and gently scooped his wife up into his muscular arms.

"Kids, why don't we go watch a holomovie?" Mrs. Landry asked as she shooed the children out of the room.

Gideon carefully lowered her back down onto the couch and laid her down with a pillow beneath her head. She weakly opened her eyes and looked up at him.

"What happened?"

"You passed out."

The woman closed her eyes again and sighed.

"Listen, Mrs. Landry is going to watch the kids while we go to Benedictus."

"Nooo..." she groaned.

"Listen, they'll be fine here."

Joan again looked up. "It isn't them I'm worried about," she said as she placed her hand on Gideon's cheek.

"Listen, my concern is you getting better. Nothing else matters. I want you to lie down and rest. I'm going to go make some calls."

The wife lowered her arm and laid it across her stomach. "Alright. I'll just stay right here."

Gideon lowered his head and kissed Joan's forehead before he left the room.

The next morning came like a blur of time. Gideon had tossed and turned all night, barely getting any sleep. He decided it was more productive to do something and so he rose very early. Sunlight was just beginning to poke its rays above the tree line by the time he was nearly finished packing their bags. A nagging feeling kept nudging him in his mind, but he had been trying to ignore it.

Joan was still in bed covered up with a white sheet. She seemed so peaceful right then. That is, except for the sound she made with every breath. Gideon wasn't a medical professional, but he had been around long enough to know that she was getting worse, fast.

He walked over to see if she was awake. She remained fast asleep. Her chest rose and lowered from her labored breathing. Gideon then moved as quietly as he could out of the bedroom. He passed through the hallway. Their bathroom was on his left while a wall of pictures on the right. Pausing for just a moment, he gazed at each of the images. Some showed the children in various phases as they had grown up, while others were of him and Joan smiling together.

Life, before he met her, had felt like an eternity ago. The idea of losing her was crushing him on the inside, but he refused to dwell on the thought for long. It wasn't the first time he had lived through the death of loved ones, but this time was different.

He continued on his way through his home. The children were still asleep in their beds, and so he maintained his stealth to try and keep it that way. Eventually, he stopped in front of a brown wooden door in the kitchen.

I have finally put this away from me, and now I am thinking of bringing it with me? Am I crazy?

Gideon wrestled within himself, but before he knew it, his left hand reached out, and he was turning the doorknob. The door creaked a little as it opened and revealed the darkened path that led down below the house.

He reached in and pressed a switch, which instantly activated the light at the bottom of the staircase.

What happens if I get there, and I don't have this with me, and something does go wrong? Ugh. I wish I was smart enough to modify it so that Joan could use it...

The husband sighed. He then took a step and went down the rest of the way.

I really don't want to take this with me. What if I get caught with it? But what choice do I have?

He stood there for a moment at the base of the stairs fighting to resist going right back up.

No, I don't have a choice. Better to have it and not need it than the alternative. I'll just have to do everything I can to not get discovered.

Finally, he pulled together the strength and strode across the basement to a wall across from him. He placed his right hand on it and felt a warmth begin to grow. After a couple of seconds, he pushed, and the wall receded slightly. He then twisted his hand, and a hologram emerged with a series of numbers on it. As he rotated his hand to the right then to the left, he ultimately heard a deep *click*. The portion of the wall slid to show the small door hidden behind it.

Gideon took a breath then pushed his finger on a small screen on the face of the door. He could hear it unlock, and he twisted the small knob. The inside of the safe was dark until the door opened far enough that a light activated. A stack of Corre Republic cash was bound together and organized to the left, while on the right was a neat stack of gold coins. At the center was an old looking black box. He reached in and pulled the box out then shut the safe.

The husband studied the artistic detail that had been etched into the exterior of the cube shape. It was made of a type of rare metal and felt heavy in his hands.

A noise from up above broke him from his reflecting state of mind. He stuffed three stacks of the money into his pocket, then pressed a button inside the recessed area, and the wall slid silently back into place. After he hurried up the stairs and shut the door behind him, he stopped to find Izzie was standing in the kitchen. She nearly jumped at the speed her father was moving. Gideon hid the box behind his back but tried to act casual about it.

"Oh, sorry. I just had to check something downstairs," he said, smiling confidently.

"Uh… okay," the oldest daughter said.

The two stood there awkwardly for a moment before Gideon walked away. Izzie shrugged her shoulders then pulled a bowl down from the cabinet.

To his surprise, Joan was sitting up in her bed, staring at a picture of the couple on the wall. He was going to walk away. But she called out to him.

"Where are you going?" she asked without turning to her husband.

"Oh, I... was just finishing up packing."

"Are you bringing it with you?"

Gideon didn't see much point in lying. He walked into the bedroom, his steps *thumping* on the wood floor.

Joan looked over to see the tiny black shape in his grip. She held out her hand to view it. The husband hesitated for a second, then decided there was no harm in handing it over. He crossed the rest of the way to the ill woman and placed the container in her open hand.

She brought it in front of her face and studied the craftsmanship of the box. Surrounding the sides of it, figures in armor battled creatures of darkness. On the top was an arch with another figure standing boldly in place in front of it. Without asking, she opened the box. Gideon started to say something then held back his protest.

It's not like she can activate it anyway...

Inside was a silver-colored woven necklace with a blue amulet attached to it.

"May I?" she asked as she glanced back to her husband.

He nodded.

She delicately removed the necklace from the box and allowed the amulet to dangle from it. Joan held it up close to her face and could see that a symbol of some sort was shaped in the center of the blue gem.

"What does it mean?"

Gideon licked his lips and looked to the floor. "It uh… it's an old symbol for "truth"."

"It really is gorgeous."

Wanting to change the conversation, the husband cleared his throat. "Like I was saying, we are nearly packed. Mrs. Landry will be here shortly, and then we can hit the road."

Not yet ready to move on, Joan stared at the necklace still. "I thought you said it wasn't really working properly?"

Gideon shifted uneasily. "Well… it still works. Kind of. It just doesn't have much power left."

"Why can't you recharge it?"

"Because… look, what's important right now is getting you better. I'm almost packed, and we'll be leaving soon."

"What about the children?" Joan asked as she lowered the necklace back into its protective case.

"They'll be fine. It's better for them to be here than come with us in the Republic."

Gideon tenderly took the box from his wife's hand and abruptly shut it. He turned to the foot of the bed, where he had a duffle bag that he was filling. With some care, he packed the small cube in between some of his clothing for when they were going through customs. He would have gone ahead and worn it, but the scanners they would need to pass through would trigger an alarm.

An hour later, the children were all fed and dressed. Kev and Aiyla were at the dinner table when Joan shuffled her way down the hall and out into the central area of the house.

"Good morning, Momma!" the young girl said excitedly.

"Good morning, baby." It took a great deal of her energy to smile, but she wanted to appear like she was better than she felt.

A knock came from the front door, and Gideon appeared from around the corner. He gave his wife plenty of space to pass, then made it for the front door.

"Mrs. Landry, good morning," the husband said.

His neighbor held a container. "I made you something for the road."

Gideon accepted the dish. "Thank you."

He stepped aside, and Mrs. Landry entered. Joan knelt down to her youngest daughter's level in the seat.

"Why do you have to go, Momma?" Aiyla asked with a whimper.

"Cause, I need some medicine from the Republic."

"Will it make you better?" Kev asked nervously.

Joan smiled at her only son. "Yes, it will. Daddy and I won't be gone for very long. I want you both to be very good for Mrs. Landry."

"Yes, Momma," they both said in unison.

The mother took a moment to kiss her son first on top of his head, then her youngest daughter. Izzie walked out of her room and knew that her parents were about to leave.

Gideon moved over to his oldest child and gave her a hug. "You remember what I told you."

"I'll take care of them," Izzie whispered back.

The father released her. "That's my girl. We should be back in a couple of weeks. We'll keep you all up to date," he said as he spoke louder to the whole room.

Joan struggled, but was successfully able to stand back up. She shuffled toward the front door but stopped to go over to her oldest daughter. Izzie and her mother shared a loving hug.

Gideon said goodbye to the other two kids then went back to the front door with the duffle bag in his hand. "I love you guys."

"Love you, Daddy," Aiyla called out.

Mrs. Landry smiled at Gideon and Joan. "Everything here will be fine. Just focus on getting better."

"Thank you," the mother said.

Gideon stretched out his hand for his wife to hold. "There is an envelope with money in the kitchen. Should be more than enough to cover their food while we're away."

"That wasn't necessary," their neighbor said briskly. "I'm happy to watch them while you're away."

The married couple took their time to walk from the porch to the driveway. Gideon helped his wife climb up and shut her door for her.

All the children had moved outside onto the porch to wave to their parents. Gideon activated the vehicle and twisted his body to watch out of the back window as they pulled out. The truck had just finished reversing, and Joan reached her right hand up to the passenger window.

"What is it?" Gideon asked absentmindedly as he put the vehicle into "Drive."

"I have this strange feeling I won't see them for a long time."

A lump formed in the husband's throat as his mind wanted to run away with that exact fear. "Uh… don't say that, hun. Everything's going to be fine. We'll be in the Republic before you know it. Doctor Gallus was confident they can treat you."

Joan pressed her head on the headrest and shut her eyes. Gideon's grip tightened on the steering wheel while he fought back his emotions.

Stay strong. Don't you give in. Be strong for her.

Chapter 4

Cycle: 412 Month: 9 Rotation: 5
Corre Republic Space
Prefecture: Expansive
Planet: Benedictus
Location: Avalon Spaceport

The trip to the Republic world had been uneventful. Their ship arrived at the trader's HOP point without any issue, and now they relaxed as best they could while their shuttle finished the journey to the planet's surface.

Travel between worlds had advanced to the point that moving between planetary systems was relatively instantaneous. Using HOP technology, a spacecraft "hopped" from one location to another by traveling through the Nth dimension. Time for those in reality still continued to move on while the ship went outside of time. As such, the occupants of a shuttle feel as if almost no time has passed at all. This worked well in Joan's situation since the Doctor had told her she didn't have much time to live.

With every planet, star, and system constantly in motion, it made hopping dangerous but calculated. By utilizing artificial navigational intelligence, ships can navigate without much issue. Every now and then, you may hear about a spacecraft going missing, but that isn't nearly as common as it used to be when the coordinates were figured out by hand.

There are typically two confirmed hop points for every Republic planet. One for traders and travelers, the other for military and government officials. Using a military hop point is illegal except on official government authority. In the Corre Republic, if an unidentified craft arrives at the Military HOP Point, space traffic control will notify the Republic fleet in the system, and the ship will be destroyed. Extreme measures such as these had to be taken centuries ago when worlds began breaking away from the Corre Republic and formed their own nations.

Once the shuttle landed at the spaceport, Gideon undid his harness and slung the duffle bag over his shoulder. Joan was weak but managed to unfasten her own straps. She bent forward, her body ached greatly. The husband assisted his wife up from her seat, and together they walked out with the rest of the passengers. Gideon nodded to the Captain who politely waved to those as they exited the cargo ship.

On either side of the spacecraft was metal fencing with arrows illuminated on the ground. Gideon tried to stay as calm as he could when he spotted the overhang that all of the passengers began to line up under. Portable scanning stations were positioned behind the bag inspectors.

Travelers from outside of the Corre Republic went through stricter scanning checkpoints than citizens did. This helped to decrease violent attacks from activists, cutting down on weapon or narcotics smuggling, and other things listed as undesirable, making it into the central nation. The husband knew that this was the point when everything could fall apart. He forced his heart to calm down. With gentle care, Gideon slid his hand out from his wife's and removed his bracelet. Joan noticed him slide the piece of jewelry into his pocket, but she must have been feeling a similar concern. She gave him a quick nod.

"It'll be alright."

Gideon gave his wife his best confident smile, but his eyes betrayed him. Since the couple had left the Corre Republic over a decade ago, neither had returned. He wasn't sure what sort of advancements or changes in their foreign visitors' checkpoints were.

They together stood in line patiently as one by one, the other passengers were cleared for entry. Gideon spotted multiple camera pods arranged about the area. No doubt, his face, along with everyone else, was already running through facial recognition software.

Worrying isn't going to change anything. Just don't draw attention to yourself… they said they altered my file in the database. But I know he could always find me…

A particular scraggly looking man was stopped by security and asked to go into a different line. He began to protest when two Republic marines stepped forward. The man looked both of the soldiers up and down. Their tan and maroon colored body armor was quite the intimidating sight for most ordinary people. They each carried a military-grade laser rifle in their right hand and a large shield in their left. Their faceplates reflected the traveler's face back at him.

The man gulped then visually followed the command. Both of the marines escorted him away to the other line of passengers. Gideon knew that the second line was for those that had some sort of red flag come up about them. Yet again, he forced himself to not appear nervous.

I can't give them a reason to pay extra attention to me. Everything's gonna be fine. Just relax…

While the nine other nations outside of the Corre Republic had experienced relative peace for a while, tension had been building between some of the border worlds. Even though the Turon Commonwealth was typically behind the times for news updates because of its governments sifting programs, Gideon had heard about the possible boiling points between the Republic and the Corpa Confederation and Union of Stars. Benedictus was within hopping distance from the Confederation, and it looked like the Republic didn't want to take unnecessary risks.

Eventually the Adama's were next. Joan stepped up first. Since Gideon carried their only bag, she was waved forward and instructed to step into the scanner. She stopped on the white square, painted onto the stonecrete ground. Large hovering plates began to rotate faster and faster around the woman until they came to a stop. Meanwhile, her husband placed their luggage onto a conveyor belt that took the bag through a different scanner.

"Alright, step out, ma'am," a young security guard said. He waved her out of the scanner, and she waited behind the dotted line for her husband.

The guard operating the luggage scanner spotted something on her screen. She signaled a different guard, and he stepped over. The newcomer took the bag from the scanner and stepped over to a new counter, then he motioned for Gideon to step over to him.

"Is there a problem?" Gideon asked meekly in hopes of not seeming nervous.

"Is there anything in here that I should know about? Any weapons, narcotics, batteries, fluids, or any other restricted objects?" the guard asked sternly.

"Nope."

The guard began squeezing and feeling around the bag. While his face remained stoic, he tossed out a question to ease the tension. "How was your trip?"

"Nothing to complain about," the visitor replied calmly.

The husband's heart began to beat a little faster when the guard stopped searching and pulled out the small black box. Gideon resisted the urge to yank the necklace away, and instead watched as the security personnel opened up the case.

"Wow. Now, this is something."

"It is, isn't it?" Gideon asked neutrally.

The guard lifted the necklace out by the amulet. He held it up to the light so that the symbol inside the gem shown clearly.

"How much did something like this set you back?"

"More than I would care to admit. It was for my wife on our wedding day."

"Hmm…" the guard muttered. "Well, it is beautiful. She's a lucky lady. My husband didn't buy me anything half as nice."

Gideon chuckled, trying to hide his nervousness. Finally, the guard lowered the necklace carefully back into its box and closed it tight. He put it back into the bag and zipped it up.

"Have a nice day."

"You as well," the husband said with a smile.

Joan breathed a little easier when she saw that her husband was being waved into the scanner. He set his bag down on a conveyor belt, and it went through a separate scanning device.

Once through his own scanner, Gideon retrieved the duffle bag without any more interruptions.

"Was everything alright?" the wife asked when her husband caught up to her.

"Not a problem."

The pair followed the other passengers that were cleared through another corral that broke into three rows for identification. Gideon looked around and noticed the four marines aligned against the wall. While you couldn't see their eyes, he knew that they watched the newcomers closely. The Corre Republic always wanted to emphasize their military power and strength. Some disgruntled citizens suggested it was one way they kept their own worlds in check.

Joan again took the lead and was the first one to the scanning station.

"Chip or ID card?" the woman asked the wife.

"Chip."

A metal post with a small device and screen stood about waist-high in front of Joan. She held out her hand beneath the scanner, and the agent watched the screen for approval.

"Reason for visiting?" the agent asked while she waited for the results.

"My husband and I are here to see a doctor about some treatment."

Joan's identification and file were pulled up with a green checkmark.

"Well, I hope it all turns out good for you. Welcome to Benedictus, Mrs. Adama."

"Thank you," Joan said meekly as she walked past the female agent.

The woman looked up to Gideon as he stepped forward. "Chip or ID card?"

"Uh, card," Gideon said as he took a slender card from his wallet and handed it over.

The silver card had his picture, basic information, and had the green flag of the Commonwealth holographically set in the plastic rectangle. Like she had done thousands of times before, the agent scanned the card and held onto it for clearance. Gideon's file ran through the system instantly. However, an error occurred.

Up above the scanning station was a small booth with darkened glass so that the visitors could not see inside. A slim woman with curly hair sat at her screen when the error message appeared.

"What's this?" she asked herself.

Her fingers danced on the keyboard as she typed commands into the computer console. Gideon's record was there, but what was strange is that even though he had official documentation, there was no record of him visiting the Corre Republic before. There was something about the man's face in his file that also caught her attention.

The agent stared for a few seconds then decided to pull out a device from her uniform jacket. She looked to her left at the male agent as he did his own work. Trying to be nonchalant, the agent held up the object to the screen, and it scanned the image. After lowering her arm, she played with her hair while she waited for the program to process its own scan.

"Is something wrong?" Gideon asked the agent down with him.

"Well, um, maybe. I'm sure the booth is checking it out, and you'll be on your way momentarily."

The husband glanced over at the soldiers against the wall, they still were standing where he last saw them.

At least they haven't moved. I really don't want to cause a scene here...

Finally, the small scanner refreshed and confirmed Gideon's results. The agent in the booth got very excited about what she discovered.

"Well, would you look at you," she whispered mockingly.

To not act further suspicious, she reached over and pressed the "Override" button on the main screen.

"Alright, here we go, Mr. Adama. You are cleared for entry. Enjoy your visit to Benedictus," the agent below said.

Gideon nodded appreciatively and walked over to his wife. He slid the bracelet back over his left hand. Joan extended her hand, and the two exited the facility. Meanwhile, the agent up above gathered her purse.

"I'll be right back. Got to hit the ladies' room," she said to the other agent.

Once she reached a quiet place, she dialed a number on her communicator. Several rings later, and a very gruff voice answered.

"Who's this?"

"Uh hi, this is Claire. I think I might have found someone you'd be very interested in."

"Oh?" the man said sarcastically. "Don't waste my time. Get to the point!"

Claire absent-mindedly played with her hair again as she looked around to be confident she was alone. "Yeah, alright. I just located Spectre. You know, the bounty hunter."

"Where are you?"

"Isn't there a big price on his head and all?" the agent asked nervously.

"You just tell me where you are. You'll be paid for your information."

The Adama's took a taxi together to the Avalon main hospital in the downtown area of the major city. Gideon had attempted to call ahead of time while they were on board the shuttle, but his calls kept dropping. He had avoided upgrading his communicator for quite some time, but the technology of Benedictus was much more advanced than Antioch was. As the communication companies improve and grow, they phase out the older tech to inspire their customers to upgrade.

"I can't get through," Gideon finally relented.

Joan gave her loving husband a soft smile. "That's alright. We're almost there, anyhow."

She could tell that he was much more anxious than she had ever seen him. Hoping to try and interrupt his concerns, she said, "The city sure is different than I remember."

Gideon looked outside of the window and peered upward as high as he could see. "Yeah... it sure has changed."

"I imagine you've seen many cities change over the cycles," Joan said kindly.

The husband pursed his lips and struggled against the surge of sadness that tried to boil up within him. "Yeah, I have," he said finally.

After a few minutes of silence, the taxi pulled up in front of the primary medical building. The hospital had multiple different wings built off of it, each specializing in some separate area of medicine. Since they had never been here before, Gideon figured walking in the front door was the best bet.

Joan managed to get herself out of the hovercab before her husband made it to the other side. Gideon reached back into the vehicle and scanned his paycard. He shut the door, and the cab pulled off to find its next passengers.

An elderly couple up ahead of the Adama's walked into the foyer. The double sliding doors opening and closing automatically as they passed through the entrance.

"That'll be us one day," Joan joked. "Well, except you might not look quite like him."

"It doesn't matter how old you get, you are my wife. I love you, no matter what."

The wife reached up and touched the side of her husband's head. "You say that now. I'm not quite all wrinkly yet. Although I have aged some since you first met me. I definitely have some more lines since the babies."

"No amount of change will turn me away from you. I will love you forever," Gideon said lovingly.

Joan glanced down to the ground beneath her. "How I wish I could spend much more time with you."

Knowing the conversation was entering a dark place, the husband kissed his wife on the lips then nudged his head toward the door. "Let's deal with this problem first."

A rush of fresh air met the couple as they entered the hospital.

Yep, same smell everywhere…

To the right of the door was a pillar. A round bulb had been installed above head level and emitted a holographic projection of a pretty woman dressed as a doctor. "Welcome to Avalon Regional Medical Center. We hope that your visit with us will be enjoyable. If you have any concerns, please speak with our Patient Experience Specialist."

"You don't see those in Turon," Joan remarked as they passed the impressive display of technology.

Three receptionists sat behind a big circular desk at the center of the open space before them. Gideon helped his wife up to the station where an older woman greeted them.

"Hello, how may I assist you?"

"Yes, my wife needs to see a specialist," the husband said boldly.

"What sort of specialist, deary?" the woman asked Joan.

"Well, uh... I have Yokum's Disease."

"Oh, dear. I'm sorry to hear that. I know that it is an unbearable experience. Had it myself about a decade ago. The same doctor that treated me actually still takes patients here."

"That's fantastic," Gideon chirped.

"Unfortunately, you will need to schedule an appointment."

The husband stood for a moment in shock.

"But, I was told by my physician in the Commonwealth that I don't have long to live," Joan pleaded.

"I'm really sorry. I don't make the protocols here, but it is procedure."

Gideon's blood began to boil. "So, you're telling me that we came all this way from Turon for life-saving treatment to just get turned away?"

"I'd be more than happy to assist in you scheduling your appointment. Other than that, there is nothing that I can do at this time," the receptionist said coldly.

Joan took a few steps back from the desk. She put her right hand to her forehead and started to freak out.

"This is insane. Hospitals are supposed to treat people!" Gideon shouted.

"Sir, you are going to need to calm down," the woman said politely.

"No, I want her to see a doctor. She is very sick!"

One of the other receptionists noticed the conversation breaking down and slowly reached beneath her station and pressed a button.

Several burly men dressed in dark uniforms headed toward the visiting couple.

"Sir, please, lower your voice, and I can assist you."

Gideon was a hair's length away from snapping. He clenched his fists, and a vein began to pop out from his neck.

Before the armed guards made it the rest of the way to the confrontation, Joan collapsed to the ground. Gideon heard something behind him and turned in surprise to find his wife sprawled out on the hospital floor.

"Joan!" he shouted as he darted beside her.

He gently shook her shoulder, but she remained motionless.

"Joan. Joan, talk to me."

The receptionist placed a hand over her mouth in shock while one of the guards radioed for assistance. One of the other guards knelt beside the woman.

"Sir, help is on the way. I'm going to need you to stand back."

"I'm not going anywhere until I know she is alright," the husband growled.

A team of men in hospital scrubs rushed over with a hover stretcher. The guard stood up and stepped aside, giving the duo room to work. One of the medical staff lowered the bed beside the woman while the other checked her heart rate.

"Please, sir, give her space," the older of the two said.

Gideon wasn't pleased, but he complied. He gripped the strap from his duffle bag while his other hand clenched tightly.

Other people passing by in the foyer stopped to watch the incident unfold. After Joan was delicately placed on the stretcher, the team led her out, and Gideon followed behind.

They walked through what felt like door after door until they arrived in the emergency room. There was another set of doors that they walked through when a woman called out to Gideon.

"Sir! Sir! Are you with her?" an overly thin man in white scrubs asked.

He rushed over to the husband, but Gideon had no intention of stopping. The male nurse carried a tablet in his hand.

"I need to ask you some questions."

"After," the husband said bitterly.

"Gah!"

The nurse walked faster until he could catch up to the team escorting her.

"I need to scan her in."

Both of the men came to a halt, and the nurse gently lifted Joan's hand up so that he could scan her chip with his tablet. A *ding* sounded from the device, and he returned her hand with care.

"Turon?" he said inquisitively as her record pulled up.

The team heard the question and came to a halt. Gideon looked at the three men, confused.

"Why did you stop?"

"Sir, I don't think you understand. I need to get information from you about her. Protocol for foreigners is that we need vital payment information before we can begin treatment," the male nurse said sternly.

The husband was angered and was not able to hold himself back. "This is absurd. We both are from the Republic!"

"Her record indicates she is living in Turon, and that makes you both tourists. Are you able to pay for this treatment?"

"What? This is about money? Yes… yes, I can pay. I have cuso!"

Gideon unzipped his duffle bag and showed a handful of money.

"Ew, cash," the nurse remarked.

"What, does this hospital not like money all of a sudden now?" the enraged husband growled.

The nurse stood up straighter. "No, it's not that." He nodded to the other two hospital workers, and they continued down the hall.

Gideon followed after them, and the nurse remained on his heel.

"Does she have allergies not on her record? What are her symptoms? Why are you here from the Commonwealth?"

"No allergies. She has Yokum's. We traveled here so that she could receive treatment. While we were in the main lobby, she collapsed," the husband answered with a bitter tone in his voice.

"I see. Well, you're in luck. Doctor Theera is in today. She will be in good hands. Would you please follow me to the waiting room?" the nurse asked as he raised his free hand back the way they came.

"I'd rather not."

The other man sighed. "Alright. But you can't go into the room. Since you are from out of the country, she will have to go through isolation until we can confirm her condition."

"Isolation? Why?!"

"Because," the nurse started to say while trying to remain calm, "you both are visitors from out of the country. My record indicates you just arrived here moments ago. That may look suspicious to the monitoring systems."

Gideon understood the logic and didn't want to waste more time arguing. "Fine."

"Alright. This way."

The nurse led the disgruntled husband to the set of doors before the isolation hall. A trio of uncomfortable looking chairs was arrayed against the wall.

"You will have to wait here. Someone will come to get you when they are ready."

Gideon didn't say a word as he sat down. His mind swirled with thoughts.

What if we got here too late? What am I going to do if she dies? I'm not ready to lose her...

The hallway became eerily quiet after the nurse disappeared around the corner. All that was there to comfort the anxious man was the cold chill of the hospital air. That and his darkening thoughts of concern.

Chapter 5

Cycle: 412 Month: 9 Rotation: 5
Corre Republic Space
Prefecture: Expansive
Planet: Benedictus
Location: Avalon Space Port

Down in a dark alley not too far from the Avalon spaceport, a lone hovercar rested on the moist pavement. The driver mindlessly flipped through screen after screen on his communicator while the other man in the back stared out at the darkening sky.

"So, Saul, do you really think this chick saw who she saw?" Bruce asked from the driver's seat.

"We're about to find out."

Saul Corbo stroked his chin while his mind played with the idea of locating the ex-bounty hunter that killed his brother. After Frankie had been murdered, his entire family grieved for a month. The loss of his oldest brother was exceedingly painful for his father to process. Being the one to deliver his brother's killer would be a significant boost for Saul and his reputation.

A tap came at the right-side passenger window. While the driver jumped, frightened by the noise, Saul remained stoic. The car unlocked, and Antonio opened his door. He slid in while the leather seat squeaked from the other man's entrance.

The thug leader waited for the door to shut before he spoke. "Did she show you proof?"

"Yeah, boss, she did. It's him alright He changed his last name, though. Goes by Gideon Adama now," Antonio said as he got situated.

"Did she have any idea where he is heading?"

"Yeah. Turns out that he is here with his wife."

"I wouldn't think someone like Spectre with his reputation could love anyone," Saul said spitefully.

"Well, I guess she is sick or something. She told one of the agents that they were here for her to see some doctor."

Corbo brought his left hand up to his mouth while he thought about what to do. "Spread the word. I want someone to check out every single hospital in the city. Keep it quiet, though. I don't want my father to find out about it."

Both of the other men looked at Saul strangely. He returned their confused look with a bitter stare.

"What?" he asked, surprised by their stunned faces.

"You aren't going to keep your father in the loop on this one, boss?" Bruce asked nervously

Saul leaned forward. "Here's the deal. This piece of trash killed my brother. I want to bring his head to my father myself. So, keep it quiet."

"Can do," Antonio said confidently. "I'll get a crew together."

"Bruce, let's get outta here. We got work to do."

Several hours passed while Gideon waited for any sort of update on his wife. He had wanted to walk away to find someone to get information from but was worried he would miss a nurse looking for him. The pervasive thought kept him stuck in place as time continued to tick on by.

When the locked doors swung open, he jumped right to his feet.

A man as tall as the husband smiled at him and walked over. The overhead lights appeared to roll across his glasses with every other step.

"Ah, you must be, Mr. Adama?" the Doctor asked confidently. "I'm Doctor Theera."

"Yes. How's my wife?"

"It's a very good thing you brought her here when you did. Her condition is severe."

"Can I see her?" Gideon asked.

When he was a bounty hunter, he was used to going on dangerous assignments. This situation made him feel entirely helpless, though, which was very strange indeed.

Theera nodded. "She just got out of her initial treatment. We rushed her straight in when I saw her. I apologize someone hasn't been out here to speak with you."

Gideon waved away the concern. "Is she going to be alright?"

"Yes, I think she will. While her conditions were severe, she is responding well to the treatment thus far. She will have to stay here for a week or so for observation and additional doses, but I am confident she should be just fine."

A great sigh of reprieve let out of Gideon. His thoughts had haunted him all the while he had remained in the hallway. Now there was real hope.

"That's fantastic news… but, her physician in Turon made it sound much worse. It sounds like it wasn't a big deal at all to cure her," the husband said in dismay.

"Several cycles ago, there was a huge breakthrough in treating Yokum's. It isn't quite a "cure," but it is awfully close. Basically, she will have flair ups every five cycles. However, we will be able to continue her treatment at that time, and she will live a long and happy life."

A sensation of relief washed over the anxious man.

Long and happy life… that sounds nice.

"Thank you, Doc," Gideon said gratefully.

"It's my pleasure. If you'll follow me, I'll take you back to her."

The Doctor held up his hand to the door panel. Automatically his embedded chip was scanned, and the doors again swung open with a *whoosh*. Gideon followed close behind, his mind swirled with happiness and disbelief. It wasn't but a few minutes ago that he was worried for her life. Now, it all looked like it was going to work out just fine.

To his surprise, Joan was sitting up in her bed. Her complexion had significantly improved, and she was beginning to look like herself again She smiled widely at the sight of her husband. He couldn't contain the joy from within himself, and it spilled onto his face.

Doctor Theera gave the couple a moment and walked down the hall to check on other patients.

Gideon rushed forward and kissed his wife on the lips. "The Doc says you're going to be fine."

Joan nodded happily. "Yeah, I can't really believe it. I feel so much better."

"I was so worried when you collapsed. I...I didn't know what to think," the husband admitted as the feeling of helplessness again fluttered in his mind.

"Sorry about that, my love," Joan said uneasily. "I uh… kinda faked it a bit."

Gideon blinked his eyes in shock. "You what?"

The wife played with a portion of the blanket covering her legs. "Well, we went through a lot to get here. I was scared of what would happen if we had to make an appointment if I didn't get looked at in time. So…"

"So, you faked them out," Gideon said in amazement.

"I'd say it was more of subtle encouragement."

The husband grinned at his wife. "Hun, there wasn't anything subtle about that."

Joan grinned mischievously.

"I was told you are going to have to stay here for about a week for more treatment."

"Yeah, they mentioned that," Joan said in agreement. "It's crazy the difference I feel right now."

"I'm just happy to see you smiling again." Gideon gently sat down beside his wife and placed his hand on hers. "I… I don't want to lose you."

"Well, sounds like I'm going to be sticking around a lot longer now," the woman said with a cheerful tone in her voice.

For whatever reason, Gideon didn't know what else to say for the moment. A strange stillness fell over the room. Joan studied her husband's face in the bright white light of the hospital room. His rugged beard covered most of his face, but she fixated on his eyes.

"You know, it's still weird to me. You look exactly like you did when we met, but that beard does a good job of making you appear older. Your eyes though and around them, look as youthful as ever."

The ex-bounty hunter didn't want to linger on this conversation. "Are you hungry?"

Joan nodded.

"Let me go see if I can find a nurse, and we can get you something to eat," Gideon said as he stood back up.

The wife pointed to a panel built into her bed. "This is the Republic. I can just push a button, and they'll bring me food."

"Yeah, but you may have to get cleared from the Doctor. I'll see if I can find him in the hallway. I'll be right back."

Before Joan could suggest otherwise, Gideon was out the door.

What in the 'verse is my problem? Don't focus on the future so much. Just enjoy the time you have together...

While Gideon strode past a group of nurses working on their individual mobile computer terminals, one in particular paid close attention to his face. She leaned forward to watch as he walked away, then pulled out her communicator.

Saul Corbo sat at a small metal table in his lavished hideout. His personal pistol had been disassembled and its parts neatly organized as he cleaned each one individually. He held up the heavy barrel and finished cleaning it with a pad.

"Boss!" Antonio shouted.

"I'm in here!" Saul loudly answered back.

His right-hand man rushed into the room excitedly. "We found him."

"Spectre? Where is he?"

"He was spotted at the Avalon Regional Medical Center," Antonio said while he strode over to the table. "I was told that his wife is going to be there for like a week or something."

"Dammit. Well, I want a team waiting there around the clock to notify me if he leaves," Saul growled.

Antonio scratched his head. "But boss, I thought you wanted to be the one to kill him?"

The criminal leader set down the piece of his gun and looked up at his thug. "Oh, I am going to be the one. But I'm not going to sit my happy self down there for rotation after rotation. If he leaves, they can tail him."

"Gotcha."

Saul leaned his head to either side, and his neck made a loud popping sound both times. "We've waited for cycles to find this bastard. A little bit longer ain't gonna kill us."

"But it will kill him," Antonio said jokingly

Saul allowed himself to chuckle as he got back to work, assembling his firearm. His henchman left to make a call.

"It won't be long now, Spectre. You're going to get what you've been owed for a long time," Corbo said quietly to himself.

Chapter 6

Cycle: 412 Month: 9 Rotation: 13
Corre Republic Space
Prefecture: Expansive
Planet: Benedictus
Location: Avalon Regional Medical Center

Joan was fast asleep in her hospital bed while Gideon watched her from across the room. He had elected to remain by her side the entire time that she stayed at the medical center. Thankfully, the staff had no problem with his presence in the room.

Unlike hospitals in Turon, this one had actual sofas for patients' family members to sleep on. It wasn't home by any stretch, but it was certainly better than a hard chair.

With each treatment, it seemed as though Joan was getting stronger and healthier. Her appetite had returned with a vengeance, and she was able to now walk on her own more like she used to.

A knock at the door disturbed Joan's slumber.

"Come in," Gideon said, standing up.

Throughout any given rotation, various nurses and other staff would introduce themselves whenever their shift began. This didn't include the multiple visits from Doctor Theera or the team that would transport Joan from her room to the treatment area of the hospital.

Dr. Theera smiled widely when he saw Joan's groggy face. "Good Morning, Mrs. Adama. I hope I did not wake you."

She sat up straighter in her reclined bed. "No, no, it's fine."

"Well, I have good news," Theera said as he held up a tablet. "You are going to be cleared to leave today."

"That's great news," the husband said excitedly.

While he had no desire to be away from his wife, he wasn't exactly enjoying his time in the hospital either. By now, the couch had worn out its allure, and his own weariness was catching up to him.

"Yep. I just wanted to stop in and let you know. Your discharge orders should be in, in about an hour. Until then, just relax."

Joan gave her physician a kind smile. "Thank you for everything you've done. I don't want to even think of what would've happened without you."

"Well, thankfully you got to us in time. Now, remember, you are going to need to schedule a visit in the next couple of weeks."

"Does she need to see you specifically, or can she see our family doctor back home?" Gideon asked.

"Oh, that's right. You are from the Commonwealth. Well, I suppose it won't be a problem for them to see you. I'll check your records for how to contact them and then send some information over to your primary physician, so they know what to look for," Doctor Theera said plainly.

Joan burped quietly when she sat up further. "Oh, excuse me. What happens if I get worse again?"

"You should expect a flair up to return basically every five cycles. When that happens, you would need to again find a physician in the Republic that can give you the treatment. If you can get it quickly enough, you shouldn't even have to be hospitalized. Who knows, maybe by then the Commonwealth will have something of their own to treat you with."

"Thanks again, Doc," the husband said gratefully.

"It was my pleasure," Theera said with a nod. "I'll get the discharge orders in. Since you're in town anyway, you should go see some of the sights here before you return to Turon."

Joan grinned, excited to be leaving the hospital in better condition than she entered it. "Yeah, maybe we will. That sounds nice."

After the physician left the two behind, Joan picked up her communicator and typed on it furiously.

"What are you doing?" Gideon asked.

"I'm sending the kids a message, so they know we will be leaving here soon."

The husband rubbed the back of his head. "To be honest, I'm looking forward to getting back home."

Joan smiled cheerfully. "Yeah, me too!"

Back at Saul's personal hideout, Antonio, Bruce, and another one of his men were playing a card game. The thug leader grinned devilishly when he saw his hand. He laid the cards out methodically as to draw as much attention to them as possible.

"Boom!"

The others tossed their cards down in defeat, and Saul laughed heartily. He reached across the table and scooped up the tokens.

"Sorry, boys, better luck next time."

Antonio's communicator sat beside him next to his ale. The screen lit up, and it vibrated. He leaned over to read the text message, and his eyes got wide.

"Boss, I guess Spectre's wife is getting discharged. They'll be leaving real soon."

Saul smirked. "It just gets better and better. Let's roll. This fraggin' bastard is gonna get what's coming to him."

The wait to leave the hospital zipped right on by for the couple. They walked out of the same sliding doors they had come in through a week ago with a skip in their step. Each felt like they had been given a second chance.

"There's a place I know up the street that has awesome food," Joan suggested, holding her husband's hand tightly.

He adjusted the duffle bag's strap on his shoulder and looked at her cheerfully, but still a bit hesitant. "I don't know, Joan. I think maybe we need to go and get a room or something before our flight out tomorrow. Lay low."

While her eyes remained happy, his wife puffed out her lower lip and sulked. "Come on, my love. How often do we get to eat at Ziko's?"

"Oh, you wanted to go there? Well, how could I turn down Ziko's?"

Joan thrust up her free hand in a fist. "Yes!"

One of the women walking by the pair on the sidewalk turned and looked at her inquisitively. The wife just giggled at her own silliness.

While his life with his family had been great, it had been quite a while since Gideon had felt this relieved. Leaving his life of hired death and brutality behind had been one of the best decisions of his life. Doing it for Joan was another one.

Across the street in a parking lot sat Saul and his crew. They watched the pair continue their way Southward from inside their dark vehicle.

"Is that them?" Bruce asked curiously.

"Yeah. That's him, alright. It's crazy that the frickin' guy still looks the same as when I was a kid," Saul said in amazement. "Here he is. Without his famous armor to boot."

He reached into his jacket and unholstered his pistol. A loud metallic *shink* rang out as he wracked the weapon and slid it back into his holster.

"You don't know this guy, Skinny," Saul said to the youngest member of his crew in the backseat. "This guy used to be something of a legend."

"Used to be," the kid said bluntly.

The thug leader recalled several stories his father used to tell him about the renowned bounty hunter, but none of that mattered now. Today he was going to get his own version of street justice.

Saul took a deep breath and nodded, trying to pump himself up for what was next. "Let's get this bastard."

Bruce put the vehicle in reverse, and the dark sedan followed after the ex-bounty hunter.

Joan and Gideon waited patiently for the traffic lights to change along with the other pedestrians. Avalon was a bustling city at this time of rotation, as many of the office employees were going on their lunch break. The vehicles came to a stop, and the signal on the opposite side of the road changed to confirm they could cross safely.

Another group of pedestrians walked across the stonecrete road as the Adama's group did the same. Bruce stopped behind a silver semi while Saul stuck his head out the passenger side window to watch. He was not about to let his brother's murderer walk away scot-free. Not when he was this close to avenging him.

The light changed, and the large truck began to pull through the intersection.

"Follow him. Follow him!" Saul said, nervously.

Their car started to pull forward when the leader got an idea.

"There's an alley just up ahead. Pull down there, and we can lure them in."

Bruce drove past the unsuspecting targets as they excitedly drew near to their destination. The thugs' hovercar narrowly missed a businessman. He dodged to the side, barely avoiding being run over.

"Hey, watch it!" the guy shouted before continuing back on his way.

The car drove for a few seconds then came to a stop. Each of the four men got out and shut their doors.

"Alright, Antonio, you need to pretend you're mugging Bruce," Saul said pointedly.

The crew's driver looked insulted. "Why is he mugging me?" Bruce whined.

"Shut up, would ya? We're running out of time. Skinny, you watch for when they're close. You need to hop out and ask them for help for your friend. We are gonna ambush them and kill 'em quickly. We might only get one shot at this. No screwups!"

"Sure thing, boss," the youngest member of their team said.

He was barely even twenty, but he was desperate to show his value to the gang. His nickname had been given to him for obvious reasons, but it didn't faze him.

Saul stepped around the corner at the back to conceal himself. The ex-bounty hunter may not know his crew, but he would likely recognize the younger Corbo.

Joan took a deep breath and smiled widely. The city may not smell wonderful, but she was overjoyed to have her life back. So many scary thoughts had bombarded her constantly on the trip to Benedictus, but now everything was different. It was like experiencing the 'verse for the first time.

Skinny finally spotted the approaching Adama's and turned back to the other two men.

"Yo, they're almost here!"

Bruce faced his old friend. "Now look, Tony, don't hit me. I wouldn't want to have to beat you up after this is all done."

"Don't worry, I won't hit your face," Antonio joked back.

They both waited anxiously for Skinny's signal. The young thug waved his left arm to Antonio, and he began fake punching the driver.

Skinny jumped out as Joan and her husband were just reaching the opening to the alley.

"Help! Help! Please, help my friend!" the young man screamed at Gideon.

"Get away from me!" the husband shouted, not interested in the situation.

Joan peered down the alley and saw the other two men fighting. One appeared to be losing the brawl, and she looked to her husband.

"You gotta help him," she implored.

Gideon reluctantly stared at his wife. "Fine."

"Oh, thank you!" the gaunt man said enthusiastically.

He stepped aside, giving the ex-bounty hunter plenty of room to enter the trap.

"Hey, what's going on here?!" Gideon shouted as he approached the other two men.

Skinny stepped behind the woman and smirked.

Antonio turned to face the newcomer and pulled out a knife handle. Its blade flipped out, and he gripped the weapon tightly. Bruce pushed himself off of the car he had been pressed against and slid a set of silver-colored stun knuckles over his hands.

Frag! It's a trap... I have to get Joan out of here!

He remained in place as the two thugs drew closer.

Bruce grinned while Antonio got very serious. The ex-bounty hunter slid his duffle bag from his shoulder and let it hang down from his right hand. He needed to check on his wife, but he knew it was unwise to look away from the two-armed thugs being so close to him.

The stun knuckles crackled loudly as they powered up. Antonio dashed forward to jab at Gideon, but he swung the duffle bag so hard that it launched the other man back hard into the wall. Undeterred by his buddy's failure, Bruce moved up and swung with his right hand. There was a whirring sound as the ex-bounty hunter ducked under the attack. Bruce swung with his left and punched the wall behind his target. The stun knuckle discharged electricity from the attack, and sparks shot out.

Gideon used his left elbow to strike his attacker in the head. He followed that with his right knee, knocking the wind out of the driver.

Joan shouted as Skinny forced her down into the alley by grabbing a handful of her hair. The sound of his wife in pain distracted the husband long enough for Antonio to get back in the tussle. He sliced the air with his knife. Gideon barely stepped back in time to avoid the strike. He blocked a follow-up jab with his left forearm to the thug's surprise. Antonio flew backward from a kick to the chest, smashing into the rear of their car.

With his two assailants down momentarily, Gideon turned to face Skinny when a shot rang out. He staggered backward and gripped his right side. His hand was covered in blood.

"Look at you, Spectre," a voice mocked him from out of sight.

The ex-bounty hunter leaned up against the wall to look at the shooter from behind him. He recognized the other man's face right away.

Saul Corbo... this is bad...

Saul held a pistol in his left hand while he grinned cruelly. "I've done it. I've actually shot the ghost that killed my brother."

Joan screamed again when Skinny shoved her closer. "Aaaaah!"

"Let... let her go," Gideon pleaded.

"You are in no condition to be making demands," the thug leader hissed.

He moved wide out of range of the injured man but got more in line with him straight on. "Fifteen cycles ago, you killed my brother in cold blood."

Gideon eyeballed Bruce and Antonio getting in place on either side of their boss.

Can I get to my bag fast enough to get the amulet?

"I did what I had to so that I could leave this life behind."

Saul covered his mouth mockingly. "Oh, was it for love? Was it for this tramp?! Is she the reason you killed my brother?"

"Wait!" the husband shouted as Saul raised his weapon toward the woman.

"Don't be mad at her. She had nothing to do with it. You're angry at me."

"You're right, I am."

The thug leader nudged his head toward the wounded man, and the other two moved in. Gideon had made himself appear like he was weakened, but he was simply luring them into feeling safe. He boosted forward and struck Bruce so strongly with his left fist that he dropped, hard. Antonio shouted something angrily as he attempted to stab the ex-bounty hunter.

Gideon caught the man's arm and broke it in a swift move. In one motion, he took the knife, spun on his heel, and he threw the knife as hard as he could. Joan felt the gush of wind when the bladed weapon passed right by her face and impaled Skinny in the eye, killing him instantly.

Antonio screamed in awful agony as he fell to the ground. Watching everything falling apart, Saul raised his pistol and fired at the large man. The shot grazed Gideon's left arm and sent a burst of the wall to his side into the air when the bullet impacted it.

"Noooo!" Joan shouted as she ran forward.

The ex-bounty hunter spun to his left, dodging the next shot. Saul fired again, this time hitting his target in the left thigh. Gideon dropped to one leg as the explosion of pain shot up his side.

Before Saul could finish him off, Joan stepped in front and blocked the next shot with her back. The husband's face was in total shock, watching his wife's own pain on her face. She fell to her knees as her blood began streaming out of her wound.

"Joan. Joan. Talk to me!" Gideon said eagerly.

With bolstered courage, Saul raised himself up. "Do you want to know what it felt like when you took my brother from my family?!" the thug leader snarled.

He frantically shoved the pistol into the back of his pants and yanked out a knife. Gideon's eyes remained locked on Joan's. Saul gripped her shoulder with his one hand as he repeatedly stabbed into her back. Every bit of anger boiled up in the ex-bounty hunter, and he forced himself to stand. Before he could take more than two steps, he was hit near his leg wound with one of Bruce's stun knuckles.

The surge of electricity raced through his leg, and his muscles gave out. He fell forward and caught himself just in time from smashing his face on the alley floor. Joan was eerily silent as Saul screamed one last time and stabbed her. The thug leader let go of the knife, the woman's blood drenched his hand and clothes.

With so many injuries, Joan slumped over onto her side.

"No, Joan. Joan! Talk to me," Gideon begged as he forced his arms to pull himself over to her.

Adrenaline and rage coursed through his veins so much so that he couldn't barely feel any pain. The light in Joan's eyes began to grow dim, and blood began to drip from her mouth.

Antonio managed to get himself to his feet. He desperately tried to keep his broken arm still, but every movement made him wince.

"No. No. No, no, no, no..." the husband's own eyes began to swell with tears.

This can't be how she dies... no. This can't be.

"Ha!" Saul shouted as loudly as he could. He jumped up and down in victory. "This is what you deserve, you piece of poosh!"

Gideon's hand trembled as he reached out to brush his wife's face. His heart ached like it never had before. The love of his life died right there in front of him. Their renewed future snuffed out in some dirty part of Avalon.

He clenched his jaw so hard that his teeth hurt. With an inner rage that rivaled a sun, he glared at Saul Corbo so intensely that he stopped cheering. Still, with some elation within him, the thug leader spat on the woman's corpse.

"I'll kill you," Gideon said quietly.

Saul threw his right hand behind his ear. "What was that? I couldn't really hear you."

"I said... I'll kill you. I swear it. I will take your life."

"Yeah, well, I don't think that is about to happen."

There wasn't anything the husband could do as he watched Saul reach back and draw his pistol again. He fired two more times into Gideon's chest. With his body now in shock, the ex-bounty hunter couldn't feel much, but he knew that he was in bad shape. He could taste his own blood in his mouth.

I'm not dying here. Not today…

Sirens wailing down the street were drawing closer.

"Boss, we gotta go!" Bruce said anxiously.

The alley looked like a warzone. Blood and debris were scattered everywhere. Skinny and Joan's bodies were sprawled out where they had fallen. Gideon lay next to his wife, his own blood spilling out.

Saul wanted so badly to continue gloating at the moment, but he wasn't about to get nabbed for murder. The three remaining thugs quickly ran for the car. Bruce had already started the engine when Gideon called out.

"Saaaaaul!"

The sheer anger in the man's voice made the thug leader stop in his stride. He turned back to the bleeding ex-bounty hunter.

"I'll kill you. I'll kill all of you… your whole family. I'll finish what I started!"

Before the thug leader could retort, a patrolman's cruiser pulled up, its lights flashing brightly. Saul got in the car and slammed his door shut as it peeled out.

Gideon watched the vehicle disappear down the alley, but not before he memorized the unique plate on the back of it. He could hear the officers approaching him from behind. Everything was getting dark, and his body was getting numb.

"Oh Joan…" he mumbled as he looked back at his wife's body.

Her lips had already begun to turn a shade of blue.

What am I going to tell the kids?

Using all the strength he could muster, he tenderly caressed her face then slid his hand up to close her eyes. His focus moved to the knife still stuck in Joan's back, and his anger was rekindled.

The first officer carefully stepped up with his gun drawn. He leaned over and saw Gideon moving. "We got a live one!"

Several other officers rushed over to the bleeding man. One of them tapped his earpiece.

"Dispatch, we have three wounded. We're going to need a medical unit."

The ex-bounty hunter stared at his wife's face for several long minutes until the paramedics arrived on the scene. He knew that this would be the last time he ever saw her in person, and he didn't want to let her go.

A pair of paramedics stepped through the holographic patrolman "Do Not Cross" beam with kits in their hands. Another medic brought a hover stretcher into the alley.

"Gods… this place is a mess," the lead paramedic asked the group of officers. "Has anyone ID'ed the victims?"

The officer's Lieutenant stepped forward. "Some of them. The skinny guy and the woman were dead on arrival. We were just about to do the big fella. He is still breathing, but he's in bad shape," he said, pointing over at Gideon. "Looks like a local gang mugged a couple of foreigners."

The tone in the officer's voice didn't bother the paramedics. There wasn't much love for those outside of the Corre Republic anymore. Some worlds and their local cultures were more accepting, but Benedictus was always known for being stringent and elitist. Which was ironic because of how many offworlders would visit to attend one of the renowned medical universities.

"Alright," the commanding medic said as he and his partner got to work.

Knowing his time was at an end, Gideon brought Joan's bloodied hand up to his mouth and gently kissed it.

The female medic set her kit down and squatted down while she began opening it. "Sir, we are going to begin caring for you. Can you hear me?"

Gideon didn't respond. He knew this wasn't going to turn out well for him. But he also knew he needed their help, or he'd finish bleeding out and die like a rodent in the streets.

She removed a portable scanner and held it just above the ex-bounty hunter's right hand. A bright light went up and down, but an error message appeared on her screen.

"Huh."

After repositioning her legs, she then held the scanner over Gideon's face. He squinted his eyes at the light as it moved up and down his face. The same error message came up.

"I don't understand..." the medic muttered as she reset the machine for another scan.

Gideon sluggishly removed the bracelet from his wrist while he allowed his face to be scanned once more.

A profile finally appeared on the medic's screen, and her eyes grew very wide as she read it over. She slowly stood up. "Uh… sir?"

The lead paramedic stopped what he was doing and came over to her. "What's wrong?"

She showed him the screen without saying a word.

Yep… here we go…

With his mouth hanging agape, the lead medic walked over to the patrolman Lieutenant. Gideon couldn't hear what was said, but he knew he was leaving the alley in binders. He slid his piece of jewelry into the inner pocket of his jacket, leaving a streak of blood on his clothes in doing so.

"He's who?! Officers draw your weapons!" the Lieutenant shouted.

All of the nearby patrolmen turned and drew their pistols.

Gideon heard someone stepping up to him. The lead patrolman leaned into his field of view.

"Gideon Adama, you are under arrest for the murder of eleven citizens of the Corre Republic."

The ex-bounty hunter mentally wandered away from the situation. It didn't matter what else was said. His record stated clearly that he was from the Commonwealth. His treatment was already going to be strenuous at best by the authorities. Being implicated in the murder was only going to make things worse. It didn't matter that he actually was born in the Republic, that part of his past had been lost long ago.

All that mattered now was getting his vengeance. Instead of focusing on the officer explain his rights to him, he allowed himself to remember everything he could about the Corbo's and their operation. The next part was to plot exactly how he was going to bring every single one of them down in a hail of gunfire.

Chapter 7

Cycle: 412 Month: 9 Rotation: 13
Corre Republic Space
Prefecture: Expansive
Planet: Benedictus
Location: The Corbo's Estate – Outside of Avalon

Several beautiful assortments of flowers and other expertly managed plants were arrayed around the courtyard. A bronze gate was crafted into an ornamental series of branches. Its double doors met together to create a definitive and distinct, "C" at its center when shut.

The thug's dark gray sedan pulled up to the beginning of the long driveway, and the car was immediately scanned by a hidden sensor. The wide gates swung inward, allowing the vehicle to pass through easily. Cobblestone was used for the majority of the expensive driveway but had white stones to line the path on either side. While it appeared lovely to the eye, it had been installed to give wheeled vehicles a harder time to get over them and into the rest of the yard.

"Hey, Saul, my arm really hurts…" Antonio groaned from the backseat.

"Bruce, call Doc for him, would you?" the group leader asked, annoyed by the whining.

The driver glanced up in the rearview mirror at his friend. "Sure thing."

Saul had given up on wiping the woman's blood off his hands. It had long since dried, and the sight wouldn't be a fright to anyone within the mansion's walls. Frank Corbo had built the Torrents into a dangerous gang. They began with smalltime muggings and robberies, but over time he was able to get into the back pocket of local politicians. Over the next two decades, Frank had built one of the most influential criminal organizations on Benedictus and began expanding to several other Corre Republic worlds.

To Saul's surprise, the death of Frankie Corbo, his older brother, unsettled his father greatly. Despite being fifteen cycles ago, he never fully recovered. The young thug hoped that today things would change.

A house servant dressed in an all-white uniform stood patiently for the sedan to come to a halt. He opened the front door, and Saul stepped out confidently.

"Where is my father?" he asked, eyeballing the balding butler.

"He is upstairs in his study," the other man replied stoically. "Shall I fetch you a change of clothes, sir?"

Saul looked down at his button up shirt and pants. Blood had splattered all over him, but he wanted to be the first to tell his father the good news.

"No, don't worry about it."

The Butler nodded his head. Saul quickly walked up to the front door. Before he had finished reaching it, the bullet-proof door made to look like bronze swung open. Another house servant stood by and happily greeted him.

With laser focus, Saul stormed straight through the large home. His father had a knack for antiques and a simpler time. While the young Corbo had been in plenty of homes that had all of the modern upgrades, there was a certain allure to his father's tastes. While on the surface, the mansion appeared antiquated, Saul knew of many of the hidden weapon locations, scanners, and other tech that Frank had installed.

The sound of his leather shoes echoed off the wide walls and hard floors with every step. He nearly jogged up the winding staircase and crossed the hall in no time at all.

Before barging into his father's personal study, he paused to catch his breath. He had waited so long for this moment, he wanted to be certain he delivered it just right.

His palms began to sweat while he collected his thoughts. He reached out and gripped the metal handle of the door and twisted the knob slowly. The door opened without a sound, and Saul could immediately taste the smell of cigar smoke wafting through the air.

Frank Corbo sat across from the door in his imported high-backed chair. He wore reading glasses only when he was alone in his study. It was one subtle sign that Saul had never gotten used to. The younger man saw it as a symbol of his father's age beginning to catch up with him, but Frank's mind was as sharp as ever.

"What happened?" the father asked when he saw his son covered in blood.

Saul nearly forgot all about it and again looked back down at himself. "Oh, this? It's not mine."

Frank's nose scrunched. "Then why in the void are you trapesing about my home in such a way?"

"I wanted you to hear it from me, Pa."

"Hear what?"

Saul was so confident he had his father's full attention now. He stretched out his arms, and his excitement spilled out.

"I did it!"

The father gently lowered the old philosophical paperback book he was holding and placed it on the stand beside his chair. "Enough with the games. Speak plainly, dammit."

"I killed the bounty hunter," Saul said with glee.

"Which one?"

"Spectre."

Frank's head tilted to the side as he tried to process what he just heard. "Ho… how? When?"

A wide smile spread over Saul's face. He lowered his arms so quickly that they clapped against his legs.

"He arrived on-world a few rotations ago. I wanted to surprise you."

"You mean to tell me that, that damned bastard stepped foot on my world, and you withheld that little bit of information?" Frank asked with a growl.

Saul's joy subsided somewhat at his father's tone. "I... I wanted to surprise you."

"What else have you been hiding from me?" Frank demanded as he stood to his feet.

While not quite as tall as his son, Saul couldn't help but feel a twinge of fear run through him. On more than one occasion, he had received a beating from his father when he was young. He would never admit it, but a piece of him deep down was terrified of Frank.

"No... nothing."

"Why was he on Benedictus?"

"It seems he came here with his wife to get her treatment. She was real sick. We jumped them after they left the hospital." Saul again mustered up a broad grin.

Frank brought his hand up to his chin while he thought. "A wife, you say. I couldn't believe someone like him could find a woman. Wait, where is she right now?"

"Dead. I made him watch as I stabbed his whore over and over," the son gloated.

The idea of a woman being brutally murdered by his son did not bother the crime boss in the least. But his mind was still not at ease.

"Is that her blood then?"

"Yeah. All of it."

Frank pursed his lips, and his eyebrow raised. "So, you're sure that Spectre is dead?"

Saul's eyes bulged for a split second. He suddenly became very quiet. The father caught the change in attitude, and he closed his eyes.

Frank lowered his voice to a rumble. "Son, I need you to tell me that you know beyond a shadow of a doubt that the bounty hunter is worm food. That he is most certainly one-hundred percent dead."

"I shot him multiple times..." Saul began to explain.

The father's posture obviously stiffened. His son took notice and stopped speaking. There had been plenty of times he had seen his father get like this right before he snapped. Saul's mind raced, trying to figure out how he could spin the situation to make his parent happier with him.

"Saul, I need to hear you tell me explicitly that Spectre is dead," Frank said before he began to cross the room slowly.

Saul averted his eyes as he continued. "Like I said, I shot him..."

"But. Is. He. Dead?!" the father screamed incredibly loudly, his face becoming bright red in rage.

"I uh... he..."

"You mean to tell me that you set up an ambush for the most dangerous bounty hunter that may have ever lived. And not only have you butchered his wife right in front of him, but you utterly failed to kill him?"

The young Corbo shifted uncomfortably in place. His right shoulder rolled while his mind replayed the events in his head.

Frank carefully reached up and touched the side of his son's face. Saul flinched but forced himself to relax. His father's approval meant so much to him, and now it was all falling apart.

"Son… what have you done?" the criminal leader said quietly.

"I wanted to avenge Frankie, Pa," the son said softly. "The authorities showed up, and I didn't want to get nabbed for murder."

"It would have been far better for you to have finished the job. I could have sprung you from jail, son," Frank said as he turned away and wiped his face.

At that moment, Saul felt like a child again. He felt overwhelmed by his failure in the eyes of his father, and he knew he had made a tremendous mistake by leaving Gideon alive. The bounty hunter's bitter roar played again in his memory.

The crime boss swung back around and stared deeply into his only child's eyes. "He will come for you," he said, lowering his voice further. "He isn't like normal men. He's more like… a ghost. In all my cycles, I've never once seen a man like him. I… I don't know if I can save you."

Saul saw real pain in his father's own eyes, maybe for the first time in his entire life. The enormous weight of the situation set itself upon his shoulders, and he wasn't sure of what to do.

"I… I left him bleeding to death. There's no way he could've survived. No way."

Frank's rage again returned from his son's stupidity. He lowered his hand, then backhanded him as hard as he could. Saul spun to the floor and looked up at his father in raw confusion.

"You have made some stupid decisions in your life, but this one takes the top of the list," the father spat angrily. He shook his head and walked away.

In desperation, Saul quickly stood back up. "Pa, if you really think he is alive, then I will finish the job."

Frank spun back around and glared at his only child.

"Let me do it…"

"Never!" the crime boss barked. "You can't handle him. He's too much for you."

"He's just a man, father."

"Just a man?" Frank asked, mockingly. 'You have no idea who he is."

Saul shook his head in disbelief.

"What hope do you have against a trained killer like him?"

The son puffed his chest out. "I have my own crew, you know. My own connections. Let me do this for you, father. I can kill this beast."

Frank shook his head, adamantly. "No, son. You are going to go into hiding until I can figure out what to do. If we are to have any chance of killing him, then I will have to call in a lot of favors."

"I don't think he has his armor," Saul said excitedly.

"But do you know that for certain?"

Saul shook his head awkwardly but then got an idea. "Even if it is here on Benedictus with him, he's gotta be locked up in some hospital or something. We can get him, pa."

Frank pursed his lips while he formed a plan.

"Okay. I need to make some calls..." Frank's voice trailed off as a plan came together in his head. Then he turned his attention back to his son.

Saul stood there for a moment in the awkward silence. His failure gnawed at him, and now he desperately regretted wasting so much time with the bounty hunter and his wife. The occasion was just too delicious to not gloat. However, now that one split second decision could result in some serious trouble.

"Go on, get out of here," the crime boss growled before he reached into his suit jacket and pulled out his communicator. He pressed a button and held it up to his ear. After a few moments, the recipient picked up.

Saul shuffled out of the room, feeling entirely deflated. His big surprise was now a massive mistake.

"Hey, it's me. I need you to handle a problem," the crime boss said as his eyes tracked his bewildered son leaving the room. "I need you to find someone for me. And you're gonna need your badge."

Chapter 8

Cycle: 412 Month: 9 Rotation: 13
Corre Republic Space
Prefecture: Expansive
Planet: Benedictus
Location: Patrolmen Central Station - Avalon

With his eyes shut, the ex-bounty hunter listened to the officer's finish securing his battered body to the medical bed. Once they were satisfied with his condition, the patrolmen exited the room. Gideon Adama listened carefully as the sound of the boots trailed off, and the door slid closed. He opened his eyes to see that he had been placed in some sort of dull gray medical room. A health monitor stood beside his bed and monitored his condition, while other equipment remained dormant beyond that. He tugged on the restraints around his wrists and ankles.

His body ached, but he was now in stable condition. There were a few minutes where he wasn't sure what would happen, but the medical staff at the precinct seemed to be very experienced with gunshot wounds.

Lucky me...

Once the officers realized that Gideon was a wanted man, protocol demanded that he be apprehended. Not all worlds in the Corre Republic had a medical wing within a patrolman station. Still, Benedictus just so happened to be one of them.

Another benefit of being on the world best known throughout the nation as being an experimental medical research location.

With nothing but the occasional noise from the monitor beside his hospital bed, Gideon's mind wandered to a dark place. His heart ached heavily, but he forced himself to focus on the anger instead of the pain. He knew that his wife would die eventually, but he wanted more time before that moment arrived.

A knock at the door startled him from slipping into further madness.

"Hello, Mr. Adama," the female officer said kindly.

She was dressed in a more professional looking uniform compared to the other patrolmen. However, she still appeared to fit with their overall style. Her pantsuit covered her body, but still had that feminine feel to it.

"I am Special Lieutenant Daykers. I need to ask you some questions."

Gideon's eyes followed the officer as she pulled out a chair nearby and turned it around backward. She sat down in the chair, facing him directly.

The ex-bounty hunter looked away and stared at the wall straight ahead of his bed.

"Look, I went down to the crime scene. I'm sorry about your wife, but I need you to fill me in with some details about what happened so that I can do my job and locate the murderer."

Gideon licked his lips but continued to remain silent. His mouth was dry but still had a twinge of the taste of blood in it.

Daykers sighed. She shook her head and decided to change tactics. "Do you have any reason to believe that this was an attempt on your life?"

"Isn't that obvious?" the prisoner growled.

"He speaks!" the Special Lieutenant joked to the otherwise empty room. She held up a small device in her left hand. "I have your file pulled up right here. Well, the one that you probably didn't want us to find. Looks like you went through some trouble to have some of your previous history erased in the B.C.I.'s database."

Gideon inhaled through his nose but kept his gaze fixed on the wall. He hated dealing with patrolmen. They acted like they knew what was going on, on the streets, but they had no real idea of what was happening in the shadows. In his previous line of work, the ex-bounty hunter had witnessed things that would make even his skin crawl.

"You have quite the list here of murders you are linked to. None of them quite concrete, but you're a suspect, nonetheless. Charges for assault, grand theft auto... the list goes on and on."

Daykers paused for a dramatic effect. "Either way, what happened to Mrs. Adama was not right. I want to find out who tried to have you killed. Maybe I can make her death mean something."

Gideon's eyes glanced over to the officer's. He stared at her for several heartbeats before he started to open his mouth. However, before he could even get a word out, another knock came from the door.

The Special Lieutenant twisted around in her chair to see two men dressed in all black armor. They each wore leather belt capes and had a certain air about them that they meant business. Both had short cropped hair and were in peak physical condition.

"Special Lieutenant, I am Inquisitor Shawl," the first man said.

He presented a device that holographically projected his badge.

"Woah now, this is my prisoner," Daykers said defensively.

Shawl's face stiffened. "And now he is the Bureau's."

"This is poosh, you know that? My guys brought him in, and now you want to swoop in and swipe him out from under us?"

Gideon watched the conversation intently, but something felt off.

There's no way that inquisitors would be assigned to me this quickly. Something's wrong...

Daykers glared at the lead lawman angrily but knew there was nothing that she could do. Inquisitors were the people the government sent in when an issue got beyond the local patrolmen's control. They had the authority to be judge, jury, and executioner when in the field. There were many stories of the men and women in the order, but many of them were not good. Maintaining law and order sometimes was a messy business.

Gideon had run into his fair share of inquisitors in his past. They didn't intimidate him, but he fully realized the situation and the enormity that someone important noticed him.

Maybe my file didn't get as wiped as I was told. What a waste of money...

With a great deal of reluctance, Daykers lowered her head then looked over at the prisoner. She shrugged her shoulders.

"Fine. He's your problem now."

The patrolwoman left the room in a hurry. Both inquisitors looked at one another before turning their attention to Gideon.

"Hello, Mr. Adama. As I said, I am Inquisitor Shawl," the man said, sticking a thumb at his chest. "My associate over there is Inquisitor Carno."

The other lawman glared at the ex-bounty hunter.

"We have been assigned to your case. However, I do need to ask you some questions."

Shawl stared at Gideon while he waited for a response that never came.

"Okay..." the Inquisitor took a deep breath, then tucked his hands behind his back. "Do you know who it was that attacked you and your wife?"

The prisoner clenched his jaw tightly but refrained from speaking. Shawl again turned to his companion. Carno tilted his head in a manner that he too didn't know what was going on.

"Let's just go ahead and cut the tough guy act, Gideon," Shawl said harshly.

"Explain to me how not only one but two inquisitors would be assigned to my case in just a few hours? I'm thinking that you're both dirty lawmen then? Am I right?" Gideon asked sarcastically.

"Hey now, let's not throw around labels, alright? I prefer the term that I'm... opportunistic."

The ex-bounty hunter smirked. "Is that what they call traitors nowadays?"

"Traitor?" Carno took a step forward but Shawl held out his hand.

The other inquisitor came to a stop with his hand on the grip of his pistol.

"I would say that it is a mighty big statement coming from some lowlife bounty hunter," Shawl said with a hiss. "Now, let's get down to business."

Gideon watched Carno relax somewhat while Shawl pulled a silver-colored communicator out of his pocket. The Inquisitor pressed a few buttons then set the device down on the small table beside the bed. He propped it up so that the prisoner could easily see the screen from his shackled position.

An older man with gray hair and deep wrinkles displayed on the screen. He smiled deviously at the sight of the bound man, but his smile was more like a predator just before striking some small creature.

"It's been a long-time, bounty hunter."

"Frank Corbo," Gideon said with a growl.

"I wish that our paths had not crossed ever again. While I was furious that you killed my oldest son, I was willing to look the other way if you stayed away from the Republic. Yet... here you are."

The ex-bounty hunter's blood began to boil. He wanted nothing else than to reach through the screen and strangle the father of the man who took his wife from him.

Stay cool. Getting angry won't get me anywhere... I need to make him squirm. Throw him off.

Frank sighed. "Even still, I am sorry for what happened to your wife."

Gideon tried to hold back his rage, but his face betrayed his internal thoughts.

"No doubt you are thirsty for blood after what has occurred. However, I wanted to reach out to you to offer a truce."

"A truce?" Gideon snarled quietly.

"Yes. I lost a son... you have lost your wife. This is justice from the gods."

Both inquisitors could sense the raw fury emitting from the prisoner. Carno was ready to react at the slightest sign of a problem while Shawl remained at ease.

"There hasn't been justice. Not yet. But there will be. And your "gods" won't be able to save you from me!"

The crime boss' eyebrow arched. "I feel that there has been enough bloodshed, Spectre. Take this as a professional courtesy and walk away." Frank made sure to really emphasize his last point.

Gideon, however, did not waver. "Give me your son, and I will leave you and your people alone."

"You would ask me to just hand over the last of my sons to you? What is a father's goal but to hand down his empire to his offspring? You have already stripped me of one child, I will not allow you to butcher my lineage," Frank said definitively.

"Then, you and all of your people will die."

Frank adjusted himself in his chair and smacked his lips while he thought. "You know, I wanted to handle this like professionals. But you are acting more like an animal."

Shawl carefully drew a syringe from his pocket and held it up so that the prisoner could clearly see it. A faint orange liquid sat within.

Undeterred by the sight of the probable poison and his predicament, Gideon breathed heavily in anger. He glared back down at the communicator.

"Know this, Frank, I am coming for you. Nothing will stop me. All of you will die! I will wipe your bloodline from existence!"

Carno shook his head at the man's helpless situation. He had seen plenty of things in his time as a lawman and plenty of violent men that acted out when they were trapped in a corner. Gideon was no different in his eyes.

Shawl, too, was unphased by the ex-bounty hunter's ridiculous claims. He yanked off the cap, revealing the needle.

Gideon glanced at the syringe and appeared to breathe heavier.

"It's a pity. Know that I really was going to let you leave if you took my offer. Goodbye, Spectre," Frank said just before the connection was cut.

The lead inquisitor took several steps forward and brought the needle down toward the prisoner's arm. Carno glanced behind him at the door to see that no one was watching them.

"Have a nice nap, big guy."

Gideon waited until the Inquisitor was very close to his left forearm. He smirked devilishly and yanked his both of his arms free with such strength that the braided restraints snapped. Before Carno could react fast enough, the prisoner gripped Shawl's wrist and forcibly twisted the needle around. The ex-bounty hunter used his right hand to push the syringe into the lead inquisitor's neck, also slamming down on the plastic plunger at the same time. Almost immediately, Shawl's mouth began to foam up with orange and white bubbles.

"Poosh!" Carno exclaimed as he reached for his pistol.

He drew it out, but Gideon pulled the other Inquisitor in front of him, blocking the multiple shots that were fired in haste. The ex-bounty hunter yanked Shawl's pistol free and leaned around his human shield to fire his own shot. With expert precision Gideon shot straight into Carno's face. As the younger inquisitor slid to the floor, Shawl continued choking on the foam.

Gideon looked him in the face. "You were dead the moment you walked into this room."

With incredible strength, the prisoner shoved the Inquisitor over. He tumbled to the ground and died from the poison within seconds.

One of the patrolmen standing guard outside the room overheard the gunshots and ran down to hit the alarm while the other officer drew his own weapon. He peaked in the window to see Gideon finish ripping the restraints from his body.

"What the…"

The sight was surely incredible as no normal human would be capable of such a display of strength. Seeing Shawl sprawled out on the floor brought the patrolman back to his senses. He swung his hand over the panel, and the bulletproof door slid open.

Gideon winced in pain from his injuries. Medical care in the Republic was advanced, but his previous bullet wounds would need some time to fully heal.

Not wanting to kill the patrolman, the ex-bounty hunter fired twice into the officer's chest. Both shots hitting the man's vest he wore under his uniform. The concussive force from the deceased Inquisitor's firearm was still enough to disorient the officer, and he fell into the growing pool of blood from Carno.

Wasting no time, Gideon quickly yanked out the connections for monitoring his vitals from his body. His window for escape would be closing very soon.

Okay, quick plan. Find the evidence room. Get my amulet and my bracelet.

Gideon leaped down from his bed and searched Carno for a spare mag. He found it on his duty belt and held it tightly in his left hand.

An inquisitor's standard-issue pistol fired ballistic rounds but could alternate between varying ammo types, and had an extended ammunition carrying capacity. This allowed agents to engage in more prolonged firefights and come out on top.

A loud alarm blared from the building's speaker system throughout the structure. Officers from all over would be rushing to Gideon's room. He needed to get distance between himself and the bloody mess around him.

The officer who had been shot was trying to raise his weapon to shoot the escaping prisoner. Gideon swung hard and batted the man across the head with the pistol. He passed out from the blow, a trail of blood streaked down his face.

Trying to be careful, the ex-bounty hunter poked his head out to the left to check if it was clear. A burst of the door frame broke off from a missed bullet. He quickly pulled his head back inside then dove out the door, aiming his gun in the opposite direction.

The other guard was returning after sounding the alarm. He fired four times before Gideon struck him in the left thigh and right arm with his own shots. Screaming in pain, the officer rolled to the floor in fear of his life.

"Freeze!" a voice shouted from behind the prisoner.

In a flash, the ex-bounty hunter spun on his heel into a squat and fired a shot into each of the three officers charging at him.

Medical staff in the area took off running in all directions. Their terrified shouts could not hide the sound of more boots coming down the hallway, echoing off the walls. Gideon bolted down the opposite direction, trying to buy himself an opportunity to find the evidence room.

Another officer bumped into him and was shocked to see the large man in what remained of his restraints and medical gown. Before he could even react adequately, Gideon pistol-whipped him into the wall, knocking him unconscious.

Special Agent Daykers had heard the alarm sound and jumped to her feet. The order came out over the radio that the prisoner escaped, and she cursed as she ran off. The dull booming sound of gunshots could be heard through the walls.

"Damn those inquisitors!" she snarled.

Two more officers rounded the corner in time to find Gideon barreling straight at them. The ex-bounty hunter fired twice into the one on the right, and she slammed into the wall behind her. In the heat of the moment, the other patrolman hesitated just long enough for the ex-bounty hunter to switch targets and fire three more rounds into the other standing officer.

Daykers saw the prisoner standing over two downed officers.

"Gideon!"

The fugitive turned back to see the Special Agent but disappeared to the left of the end of the hall.

"Frag!" Daykers growled.

The prisoner continued running until he finally saw what he was looking for.

There it is!

He ran up to the evidence room but was surprised to find it had a scanner outside of the door. Gideon breathed angrily before he got an idea. He stepped aside, concealing himself from the direction the Special Agent would be coming from.

Daykers was upset with herself for losing her prisoner, especially if it meant that something also had happened to the inquisitors. She charged down the hall but felt like something was wrong. Before she could fully figure out that she had stepped right into Gideon's trap, he was all over her.

He first chucked the spare mag so hard that it whacked her square between the eyes. She grabbed her face in pain, and he struck her with the pistol across her forehead.

Gideon reached out and caught the knocked-out woman in his arms. He dragged her over to the scanner and held her head up to the terminal. A bright red light emitted and moved over her face. The door unlocked, and he pulled the Special Agent inside with him.

He quickly lowered her to the floor, and the door shut behind him. Rows of shelves were lined up as far as he could see. The ex-bounty hunter sighed then began jogging up aisle after aisle until he found an area that stored the items by those held at the precinct. His duffle bag was left open with some of the clothes left carelessly tossed aside.

Oh, please still be here…

Gideon set the pistol down on the table and began rustling through the remaining contents of the bag. Just before he was about to panic, he found the small box. He let out a sigh of relief and lifted it up to see.

Daykers let out a low moan as she began to regain consciousness. Her head throbbed intensely, and she managed to pull her left hand up to comfort the pain. She heard a noise come from deeper in the room, and the memory of the prisoner rushed back to her.

In a flurry, she got to her feet and looked around for her firearm.

Meanwhile, Gideon also located the clothes he had been wearing when he was taken into custody. He tore open the clear plastic bag and dumped his bloodied clothes onto the table. In a flash, he pulled out his jacket and felt around in his pocket and discovered his bracelet was where he left it.

"Yes!" he exclaimed.

"Dammit!" the female officer whispered.

She leaned around one of the stacks of evidence in time to see Gideon slide the jewelry on his wrist and then open the small container in his hand. He delicately pulled out the necklace and lifted it up to inspect the amulet. The ex-bounty hunter placed the metal chain around his neck, then pressed his left hand to the stone that hung from it. Immediately a swarm of neon blue mist covered his body and formed into a suit of power armor.

Daykers' eyes grew very wide at the sight, and she ducked behind cover. Gideon's helmet pulled up his HUD and automatically began scanning the area. He looked to his right to see the Special Agent hiding around the corner, along with her heart rate and other information displayed on the side of the screen inside the helmet.

A countdown appeared in the upper corner of his HUD, starting at "12:00."

"Do yourself a favor, Daykers, don't come looking for me," he said boldly through his helmet's external speakers.

The officer saw no reason to confront the man. She remained as hidden as she could when the ex-bounty hunter spotted heat signatures of more officers starting to pop up on the other side of the evidence room's door.

Gideon slung his bag over his shoulder then picked up the Inquisitor's pistol. A mist of the same type of particles created a holster on his right hip. He secured the weapon to his thigh then stepped up to the wall to his left. Using the modified burner on his left wrist, the ex-bounty hunter quickly cut a hole in the wall large enough for him to fit through.

The door to the evidence room slid open, followed by a metal cylinder that was tossed inside. Daykers barely had time to shut her eyes and look away when the flash grenade went off, filling the evidence room with a blinding light. The officers rushed inside, wearing thick body armor and guns raised.

"He's trying to escape," the special lieutenant shouted. Despite her eyes being shut, she still saw spots everywhere she looked.

Several of the patrolmen rushed into the room while the Daykers stopped one of the others not wearing armor.

"Lockdown the building. He can't escape. The suspect is wearing power armor."

Gideon stormed down the hallway as the armored officers tactically approached the hole he left behind. One of them spotted him running off and fired her scattergun. The powerful slug slammed into the ex-bounty hunter's armor and thrust his shoulder forward, but it was unable to pierce it. He shrugged off the attack and rounded another corner.

The alarm continued to sound as Gideon fought his way out of the precinct and disappeared into the night. Daykers finally made it back to her prisoner's room to find both inquisitors had been killed. While she was not a fan of the two lawmen, they didn't deserve to die like this.

Knowing she was going to have a stack of paperwork to fill out, she slunk down the hall toward her office, her head still throbbing.

Chapter 9

Cycle: 412 Month: 9 Rotation: 13
Corre Republic Space
Prefecture: Expansive
Planet: None
Location: Drifting in space

A chill coolness was in the air aboard the mysterious sleek vessel that drifted through the vastness of space. The sound of a beautiful melody played throughout the spacecraft, with the lights dimmed low. Only a few sources of illumination shined, mainly from above a workstation at the back of the ship.

The area around the table was in the sense of organized chaos. While it appeared as a mess, the boxes and other objects had a semblance of being stacked a certain way. The only additional glow in the vast space was that from an array of monitors and hologram projectors that displayed content from all over the Corre Republic. Some showed newscasts from individual worlds, while others played clips taken from the stream posted by random citizens.

There was no noise from the moving images, only the gentle music playing through the sound system. The sole occupant of the ship sat in the darkness of the room. His armored finger swayed with the beat of the instruments. With closed eyes beneath his helmet's blackened faceplate, the armored man allowed the rhythm of the music to flow through him. It had been ages since he just sat and enjoyed his favorite composer, who had long since passed away. However, that wasn't to last.

A bright red light flashed from a chrome-colored console off to the right of the multitude of screens. The man was disturbed from his peaceful moment, and he spotted the glow. He took a deep breath, knowing that it was time to get back to his job.

The Keeper of Knowledge stood up and rolled his right shoulder. As his body rose, all of the cables connected to his suit disconnected and retracted automatically into the chair.

Despite his armor, the defender of the Corre Republic was a very tall yet slender man. His suit was a very dark blue with orange lights shining across his armor to add to his ethereal appearance. On either side of his eerie helmet was a jagged bulb. While they seemed out of place to an ordinary passerby, the spheres were used as data storage for the Keeper to access when he was in the field.

Generations ago, the rank of Knowledge, along with six others, was created by Prefect Major Magnus II. After the war with the Synthetics nearly extinguished all of humanity, they were assembled to be the ones to protect the Republic from all threats. Both from within and outside of its borders.

Gone was the man that once became known as Knowledge. Now all that remained was the never-ending job of saving his nation from disaster after disaster.

There wasn't a single other person within the Corre Republic that was as connected to information as Knowledge was. He had constructed unique sifting algorithms that scoured the stream for new information. Various antennas and dishes were installed on the outside of his private *Sparrow* spacecraft to enhance his ability to receive signals no matter where he was within the nation.

Each keeper was set to oversee particular areas of the Republic and her people. Knowledge's role was to monitor and process data and information. That task, while simply written, was one that involved constant modifications and alterations to his database. It was a hard job that would never cease, but he was up to the task. There was no one else he knew that could do it. And he essentially knew of nearly every single citizen through his records and databases, even though they had never met.

Once a week, Knowledge would download a master copy of all data that was collected on every single of the sixty-five Republic planets. It would be compiled, processed, and reduced in size before being sent to him without anyone else being the wiser. The size of the information was beyond the capabilities of all computers within the Republic, except for his own. In his previous line of work, the keeper was a master data processor and scientist. Constructing a series of computers able to handle the monumental task took him time. Still, he was finally able to figure it out.

The more complicated feat was setting up the secret data collection points on all sixty-plus worlds of the Republic without anyone else knowing. Now all he had to do was go through the weekly task of sorting all of the information so that it could be stored appropriately into his helmet. No data was kept on the ship itself. Everything was stored within the experimental infrastructure that ran through his power armor. Using sophisticated algorithms and custom-built software, the keeper was able to tackle the task all in one rotation. Nonetheless, it was disseminating the data that was hard. He learned to heavily rely on his own secret artificial intelligence, named Catherine, to assist him in his duty as a keeper.

He strolled across the room and pressed a key below the strobing light. The glow deactivated, and the screen for the station came to life. A criminal profile, along with the facial scan of the individual displayed brightly against the Keeper's armor. Knowledge stared at the image of the man he had not seen in quite a long time.

Wanting to confirm his system's initial result, his armored fingers danced across the keyboard. He had to be certain who the man was. Sometimes people just looked like someone else due to biology or from reconstructive surgery. The universe was a tricky place sometimes, and there had been occasions when particular persons very closely resembled another individual for a variety of reasons.

A secondary monitor to the left of the screen activated, and a swirling icon spun in place. Within seconds the machine showed confirmation of the Keeper's suspicions.

Internally he felt a mixture of anger and regret, outwardly he remained perfectly still.

"I found you…" he said sternly. "On Benedictus no less."

"Is it just me, or does that look like Gideon?" Catherine asked with her kind sounding female synthetic voice.

Knowledge continued to stare at the image of the bearded profile picture of Gideon Adama for longer than was probably necessary.

"Catherine, I want you to run a confirmation check on his profile from Benedictus and compare it to every image we have of him. I need to be absolutely certain this is him and not someone else."

"Of course."

Catherine got to work, and Knowledge tapped rapidly on the keyboard. He then took several steps to his right to work on another station while the first terminal processed.

Within moments the Keeper was in the internal network for the Avalon patrolman station and had access to any system he wanted. He scoured through sensitive details of multiple operating systems, searched through recently detained suspects, and much more. There was simply too much for him to process at that exact moment, and he needed to keep moving. More than once, he had cursed the limitations of his natural body.

He pulled out a cable built into the right forearm of his armor and connected it to the console. While the station began downloading the information, the Keeper's heads up display showed the files being loaded onto his suit's data network. He raised his left arm, and a hologram appeared. It transformed into a broken-down separation of data based on its purpose. Knowledge thought for a moment, and the suit's neural link sent a command to the display.

Within seconds most of the data was placed in folders and other locations in the bulbous database, leaving only the information on Gideon Adama behind. One particular file caught the Keeper's attention. He disconnected the wire from the console, and it slinked back automatically.

"I can confirm that this is him," the AI said neutrally. "He was apprehended by the local authorities after an incident with some gang violence, but it appears that he has recently escaped custody."

Using his right hand, Knowledge scrolled through the file when the fugitive was apprehended and the report that was submitted. He then pulled up an additional screen and accessed the patrolman station's security footage. He fast forward through feeds of him running through the station firing at the patrolman, and then when he was at the evidence table.

Moving at the same speed, he kept scrolling but realized that Gideon had suddenly vanished from the security video file.

"What the…"

Rotating his right hand backward, the footage slowly reversed until Gideon again reappeared. Carefully twisting his hand clockwise, Knowledge watched the fugitive slide the bracelet on, then he disappeared. The camera feed continued to record, but the man vanished.

"How is that possible?" Catherine asked as she, too, was dumbfounded.

"I have no idea," the keeper muttered under his breath.

He once again replayed the footage and slowly went frame by frame. But he had no explanation of how Gideon could just disappear from the camera's sight.

"Set the coordinates to Benedictus," Knowledge said distractedly.

"Right away," Catherine confirmed before invisibly jumping from his suit and into the ship's internal network.

Knowledge took a moment to read all about Joan Adama's injuries, but he was not bothered by the brutal description. His life as a protector of the Republic brought along with it several lifetimes worth of bloodshed and chaos. He had seen more than his fair share of cruelty. So much so that he wondered at times when he was alone if he was numb to it by now.

Without another word, he headed for the bridge of the ship. His boots clanked against the metal grates with each step. Decorative ribbons that hung from his armor swayed back and forth.

The door to the bridge had been left open, but recognizing its pilot approach, a series of lights automatically activated. He sat in his chair and flipped several switches above him. The engine roared to life and began to rumble further back in the ship, but the gentle vibrations could be felt through his armor.

"Coordinates set. Engines powering up. Kay, should you possibly call in some backup for this? Your last encounter with Gideon didn't go so well," Catherine pointed out through the cockpit's speakers.

He knew there was no point in arguing. Her logic was sound. A cluster of small monitors was built into the dash on Knowledge's right. One screen turned on, and a holographic icon floated above the assembly. The keeper tapped the symbol, and it transformed into a straight line.

"This is Knowledge. I found him. Requesting any available assistance."

As the Keeper spoke, the line moved up and down, displaying his speech volume while simultaneously recording the message. The broadcast was sent out with the high priority transmitter. While he waited for a response, Knowledge rotated his chair to the left to face his HOP drive console.

Generations ago, the invention of HOP technology allowed the only known sentient race to leave its homeworld, Prime, and spread about the stars. While virtually all artificial intelligence was illegal widely throughout the Corre Republic, it was still necessary for a ship to safely calculate the path through the Nth dimension and arrive at its destination. Knowledge despised all AI with every fiber of his being, except for Catherine. He just couldn't trust them after what happened during humanities struggle for survival against the Synthetics.

Every modern AI was slightly different than its counterparts, but they all obeyed their fleshy masters without question. Knowledge had personally constructed Catherine and was well aware of the destruction unbridled machines could accomplish. As such, he was cautious about which systems his personal AI could interact with. The last thing he would tolerate would be an unchained program running about on his ship, or even worse, through his power armor.

He was in the middle of putting the finishing touches on his trip to Benedictus in the nav computer when a chirping sound came from behind him. Spinning the chair back around, Knowledge was surprised to see the unlikely helmeted face of the Keeper of Life.

Unlike Knowledge, Life had a brightly colored suit of power armor. As if to play into her position's trope, she had chosen to be white with bright blue highlights.

The dark blue Keeper stared for a heartbeat too long, and Life chuckled.

"You didn't think I'd answer?" Life joked.

"Honestly, I wasn't sure who would."

"I'm sure Peace would if he could. However, this isn't the first time you said that you found the Erravi," the other Keeper pointed out with a passive-aggressive tone in her voice.

Knowledge bobbed his head. "True. This time is different, though."

Before Life could counter, another Keeper interrupted the conversation appearing on another one of the screens.

"Death, you are coming along as well?" the white Keeper asked her darker colored counterpart.

"His sudden appearance is too coincidental to ignore," Death said with his deep brooding voice.

It may have seemed odd for anyone outside of their order of why each of the keepers wore their helmets, but it did not bother them at all. The risks they faced were boundless, and it paid to be cautious.

"Do you think Liberty is available to help us?" Life asked Knowledge.

He shook his head in response. "She is investigating some incident out on Calvary. Last I heard, War is also locked down fighting against some scout forces from the Faust Union."

"Does he have the suit?" Death asked in reference to Gideon.

"I believe he does. But I may be onto how he has been able to avoid me for all these cycles," Knowledge said calmly.

"We are more than capable of bringing down one traitor," Life said, puffing her armored chest out.

Knowledge wanted to agree, but the memory of his last encounter flashed through his very filled mind.

"His suit has to be low on power by now, right?" Death asked the others.

Life looked to Knowledge. "Kay?"

"Honestly, I can't say for 100% certainty. Based on my understanding of how our suits work, yes, he should be low. But honestly, I would have thought his amulet would have been at low power mode for over a decade now."

Life quietly scoffed while Death shook his head.

"It makes no sense how a traitor like him could be running around all this time, but Peace is locked away to keep him alive," the black colored keeper growled.

Knowledge saw no point in continuing the back and forth. Time was precious if they were going to track Gideon down.

"I'm transferring coordinates to his last known sighting now. I also have access to a highly classified HOP point for the planet. I'll send that over too."

"Is this a safe HOP point, Kay?" Death asked suspiciously.

"I haven't tested it myself exactly, but I reviewed the math. It all checks out."

Death began to protest, but Life cut him off.

"We can't risk our target getting away again. We do this for Peace. He will finally be able to get out of that damned chamber."

Knowledge said nothing, but the black colored keeper nodded in approval.

Wanting to move the conversation forward, Knowledge jumped back in. "I should arrive before both of you. I'll do some investigating to see if I can locate him."

"See you there," Death said before his screen went dark.

Life, on the other hand, just cut her feed.

She's a bit arrogant for being the keeper of life...

Knowledge turned back to his navigational console to continue his preparations. He transmitted the data the other two would need, and his thoughts began to wander.

Memories of Gideon and the blue Keeper played through his mind. While the two had been at odds together on more than one occasion, at one point, they became close friends. However, duty came before relationships. A keeper could live no other way.

Catherine hadn't wanted to disturb the meeting between the convening keepers, so she had held back her own thoughts. "Oh Kay," she said tenderly. "Are you sure about this? Gideon was your friend. Are you going to be able to kill him if need be?"

Knowledge licked his lips and looked away from the screen, hoping to clear his head.

"He was given a death sentence from Peace, but I'll do what I can to keep him from getting killed. Especially since this is all my fault..." Knowledge said as his voice trailed off.

Chapter 10

Cycle: 412 Month: 9 Rotation: 14
Corre Republic Space
Prefecture: Expansive
Planet: Benedictus
Location: Downtown Avalon

While nightfall still darkened the early morning sky, the ex-bounty hunter had finally rid himself of the patrolman. It had taken him much longer to ditch them then he thought it would have, but at least he finally had a moment to catch his breath.

He had powered his suit down as soon as he was clear of the station so that it could save what little power it had left. It would have been easier to blend in if there were more crowds around, but it was much too early for pedestrians to head for work.

Gideon ducked into an alley while a patrolman cruiser drove by with lights flashing. After checking to see if anyone was following him, he unslung his bag and sat up against the brick wall behind him.

His body ached from head to toe.

"Frick!" Gideon exclaimed.

Using his left hand to prop him up against a wall, he cupped his right side with his other hand. His lungs suddenly fought to inhale.

I'm overdoing it…

The power armor that he wore was unlike almost anything else on any of the colonized worlds. It ad the ability to do some pretty amazing things including beginning to heal the wearer. This, of course, only applied when inside the suit. Other features such as advanced surveillance and information gathering, along with enhanced strength, worked together to help the ex-bounty hunter become a fearsome hunter in his past line of work.

Somehow, after using his suit extensively for many cycles, Gideon discovered that his own body had lasting effects of the suit, including an enhanced level of physical strength and increased endurance. On more than one occasion, he had wished he better understood precisely how his power armor worked.

Unfortunately for Gideon, strolling around a world like Benedictus in full armor would only continue to draw attention to himself. As it was, most of the planet was already probably looking for him.

Okay… focus, Gideon. Don't get caught up in the problems. What's next?

A distracted couple walking the sidewalk passed by the alley entrance. The fugitive half-ducked down, but they did not turn his way.

I haven't been back here for a long time. How do I know where the hideout for the Corbo's is anyway? I need intel before I go charging in…

While he didn't want to agree, deep down, he knew it was the smart choice. A piece of him simply wanted blood for the death of Joan. The throbbing pain in his leg, though, kept him from getting too far ahead of himself.

He forced himself to stand and slowly walked several blocks, trying to be as nonchalant as possible, eventually locating a pharmacy. Since it was closed for the night, he figured he had a good chance of not being spotted. Using his suit, he overrode the business's security system and snuck inside. He grabbed several packages of bandages and other medical items, storing them in his duffle bag. On his way out, he spotted a brand of chips that were only sold on the very planet he was beginning to loathe. Angrily he snatched a bag and limped his way out of the storefront.

Advancements in technology and culture within the Corre Republic made it nearly impossible for citizens to purchase goods without electronic payment. He had brought plenty of cash along with him from the Commonwealth. But the hospital bill took a substantial amount of it. Still, he would probably need that very soon, then would be low on monetary options. Since the visit back to his old home had turned so severely, his bank accounts would undoubtedly be on hold as soon as the Republican authorities linked his visit back to Turon and notified their government.

After thirty minutes of hobbling down the more dangerous side of town, a single bead of water tapped him on the top of his head. He held out his hand and felt another droplet, followed by more.

Oh great…

The fugitive searched around and thankfully spotted an abandoned structure to his left. It was clear that the building was condemned.

I sure hope nobody's inside…

The ex-bounty hunter limped faster to reach the door before the more torrential rain started. Just as he got beneath the overhang, a heavy downpour fell. The front door of the old building had an old-style knob. He jiggled the handle, but the door did not open. Using his enhanced strength, he kicked the door in and stood there for a moment.

Water began to pool around his boots. Seeing no lights coming from within, he decided to enter and take his chances. The sound of the rain pounded on the metal roof of the musty smelling building. It would be much easier to just put his suit back on and sit in the corner of the room, waiting for it to fully heal his injuries. Something in his mind nagged him though that, that would be a bad choice.

The glow from a nearby fast-food restaurant's sign shined through a broken window high up on the right wall. It gave the room some light, giving Gideon enough to do what he needed to. He grunted at the pain that shot up his side as he pressed his back up against one of the walls and slid down slowly. The duffle bag slipped from his shoulder and hit the ground with a *thud*. He leaned his head back and gave himself a minute to just relax. His right hand still cupped his aching side.

I can't bleed to death here… I have to get fixed enough to keep moving. I will kill Saul… I will!

A twinge of guilt entered his mind.

What about the kids, though? Would Joan want this with them waiting for me back home?

Angered at the back and forth in his own mind, Gideon smashed his left fist so hard into the wall that it shook him. A stream of dust gently fell from the ceiling, peppering the ground nearby the man's soar legs.

I can think about that when I am done dealing with Saul and his father.

"I'm gonna kill 'em. Both of them. Both for what they did to me."

A faint shred of shame tugged at him for making the focus of his rage about himself and his loss, and not for the death of Joan specifically.

Mustering the energy to tend to his injuries, Gideon opened his duffle bag and retrieved the medical supplies. Several moments later, he had changed all of the bandages out with fresh ones. The rain continued to pound on the sleeping city, adding to the dread that the fugitive felt within himself.

The man took out the bag of chips begrudgingly and pulled it open. A whiff of deep-fried vegetables puffed into the air. The first chip was incredibly salty, much more than he remembered. His mind wandered to a simpler time. He recalled the first time he ever met Joan and how beautiful he thought she was.

His eyes swelled up with tears as a rush of emotion nearly swallowed him whole. It was the sheer exhaustion that began to overtake him, though. Gideon remained leaned up against the wall as he fell off to sleep.

Chapter 11

Cycle: 412 Month: 9 Rotation: 14
Corre Republic Space
Prefecture: Expansive
Planet: Benedictus
Location: The Corbo's Estate – Outside of Avalon

Frank Corbo sat in his favorite chair within his personal office. His mansion was so large that two other members of his crew had rooms granted to them to use when on-site. Still, the crimelord made a point that his office was exceedingly wealthier in appearance.

It had been hours since he had last heard from the inquisitors, and he was getting increasingly nervous. He had messaged Shawl directly, yet there had been no response. Part of him already knew what must have happened, but he feared to learn the truth. Aggravating a man like Gideon wasn't a treat for him. Animals like that were best left undisturbed.

He held a glass of amber colored alcohol in his left hand, while his right hand played with the rim of the cup. His gaze was fixated on a statue across from him of a serpent and a mythical beast fighting. Saul Corbo leaned up against a wall off to the right. He mindlessly scrolled through an app on his communicator. Meanwhile, Deni Moore, Frank's right-hand man, sipped his own drink in the corner of the room.

A short muted clip of a fat man tripping over a plasti-crate began to play on the son's device. He let out a slight chuckle, which greatly agitated his father.

Frank's lip curled. He set the glass down and shot to his feet. Saul's eyes grew wide with confusion while his father yanked the electronic object from his hand.

The crimelord tossed it angrily through the room. It hit the wall with a loud crack and flipped to the hard tile floor.

"Hey, what was that for?!" Saul protested.

The son received a backhanded slap for his trouble.

Saul's head twisted harshly to the left. He was more in shock than upset at what just happened. Instinctively his right hand comforted his throbbing cheek.

"You are a fool!" Frank spat venomously.

"Pa..." the son started to say meekly.

The crimelord spun on his heel and threw his hands into the air. "By the gods, you are one of the dumbest people to ever exist in this 'verse!"

While the dispute between the Corbo's played out, Deni remained silent. His slicked-back hair along with expensive suit added to his air of confidence. He had been present in an innumerable amount of incidents of the crimelord's rage. This was nothing new for him. He took another sip of the neon green drink and set the glass carefully down on the stand beside his own chair.

Saul's eyes glanced over to the other man, but he quickly noticed he wasn't going to get any backup from Deni.

"Dad, look, he's dead. There's no way that in his condition he could kill two inquisitors. It… it just isn't realistic."

Frank faced his son with a hard glare. "How can you be so fraggin' dense?!" the crimelord tapped the side of his own head in his frustration to stress his point. "You are as stupid as your mother. Always talking but never actually thinking!"

The derogatory mention of his divorced mother gave Saul an ignorant man's courage. He stood up straight and stuck out his chest.

Frank spotted the visible change in his son's demeanor, and he cocked his head to the side. "What's this? Are you standing up to me now?"

"You don't need to insult mom over this, Pa."

Deni smacked his lips quietly then took another sip of his drink. He had worked with the crimelord for a very long time. In his older cycles, he had seen Frank calm down more, but there was one thing he knew that would always infuriate his boss, which was dissonance.

"You fraggin' piece of poosh. You think you're a tough guy now, huh?" Frank growled.

Saul licked his lips and looked away for a moment. "You don't respect me…"

The crimelord didn't hesitate to interrupt his son. "And why should I?! You go about this city carelessly tearing down my decades of work to show off. Now here we are, you have pissed off the

Spectre, and brought vengeance down upon this family."

Saul's eyebrows furled, and he pointed toward his chest. "I have busted my backside for you all my life."

Frank swatted away the comment and started to walk away. "You've done little more than been a pain in my side."

The son looked genuinely hurt by the retort. He sniffed and buried his feelings, hoping his father didn't see the moment of weakness on his face.

"You know what, I hope he is alive."

"Oh, you do, do you?" the crimelord asked as he aggressively came back over to shout at his son. "And what are you gonna do exactly? This is the fraggin' Spectre. He has taken more lives than some armies."

"I'm not afraid of him," Saul said boldly.

Frank's eyes burned. "Well, you should be!"

The two men's shouting match was disturbed by a calm melody that played from the crimelord's own communicator. Each of the three men looked in the direction of the sound. Frank stood still for a moment then crossed the room. He hesitated for a second while the musical ringtone continued. After preparing himself for the worst, he picked up the device and swiped his finger across the screen before placing it against his ear.

"Yes?"

Saul glanced at Deni, but the other man kept his focus on his boss.

"Alright," was all the crimelord said. He lowered the device, and only Saul didn't realize what was happening.

"So?" the son asked, shrugging his shoulders.

Frank pursed his lips. The small black communicator suddenly felt very heavy in his hand. His mind raced with trying to come up with a plan, but the chattering of his only surviving son brought him back to the here and now.

"Well, what happened?" Saul inquired annoyingly.

"He escaped. Both of the lawmen are dead."

Deni cursed under his breath, then downed the last of his drink. He winced as the intense burning sensation from the alcohol raced to his stomach.

Saul nodded to himself, then looked back to his father. "I will finish this, Pa. Just give me…"

"No," Frank said without turning back to his son. His tone was low but was clearly definitive. "You will do nothing. You will remain hidden until he can be dealt with."

"But… bu…" the son was flabbergasted by the crimelord's decision. He again glanced at Deni, who now was staring at the floor. "You… you can't be serious."

The father shook his head. "Oh, I'm dead serious. I can't take the chance of you getting killed by him."

Finding a reserve of passionate energy, Saul stepped up to his parent and locked eyes intently. "No, Pa. I will finish what I started…"

Frank moved impeccably fast. He wrapped his hands around his son's head and yanked it forward so that their foreheads touched. Saul at first raised his arms to shield himself, but then realized his father was holding him still.

"Son, I... I can't risk it. Please... obey me for once. I can't lose you like I lost your brother to that bastard."

Sensing the awkwardness of his boss being so tender at that moment, Deni adjusted his suit jacket and cleared his throat.

The son was speechless. He had never seen his father be so stern yet caring. It was a strange feeling, but at that moment, he genuinely felt loved.

"O... okay, Pa. I'll listen."

Frank released his adult child and tugged on his own jacket to correct its position. He turned toward his right-hand man.

"Deni, I want you to personally take him to the safe house."

"You got it," the high ranking thug said plainly.

"Don't let anyone know. Keep it quiet. I don't want Spectre getting a tip from some loose-lipped fragger."

Saul felt helpless. He knew he had been the catalyst that brought all of these problems down on his father's operation. He wondered how he could have screwed up so badly that this is where they were now.

"What are you planning to do?" the son asked nervously.

Frank's face became very focused and stone-like. "I'm going to track down that animal and put him down before he has a chance to come for us. His blood will be spilled for what he did to Frankie. I swear it."

Saul slunk out of the room while Deni noticed that Frank had locked eyes with him.

"Boss?" the thug asked calmly.

"Before you leave, I want you to put a contract out on him."

Deni nodded and pursed his lips. "So, you do think he is alive then?"

"I do. And we need to enlist some additional firepower. If he's out on the streets, it's only a matter of time before he makes a go for us."

Chapter 12

Cycle: 412 Month: 9 Rotation: 14
Corre Republic Space
Prefecture: Expansive
Planet: Benedictus
Location: Patrolmen Central Station - Avalon

The hustle and bustle of the previous rotation had finally settled into a relative calm. Much of the debris had been swept away or cleaned up, along with the bodies being removed. What remained though was the various bullet holes and scorch marks from the gunfight that ran through much of the station.

Special Agent Daykers had been hard at work filing the respective report on the incident. She had already been chewed out by several of her superiors, and the long stretch of hours on her body was making it difficult to focus. At this point, she wasn't even sure if she would have a job when the sun rose.

The woman typed away on her government-issued computer station while she neared the end of her extensive details of the account. None of her superiors fully understood how an injured man could kill two inquisitors then escape the station. Renowned bounty hunter or not, it wasn't adding up.

A sturdy knock at the door roused her from her internal thoughts.

"Come in!" she roared with her back to the door.

She didn't want to look at the visitor, fearing it was the Chief or worse, that someone had come to fire her.

The door slid open, and she heard the similar sound of thick mechanical steps. Her heart pounded, and time seemed to slow as fear gripped her insides. She spun around quickly to see a very tall armored figure in the doorway. In her fatigue, she thought that Gideon had returned. Her heart rate escalated further but started to subside when she realized the stranger was different than the ex-bounty hunter's appearance was.

"Special Agent, I am here to ask you some questions," the man said, his face entirely hidden by a smooth black faceplate.

A holographic icon appeared above his raised left forearm. Daykers recognized the symbol as belonging to the Keepers of the Republic. Her eyes grew wide before she caught herself. Not knowing what correct protocol was, she hopped up from her chair to stand. In an attempt to improve her appearance, Daykers smoothed her uniform and used her hand to quickly brush back loose strands of her hair.

"Sir!" she exclaimed. "Forgive me for the mess."

The Keeper looked around the office but failed to identify anything unruly except for some tablets and other devices scattered about.

"Please, have a seat."

Daykers obeyed the order and sat back down. Her eyes remained locked onto the faceplate of the visitor while he stepped into the middle of the office.

"I am the Keeper of Knowledge. It has come to my attention that you encountered a very dangerous individual yesterday evening."

"Yes, sir," she replied regrettably. "We picked up Gideon Adama after an attack in an alleyway in the city. His wife, Joan Adama, was dead upon arrival."

"Yes, I read the file," Knowledge said plainly with a twinge of arrogance in his voice.

Daykers realized that she had been nervously picking at one of her fingers with the other hand and pressed them both tightly against her lap.

"What I want to know is what is the end of that report you are typing up right now." The Keeper pointed at the terminal and held his gloved finger still.

"I am nearly finished with it, sir. But if you have any questions, I am more than happy to assist you."

For generations, there had been rumors of armored heroes that fought in the shadows of the Corre Republic. The ever-watchful guardians of the nation. Some people had posted images or clips of them in action on the stream. Still, there wasn't a real confirmation of their existence from the government until about a decade ago.

They now made more appearances in the public eye. Some had even been on operations with the military to launch attacks against neighboring nations. No one really knew how many of them there were, or what their jurisdiction was. The Bureau of Central Intelligence even still refused to comment or shine any light on specifics of the keepers' involvement in the government.

The officer never imagined she would ever get an opportunity to see one of them up close. Knowledge's armor was majestic, yet it still had an unsettling appearance to it. Her training kicked in, and she realized that he had no weapons of any kind. That seemed very odd, considering the necessity for using a power armor suit.

This entire situation with Gideon and now a genuine keeper was way above the special agent's paygrade.

"What I need from you is any sort of information about where the suspect may be heading," Knowledge said.

Daykers shook her head slightly to bring her back to the conversation. "He uh… didn't give me much. I was in the middle of interviewing him when the two inquisitors showed up."

Knowledge tilted his head to the side. "Inquisitors?"

The Keeper's tone sounded harsh, and the Special Agent wanted to not agitate him any further.

"Yessir. Two inquisitors with special clearance came and informed me that they were taking over the investigation. Before I knew it, I was rushed out the door. Several minutes later, an alarm sounded through the station. By the time I discovered the bodies of the two lawmen, it was too late."

Knowledge brought his hand up to where his chin would be. "Why wasn't this in any of the other officers' reports?"

"Uh...?" Daykers was shocked that Knowledge had even known about the other reports so quickly.

"I saw the footage from the evidence room. I want to know, did he turn invisible?"

"I'm sorry?"

Knowledge tucked both of his arms behind his back and spoke as though he were addressing a child. "After you had regained consciousness, you saw Gideon slide a piece of jewelry over his wrist. At that point, he vanished from the cameras in the room. There was a blue glow, and then I heard his voice in the replay speak to you several moments later."

The special agent blinked her tired eyes and struggled to recall the moment just before the fugitive was covered by that suit of armor.

"Yes, I remember he was putting on some kind of bracelet or something. But he never disappeared from my view."

Knowledge tilted his head ever so slightly. "I see. That is all."

The keeper began to exit the office, but Daykers couldn't pass up an opportunity like this.

"Sir, is it true?"

"Is what true?" Knowledge asked as he came to a halt.

The woman swallowed hard, sort of embarrassed by the question burning in her mind. "There are rumors and whispers that Gideon

Adama made a deal with a daemon, and that's why his suit works the way it does. I've never seen anything like that before in my life. It materialized around his body. It was incredible."

Knowledge turned his head to the side but kept the rest of his body aimed at the door. "I assure you that the suspect is still very much a human and that his "armor" is from the realm of reality. I will be assuming command of the investigation. Do not pursue him in any way."

A hologram appeared over Knowledge's left forearm. Using his right hand, he flung the invisible data to the Special Agent's computer console.

"You have my contact information. Inform me if he is located. He is to be considered extremely dangerous. Do not engage him. Contact me before you do anything else if he is discovered."

The officer swallowed anxiously. "Yes, sir. I will."

Without another word, the Keeper exited the room. His heavy steps could be heard heading down the hallway until they faded in the distance. The Special Agent stood there for a moment in disbelief. Something tugged on her mind that all of this was going to get much worse before it was over.

Knowledge strolled through the interior of the station, making his way out of the structure. A busy hustle and bustle was going on as officers went about their duties. Some were booking suspects, while others filed reports, all of them came to a halt when the dark blue power suit entered the room. A

145

small boy grinned excitedly at the Keeper while his mother looked horrified at the sight.

The eyes of everyone nearby followed Knowledge as he made his way out of view. It took several seconds afterward before they did much else besides be in shock and awe. Unless you spent time around the Republic Armed Forces or lived on a border world, most people never saw a power suit up close. Sure, designs like the Centurion were pretty commonly known through images on the stream or in holomovies. Still, the Keeper's armor was something entirely different. It made the slender man look almost mythical.

Knowledge disabled his external speakers so he could speak with his AI in private.

"Catherine, compile a list of all devices that are known to hide an individual from the view of a camera feed."

"Right away. What do you suspect he has?"

"I don't know, but possibly this is how he has been able to evade me for so long."

Chapter 13

Cycle: 412 Month: 9 Rotation: 14
Corre Republic Space
Prefecture: Expansive
Planet: Benedictus
Location: Downtown Avalon

The dank smell of the abandoned structure filled the space. A steady drip sound echoed through the empty room. Gideon had laid down against the wall and at some point had slumped over to the side. His head rested on his duffle bag, while his stolen pistol remained hidden just out of view. While his mind wrestled with a vivid dream, he rolled to the other side.

Suddenly he was awoken from his slumber by a wet nose that pressed itself up against his face. The ex-bounty hunter sat up in an instant with his weapon drawn. To his surprise, a kind-looking canine skittered across the floor in panic. It ran out of the room as it yelped.

The man breathed heavily for a few seconds while his brain caught up to what just happened. Finally, he lowered his weapon and slumped back against the wall.

Tiny beams of daylight pierced through several of the nearby dingy windows. The clouds from the storms the previous night were long gone. All that was left was a shining light green sky.

147

Gideon stood up slowly. "Uuuuh..." he groaned in pain and held his waist.

With great care, he got back up to his feet and stowed away the bits of medical supplies he wanted to take with him. Upon inspection of his bandages, he was satisfied with their condition for the moment. The ex-bounty hunter slung his duffle bag back over his shoulder and stuffed the heavy inquisitor's pistol into the back of his pants.

Alright... I need a plan. I can't just wander aimlessly down the street.

He took a moment to breathe slowly and to mentally orient himself. Somehow in his sleep, the amulet had slid out from his shirt. After sniffing and clearing his throat, Gideon put the necklace back under his clothes.

Before I can do anything, I need to secure weapons. So that needs to be my first step. Next is locating where Saul is. Then... then I'm getting off this damned rock.

Satisfied by his agenda, the wounded man headed for the door. Carefully he peeked through one of the windows to see that outside had become a hectic place. Vehicles drove up and down the street while several people moved about on the sidewalks. Before stepping outside, he took a second to briefly groom his beard and hair. He didn't want to get any extra attention directed his way.

Screw it. If some officers find me, I'll deal with it...

With that, Gideon exited the abandoned building and went left. A car up ahead honked furiously at a parked semi-truck. The driver of the larger vehicle was in the middle of climbing down from the cab when he heard the boisterous display of frustration coming from the other motorist. Unphased, the truck driver swatted his hand at the noise and went inside of the building he parked in front of.

The ex-bounty hunter looked down as he passed a patrolman that made a beeline for the loud situation unfolding. Not recognizing the fugitive, the female officer began blowing her whistle.

Avalon was the sort of city that, at one point, had tremendous potential. Unfortunately, its best rotations were behind it. After the war with the powerful artificial intelligence known as the Collector and his robotic army of Synthetics, Benedictus underwent an economic boom. Refugees from a multitude of worlds came for work while the Republic began rebuilding some of the lost worlds.

For several decades, the previously unimportant planet flourished. New highways, cities, and infrastructure were constructed. While the Anterior worlds needed to be rebuilt after the war, Benedictus continued to expand rapidly. Eventually, though, the citizens realized that they could vote in more and more social programs that benefitted them in their monetary woes. Instead of maintaining the traditions of being a hardworking people, the residents became disgruntled toward work over time, and it led to a more entitled view.

It was ironic in a sad way that where at one point in time, this planet was strengthened in many ways, it now was a husk of its former self. Crime and backroom deals helped to fill in the void that was left as decay and failure set in from the corrupt politicians. Roads and highways continued to decay, while the rich and powerful lived lavish lives up in their penthouses.

Gideon continued on his way toward a less savory part of the city. Sirens wailed in the distance while he crossed the street. His side had begun to ache some time ago, but he didn't want to stop to deal with the pain until he had reached a safer location.

He recalled memory after memory of his life when he acted as a bounty hunter on the world. Many different employers had reached out to Gideon over his career. Some had been so thrilled with his performance on his assignments that they would extend to him a contract to work exclusively for them. However, he didn't want to live under anyone's thumb. Gideon was motivated by more than money. The only problem was sometimes he didn't know why he lived that life.

Everything changed when he met Joan. Their paths crossed when he happened to be making a stop in a grocery store. Despite being incredibly wealthy from his dangerous life of work, the bounty hunter preferred to cook his own food. The future couple had locked eyes by accident, but he was much too shy to ask her out. It wasn't until after several more weeks of happening to encounter one another at that same store that he finally found the courage to approach the young woman.

My past is what got her killed...

Tires screeched, and Gideon's head shot up. He spun around to see a mustard-colored sports car swerve onto his street. The ex-bounty hunter slid his hand under the back of his shirt and firmly grabbed the pistol's grip. Thankfully, a patrolman's cruiser swung around behind the escaping car and chased it speedily down the road, lights and siren on full blast.

Carefully Gideon checked around him, then relaxed and released the weapon. He tugged on his shirt to be sure it still correctly hid his firearm then carried on his way.

He had walked these streets more times than he could possibly count when he first arrived on the planet. Now though, it seemed to serve as a punishment. Again his memories of first meeting his wife resumed in his mind. Of all his cycles across so many planets, he had never quite met a woman like Joan. Her smile, the way she would play with her hair when she was deep in thought, even how she would snort when he made her laugh, it all combined to infatuate the hardened killer to soften his heart.

Long ago, he had made a personal rule to never fall in love again. That no matter what, it was more important to protect the amulet, keep his skills honed, and to embrace what he now was. The life of a bounty hunter allowed him to make use of his extensive military training and experience. He didn't care about any of the crimelords or politicians and their agendas. They all were part of the same scum as far as he was concerned. He just enjoyed ridding the 'verse of bad guys and getting paid for it.

Everything changed when that petite woman entered his life.

Get it together. I can't dwell on this right now. Focus!

Gideon shook his head and exhaled forcefully out of his nose. Try as he might though he couldn't stir the memories again pushing through the mental wall he tried to erect.

As he passed by a small deli, the smell of fresh bread wafted through the air and instantly reminded him of their first date. Being out of the game of romance for a very long time, Gideon didn't have many ideas on something romantic to do, so he took her to get sandwiches. At the time, he was still in shock that she said yes. With his bushy beard and stern appearance, he always imagined himself to look somewhat intimidating. But Joan didn't see him as a rock, she saw something else that even he couldn't see anymore.

After that first evening together, she was all he could think about. Despite trying to keep her out of his thoughts, he wasn't capable of preventing her from invading his mind. Within a few short weeks, he made the bold decision to leave behind being a bounty hunter. He hadn't yet shared his underground profession with her, and he didn't want to bring it up until it was behind him.

It took some time, but he was able to clear accounts with several other bounty hunters and employers. All that was left was Taravis Dole, who just so happened to be a rival to the Corbo's in Avalon. Cycles before, Gideon was targeted by Frank Corbo after the bounty hunter had assassinated one of his high-level associates. Fed up with Spectre's involvement in the scene, Frank put a hit out on the bounty hunter that had him targeted by many other colleagues.

After several failed attempts on his life leaving a slew of other hitmen dead, Gideon made a deal with Taravis to have the contract broken. The reprieve was not to last. When the bounty hunter came to his old employer to inform him that he was leaving the life of a hired gun behind, the crimelord told him that he would release Gideon from owing him by getting revenge against Frankie Corbo Jr. Spectre knew that this could throw him into a world of problems, but he loved Joan too much to live in fear.

He learned of where the rival boss's son would be and dealt with him. Taravis released the bounty hunter and he went on his way. There was always a part of him that wondered if Frank would send someone after him. Thankfully though, the Adama's had been able to live in peace while they lived in the Turon Commonwealth.

After laying low for a couple more hours, the evening was nearing. Clouds began to build above the city, and the daylight was blocked. Gideon wanted to hate himself for what happened to Joan, but he couldn't figure out what they could have done differently.

She needed to get here for the treatment... but why wasn't I faster? I should have been able to kill all of them. If only I could have gotten to my armor... I knew better. I should have been wearing the damned thing!

A gentle mist of rain started to fall onto the decaying part of Avalon. There was a faint muffled sound of music ahead of the saddened man. He knew the noise probably came from the Last Shot bar.

Okay. It's time to get serious. Now is the time to act. Get serious.

Gideon licked his lips, and he shrugged off the emotional thinking that had barraged him for blocks. An impressive holographic sign for the bar rotated by the road. It morphed into a woman in skimpy looking clothes motioning with her finger for those driving by to come on in. The man wasn't the least bit intrigued by the sight of the large beautiful woman. He was a man on a mission.

Last Shot undoubtedly was going to have multiple bounty hunters, assassins, and other murderous people inside. He wasn't afraid, though. His shortlist was to get information and to get weapons. While the patrolman had conducted multiple busts and raided the establishment, they never had been able to successfully locate the hidden passage leading deep beneath the structure.

Gideon had been able to get access more than once to purchase weapons, but today could be different. He took a deep breath as he walked up to the business and spotted one hitman he recognized. Rando Baver had been standing outside to smoke in peace when he saw the legendary Spectre stroll on up.

The sight of Gideon walking confidently his way was almost enough for the killer to draw one of the pistols he had concealed on him. However, he knew that a bounty hunter of Spectre's level would undoubtedly be armed. A piece of him wondered if he could draw fast enough to take out his old rival, but he decided it was best not to try it.

"Well, as I live and breathe," Rando boasted loudly, doing his best to overcome his fear. "I didn't think I would ever see your sorry face again."

The currently employed bounty hunter hoped that by displaying strong confidence that Gideon would go on his way. Thankfully for him, Spectre strode straight on by without so much as a nod. Rando let out the breath he had been holding and took a long draw from his smokestick.

The volume of the music playing from within the bar continued to get louder and louder as Gideon drew closer. Two men standing in front of the door saw the approaching man and stepped aside when they realized who it was.

Spectre pushed open the door and was greeted by a blast of bass from the DJ's speakers. His eyebrow arched, and he looked around. Standing in the doorway drew the attention of any of the other bounty hunters that were worth any merit. Gideon spotted several well-known competitors, Crem, Cort, Sito, even Hannibal, all exceptional killers. Well, at least that is what their reputation would lend you to believe. He would have no way of recognizing any of the new hotshots that rose up while he was away.

Not being one to shrink at a threat, Spectre adjusted his duffle bag over his shoulder and headed straight for the bar.

Charlie Kenner also had seen the ex-bounty hunter enter the establishment. She finished drying a shot glass off and set it upside down on her counter. A wide smile spread across her face, and she tossed her towel over her shoulder.

"Didn't expect to see you again," she said jokingly to the newcomer.

Gideon's countenance remained neutral and hard. "Hey, Charlie."

"Can I get you something?"

"Yeah, the usual," Spectre said with his gruff voice.

The middle-aged woman bit her lip and smirked before walking off to get his preferred drink.

While at one point, Charlie was an exceptionally attractive woman, the passage of time and excessive use of narcotics had awarded her multiple wrinkles and a sag to her shoulders.

From across the bar, one of the bounty hunters observed the fugitive closely. Hannibal wore his wide-brimmed black hat even indoors. He took a gulp of his strong ale then firmly placed the mug onto his table. His guest was surprised to see his friend just stand up in the middle of their conversation. However, the bounty hunter had business to tend to.

A long scar ran the length of his face, even taking out part of his left eyebrow. He adjusted his dark trenchcoat when he stood up, being sure to keep his firearms hidden.

Crem and Sito whispered back and forth to one another while Cort appeared not interested in the scene at all. She drained her own drink and laid her head down on her arms, trying to get some rest despite the incredibly loud music from the overly enthusiastic DJ.

Hannibal made his way up behind Spectre. Sensing that he was being watched, Gideon turned his head to the left. Noticing his old colleague, he nodded.

"Hey."

The other bounty hunter froze in place. "Hey."

One of the table occupants somewhere else in the building roared in laughter from some unheard joke. However, Hannibal and Spectre kept their eyes locked. The tension between the two men was incredibly subtle, even others nearby picked up on it. Charlie stopped in her tracks when she saw the other bounty hunter just standing near the bar.

The DJ at the back of the building transitioned the song that had been playing to one that was more even more upbeat. He stuck out his tongue and bobbed his head in unison with the beat.

Eventually, a mischievous grin peeked out from behind Hannibal's own scruffy beard. Gideon too smirked and stood up from his stool.

"Come here, you big animal," Hannibal said admirably.

The two men shared a hearty hug together, each loudly patting the other man's back.

"It's good to see you!" Gideon said, genuinely.

"Same to you, my old friend."

Spectre motioned to the bar, and the pair strode over. Hannibal walked up to the man that had been sitting beside the fugitive at the bar.

"You're in my seat," the bounty hunter growled.

The skinny man turned around, searching for who was speaking so harshly. His eyes bulged when he saw Hannibal towering over him. He yanked his drink from the counter and retreated to some other empty seat.

Spectre sat down, and Hannibal's pleasant demeanor again returned. He squeezed his friend's shoulder tightly and gently shook Gideon.

"I didn't think I'd ever see you again."

The ex-bounty hunter nodded his head. "Yeah, I didn't think I'd be back."

Seeing the change in the situation, Charlie returned with Gideon's beverage. She set down a glass with what looked like some red-colored liquid.

"What is that sissy drink doing here?" Hannibal blurted out sarcastically.

Gideon smirked and took a sip.

"Can I get you anything?" Charlie asked the other man.

Hannibal again got very serious. "Yes. A dark brew ale!"

The bartender scooped up an empty mug from under the counter and pulled down on the lever, filling the glass with a rich amber-colored beer.

Foam spilled over on the sides, but the large man did not mind. She slid the drink over, and his eyes lit up delightedly. A man further along the length of the bar raised his hand, and Charlie rushed off to tend to her customer.

"You don't look like you've changed at all," Hannibal said, looking back over to his friend. "Still the same hard-headed brute I take it?"

Gideon glanced at his fellow hunter and began to notice all of the gray hairs that now littered his beard. Hannibal still looked very muscular, but Spectre did make a mental note of the way he used his right arm.

Guess that bum shoulder of his is still bothering him.

Almost as if he had an injury that made it a bit difficult to move. Many people throughout known space had been replacing injured bodily parts for generations. Gideon knew of Hannibal's leg replacements and wondered why he had never gotten a new shoulder.

Maybe he isn't doing so well financially. Better play it safe in case he is looking to cash in with me.

"You still hunting?" the ex-bounty hunter asked plainly.

Hannibal took a deep breath and pursed his lips while he swallowed another gulp of his brew. "Yep. Looking to maybe retire soon, though."

"Really?" Gideon asked, surprised by the other man's answer.

"Yeah. I'm starting to feel my age. Things don't move quite like they did. You can only push your luck for so long before this life kills you."

Spectre carefully looked to the left to check on Crem and Sito. The two men still were seated at their table, but he noticed that Cort, who had been sitting by herself, was now missing.

Hannibal again lifted his mug, this time though he just stared at the drink. Carbonated bubbles lifted up from the sides and floated their way to the top.

"So… I heard about a man that blasted his way out of a patrolman station sometime last night. Heard he had some kind of special armor or something."

Gideon glanced at his friend, then placed his eyes straight ahead. "Oh?"

"Yeah. Strange times we live in."

"It is indeed," Spectre replied neutrally.

"Yep." Hannibal finally took a large gulp of his beverage and let out a satisfying sigh.

"Let me ask you straight, Hannibal. Are you working?"

The bounty hunter smacked his lips and let out a short chuckle. "No. No, I'm not. It would have to be quite the amount of money for me to gun for an old friend."

But you still would, wouldn't you?

Gideon hid his disdain beneath his own smile.

"I did hear something about some guy and his wife from out of town being attacked in some random alley. Guess the lady got killed."

There was a long lapse of time before Spectre answered. "Yeah."

Hannibal's behavior became more solemn. "I'm sorry."

Gideon fought to hold back any real sign of emotion. He simply nodded his head several times.

"Was she the one?"

Back when Gideon still worked for hire, Hannibal was one of his closest friends. Their line of work frequently created the atmosphere for confrontations even amongst the bounty hunters and hitmen. However, the two men had worked alongside one another on several assignments and had come somewhat close in their time together. Gideon had shared his reason for leaving the business of death behind with his friend before he left.

"Um… yeah. Yeah, she was."

Hannibal stroked his beard with his left hand. "Do you know who did it?"

Spectre looked away, then turned back to his drink. "Yeah."

"And how are you planning on dealing with it?"

Gideon locked eyes with his old friend. Hannibal saw the pain hiding beneath the surface in the ex-bounty hunter's eyes, but he also saw the intense resolve.

"Ah," was all Hannibal could think to say.

Both men turned their attention back to their respective drinks and remained silent for a short time. The music continued to blare from the speakers, and it seemed that many others around the pair were enjoying themselves. That is, except for the two lowlifes that broke out into a brawl against one another near the entrance of the bar.

Hannibal drank the last of his ale and set the mug down. "Well, I can honestly say that I don't envy the guys who did it. It is good to see you again, Gideon."

Spectre raised his glass to his old friend, and the other man stood up and left. Seeing the other man go, Charlie came back over to her customer.

"Can I get you a refill?"

"Nah. I was hoping you could get me something else."

The woman tilted her head playfully. "Oh? Like what?"

She reached her hand out and gently brushed up against Gideon's own.

"I wanted to see the cellar."

"Oh…" Charlie said before she pulled back her hand.

If the woman was bothered by his response, Gideon couldn't tell. He learned long ago not to trust someone like her. Someone willing to throw themselves at a bounty hunter was always warranted to be cautious of. While some women were genuinely attracted to a man that lived dangerously, others were used as a ploy to lure a hitman to his death.

Joan never knew it, but Gideon had gone to the extreme to verify her identity. He didn't want to take any chances and had gone to incredible lengths to try and find something on her before they got serious when dating. He had more than adequate contacts at the time that could find anything on anyone for the right price.

The bartender leaned onto the counter, bringing her face closer to his. "I had heard that you were out of the game."

"I am," the ex-bounty hunter said gruffly. "But... I need to take care of something."

"I see. And you came to see me?" the woman asked flirtatiously.

Several cycles before Joan was in the picture, Gideon had a fling with the then much younger and prettier arms-dealer. The truth was he figured she would now be one of the only weapon dealers that wouldn't put a bullet between his eyes if the Corbo's put the word out. As much as teasing her would probably help his situation, the pain in his heart temporarily prevented him from even being able to put up a believable act.

"I knew I could trust you," he finally decided to reply.

Charlie stood up, her feelings were slightly hurt at being denied by the renowned killer twice in one evening, but she figured she might as well make a sale. She looked over to a bouncer that was watching the door and nodded to him. He understood the signal and kept a close eye on the front door.

"Follow me," the bartender said kindly.

Gideon didn't bother finishing his drink before standing up to follow after the woman. She led the way through the majority of the bar. Spectre noticed that Crem and Sito were still watching him as he made his way through the crowd. Sito gestured with his glass to his fellow bounty hunter. Gideon bowed his head slightly, acknowledging the greeting.

Once again, the song changed to a different beat. Those that were gathered on the dance floor jumped up and down and whipped their heads back and forth to the flow of the song. That was when he finally found Crem. She had found herself a dance partner and was moving to the beat energetically. Gideon happened to spot her toss back more than one small object into her mouth.

Probably rox.

Within the amount of time it took for the ex-bounty hunter to pass the woman and her dancing friend, her pupils dilated, and she moved sluggishly. Yet, her mannerisms also seemed quickened.

Long ago Gideon had elected to abstain from narcotics. He had simply witnessed too many instances where people he knew were forever altered by the substances. What was worse was that the drugs on the market now were much more potent than even when he was a child.

Rox was made from synthetic compounds that gave the taker an instant sensation of peace and joy. Still, it also accelerated the heart rate giving heightened awareness. Most users shared experiences that sounded wonderful, but that was mostly after the first or second use. The human body quickly built up an immunity to the substance, which, of course, meant that it would require more considerable amounts to again approach the same high. If one was not careful, it was incredibly easy to overdose.

The worst part was that if a user did want to get off the drug's extreme addictive control, they would have to quit cold. However, a potential downside to this was that they could go into cardiac arrest and die. It was a very dangerous narcotic, and it had claimed many lives and possible futures throughout the Corre Republic and several other nations.

Charlie disappeared around a corner up ahead, but Spectre wasn't worried. He had been down to the cellar on more than one occasion in his career and knew where he was headed. The only reason he needed the bartender was that she was the only one who had access to the hidden lock. Despite trying to look cute and bubbly, Charlie Kenner was actually the owner of the Last Shot. She was well connected in the underworld, but she had typically chosen to remain an arms-dealer rather than get involved in the bounties herself.

Gideon turned down the same hallway and the woman stood further away, hands on her hips.

"Are you getting slow in your old age?"

The man allowed the tiniest of smiles to break out on his lips.

Charlie sighed then opened the door to the basement. Lights kicked on automatically, and the two began the descent down the stone staircase. The overall volume of the music deadened the further they went. However, the bass still continued to penetrate through the underground walls.

The basement itself was fairly empty. Several plasti-crates were stacked up in one corner, and some old tables and chairs were arranged to the left. To anyone who was visiting the bar for the first time, they would be confused at its underworld reputation. However, Gideon knew better.

"Is there anything, in particular, you are looking for?" the woman asked while she crossed the room.

"I'm actually here for a couple of things."

Charlie walked up to a specific hole in the wall. It was so small that the ex-bounty hunter couldn't even imagine being able to stick his finger in. The bartender, however, easily could. She held her index finger up, and it split apart to reveal a slender key within. The woman inserted it into the opening, and a subtle click sound came from behind the wall.

The woman stepped back and her finger slid back together as a bright blue line formed in the shape of a doorway. She pressed it tenderly, and the secret door swung open without a sound.

"How 'bout you tell me what you are looking to accomplish, and I can get you what you need," the arms-dealer said confidently.

Gideon strolled past the woman and stepped onto the lift that was installed inside the passageway. Charlie followed, her steps clanking against the metal floor of the elevator. She gently shut the door and pressed a button on her right.

The secret elevator moved silently yet quickly.

"I need an assortment."

The woman's eyebrow arched. "Really?"

Spectre noticed that the rush of air from the speed of their descent smelled a bit stale, but Charlie's focus was strange. She just was staring straight at him.

"What is it?" he asked curiously.

"Your necklace, it looks exquisite."

He realized that the amulet had accidentally slid out from beneath the collar of his shirt. Trying to be as dismissive of the comment as he could, he tucked it back in and stared ahead.

"I wouldn't have taken you for a jewelry man," she remarked as she also motioned with her hand to his bracelet.

The ex-bounty hunter saw no reason to respond. He was in no mood for small talk.

Ten more seconds past before they reached the bottom of the shaft. The door automatically slid open, and overhead lights revealed a short passageway. At the end was a thick metal door with a scanning station to the left of it. Charlie stepped up and went through her normal routine.

Gideon adjusted the duffle bag on his left shoulder. He kept his right arm loose, but ready to respond in case she tried anything suspicious. There was no telling exactly who was going to make an attempt on his life or not. He simply had no idea what the Corbo's would do once they figured out he escaped not only the two inquisitors but the patrolman station too. It was likely they were going to send out a massive contract on his life, and a whole new flurry of problems would emerge for him.

A ding chirped from the terminal, and the door slid into the wall while an additional door behind that one also opened. The interior room was dimly lit, but the fugitive could immediately see the wall of firearms arranged by type.

Charlie grinned accommodatingly. "Alright. Well… for assortments, I have a couple of packages ready to go. They are fully customizable, of course."

Gideon looked back and forth at the wall-mounted firearms. The arms-dealer had everything from ballistic rifles to smuggled plasma weapons from the Union of Stars. In his line of work, he had used more guns than he could possibly remember. Some were used only a couple of times because he didn't care for them, while others had been used extensively. In addition to his time as a bounty hunter, Gideon had also been part of the Republic Armed Forces, which further exposed him to a variety of weapons.

He took a deep breath through his nose and calmly exhaled. Charlie placed her hands behind her back to prevent her guest from seeing her carefully push a button built into her artificial left arm. Just as the ex-bounty hunter stepped into the room, a hidden door in the ceiling popped open, and a turret dropped down. It aimed its dual chain guns at the doorway with a red laser at the center of its camera pod shined. However, instead of tracking Gideon's movements, it just stayed in place.

The arms-dealer was confused but needed to play off what just happened before Gideon shot her. "I'm so sorry about that, hun. Damned thing has been on the fritz lately. I need to get it fixed before someone ends up getting shot."

Spectre glared at the woman but stayed in place.

"What?" Charlie asked, raising her arms innocently. "I couldn't ever shoot you. I brought you all the way down here to make a sale. If I wanted to kill you, I'd have done it already."

Wanting to move past the entire mishap as quickly as she could, the woman spun around and motioned with her hands toward the weapons mounted to the wall. "Any potential hints on what your hunt is going to be like?"

Guess I might as well tell her. I need info anyhow...

"I need to know where the Corbo's hideout is," Gideon said as he walked beneath the stationary turret.

Glad I have the bracelet with me.

Charlie's eyes grew very wide. "Frag me. You actually are going after them?!"

Spectre wasn't bothered by her remarks. He stood perfectly still, like a stone.

"You are one stupid bastard, you know that, right?" She ran her hand through her hair and down to her neck. "Well, if you are going to stand a snowball's chance, you should take my assault package."

The arms-dealer walked over to the wall and pointed at the large Zan-Tec Carbine.

Gideon shook his head. "I need it to pack a punch, but I need everything to be compact."

""Compact". Alright, then you should take the hit and run set." Charlie pointed her hand at an arrangement of firearms on the other side of the display.

Spectre stepped over and recognized the Pylon 7A Commando Rifle instantly. He removed the long-gun from the rack and aimed it away from the woman. Without even thinking about it, his muscle memory took over, and he began checking over the rifle as he listened to the rest of her sales pitch.

"The seven-A is military-grade parts. Includes holographic sight and flippable zoom sight to reach out and touch someone. Being a heavier charged laser rifle, it won't have a problem with armored targets. Unless they are power armor, of course," Charlie said as she smirked.

The man pressed a button on the right side of the rifle above the grip, and it mechanically collapsed into a smaller shape. He hefted its newfound size in his hands and nodded with approval.

"Included in this package are two Storm Magnums."

Gideon spotted the two large pistols beneath where the rifle hang. He set the gun back up on the rack and removed one of the handguns. Again, he safely checked the pistol if it were loaded then played with the slide.

"As I'm sure you are well aware, the Magnums are excellent at disposing of unwanted threats. While they are ballistic, they have incredible stopping power."

"Do you have armor-piercing rounds?"

Charlie cocked her head to the side as if she were insulted. "Gideon, you may have been cut of the game for a while, but I am known for being an all-in-one supplier these rotations."

"Good. I'll need spare mags and plenty of rounds."

"Done," the woman said resolutely.

"What about for up close?"

Smoothly, the arms-dealer waved her hand toward a cabinet to the ex-bounty hunter's left. He spotted the additional display and walked over. Lying on top of a bed of velvet was a collection of knives in all shapes and sizes.

Spotting one in particular that caught his eye, he lifted up an all-black serrated blade.

"Ah, that is a good choice. Hardened steel from a mine on Nativity. The blade itself is full-tang and will not fail you during any of your... thrusts."

Spectre flipped the melee weapon back and forth in his hand until he felt satisfied with it. "I'll take three."

"Excellent. I assume you will want a supply of powercells for the rifle as well?"

"Yes, please," the man replied before setting the knife carefully back down on the display.

"Also, do you happen to carry any swords?"

Charlie grinned from ear to ear. "You sure know how to party, Gideon. Yes, over here if you would."

The woman strode over to a tall metal case, and delicately opened its double doors. It was loaded with all sorts of brutal weapons from battle axes to detailed short swords.

"Do any of them grab your eye?" Charlie asked seductively.

"Yes, that one." The ex-bounty hunter pointed to a sheathed sword that had emerald embedded into the handle.

The woman removed it from the display and used both hands to offer it to the buyer. Gideon accepted the sword then drew it from its scabbard. He inspected the handle and then moved his eyes up to the blade itself.

"This was handmade from a sword maker generations ago. I was told that it was owned by a general that fought against the Synthetics."

That last remark got Spectre's attention. "Oh?"

"I purchased it from an antique dealer that tried to spin me quite the story."

To the woman's surprise, Gideon said, "I'd be interested to hear it."

"He informed me that the original buyer for this impressive sword was General Taybard."

"I believe he led the 307th against the machines in the last battle of the war," Gideon stated plainly.

"Ah. History is not quite my forte. But alas, the seller was remiss with much more detail than that. I suppose that it has been owned by collectors on and off. Typically I don't pick up such an old weapon, but it was in such spectacular condition that I took a chance that a buyer would come by that understood its worth."

The ex-bounty hunter noticed a design in the handle that looked like it could be removed. He slid it up with his thumb, and it lifted up, revealing an old powercell inside.

"I… didn't know it did that," Charlie admitted in awe.

"I had heard about a collection of swords made for key personnel in the war that was heated to be able to cut through the Synthetic soldiers if a ship were boarded. I've never seen one in person, though. I'm sure the powercell is long since dead."

There was a certain reverence to Spectre's voice, and Charlie knew for certain he would be taking it with him. A man like Gideon had an air about him that he was drawn to weapons with a story. He softly slid the sword back into its home and held it down by his side.

"I'll take it."

"Is there anything else you require for your hunt?"

Gideon looked up as he thought for a moment. "I would like three frag grenades, oh, and a bag."

"And how would you be paying?"

The ex-bounty hunter slid the duffle bag from his shoulder, and it plopped on the ground. He then drew the lawman's pistol from his pants. For a split second, the woman became dreadfully terrified. This was the first time any of her clients had ever drawn a gun on her in her own business, at least, she thought that was what was happening. That is until he dropped the magazine out of the weapon and racked its slide to clear it.

On the outside, she was completely composed, but within she was so happy that things hadn't turned out differently.

Gideon held the weapon out. "This is an inquisitor standard issue pistol, would you be interested in it?"

"I would be happy to accept it toward your total," she answered kindly.

"Great. I also have cash for the rest."

Chapter 14

Cycle: 412 Month: 9 Rotation: 14
Corre Republic Space
Prefecture: Expansive
Planet: Benedictus
Location: Downtown Avalon

Once the two finished the transaction for the firearms, Gideon chambered a round in one of his new Magnums and slid it into the back of his pants. He placed the other two weapons and ammunition into his duffle bag, along with the grenades. The sword, however, was put into its own individual bag.

Charlie placed her new handgun and the cash from the deal into a multi-layered safe built into the wall. The door shut with a loud *thud* followed by several clicking sounds as the metal rods slid in place.

They walked together out of the showcase room and headed back for the elevator.

"So what can you tell me about the Corbo's? What has changed since I was last here?" the ex-bounty hunter asked, coming to a stop just short of the lift.

"I can tell you that it isn't going to be easy to get into Frank's estate. The place is like a compound from what I've heard."

Gideon shook his head. "I'm not worried about that. How large is their operation now?"

Charlie scratched the back of her head. "Well, I'd say that they now control about half of the city. A lot has changed, Gideon." She paused for a moment before sharing her inner turmoil. "Are you sure you want to go through with this?"

Ironic, you ask after I pay for everything…

"Yes, I'm certain. It has to be done."

"Well, alright. Frank bought his estate in the Grove district. You can't miss it. He literally owns the largest home in the city. It is going to be swarmed by guys, though, especially if they suspect you are coming."

Gideon's eyebrow arched.

"Yeah, I heard about your wife. I'm sorry."

Charlie appeared to be genuine, but he didn't care either way. Gideon slung the duffle bag over his left shoulder and held the other bag in his right hand. He stared at her neutrally. The arms-dealer got the hint, and she entered the elevator. Spectre followed and the door shut.

The ride back up to the basement was silent between the occupants, except the higher they climbed, the volume of the music above grew. Gideon began to recall the information he remembered about Frank's operation and any potential hunters that could be in his employment. However, since he had been gone for so long from Benedictus, there was no way to know who was still in the business and who was now the top hunters.

It doesn't matter how many guns he has working for him. I'm going to kill them all if they get in my way…

Charlie was the first to step off the elevator when the door slid open. She turned her head back to her most recent customer.

"It is good to see you again, Gideon. Let me know if you need anything else."

"Thanks for your help, Charlie," the ex-bounty hunter said. "Maybe your turret will work next time," he quipped.

Charlie's face turned red as she tried to hide her intention with the turret. "No, it's like I said…"

Gideon didn't care either way. He started toward the stairs as the hidden door slid shut.

Once back up inside the patron area of the bar, he saw that many people were still dancing to the beat, but Gideon realized he didn't see Crem or Sito anymore. Another pair had replaced them at their table. He looked to his left and saw Cort staring at him while drawing a pistol from beneath her loose jacket.

Gideon shoved Charlie over and dodged to the side, narrowly avoiding being hit by the burst from the other bounty hunter's weapon. The bullets tore through a man that had accidentally been in the wrong place at the wrong time. He collapsed to the floor, but the DJ didn't hear the shots due to his own headset blasting music in his ears. Several people sitting around saw the discharge and bolted out of the area, some knocking their tables over in the process.

Spectre rolled to cover behind the corner of the wall leading down the hallway to the basement. He dropped his bags and drew the pistol out from his pants.

The bartender desperately crawled away from the shooting and hid behind one of the flipped tables. She turned back in time to watch Gideon press his free hand on the amulet hanging around his neck. A burst of bright blue particles washed over him and formed into his frightening armored look.

"What the..." she stammered as her brain struggled to understand what she just saw.

Cort, in her foolish drunkenness, slowly moved up to where her target hid. She had already missed her opportunity to kill the more experienced bounty hunter in an ambush. Still, either way, she could not allow him to escape. The payday was too big for that.

She fired her pistol, shooting another burst of three bullets into the wall, sending bits of debris spraying everywhere.

A, "12:00" displayed up in the right-hand side of the Spectre's helmet's HUD.

"Commencing healing process," the suit said to him plainly.

"No, disengage. Frick!" Gideon cursed at his armor's automatic systems.

I gotta be quick this time...

The timer immediately dropped to "6:00" as it drew power to mend its user's body.

Gideon used his left hand to yank the collapsed laser rifle from the bag and magnetically connect it to his back. The female bounty hunter fired several more times as she continued to get closer.

"Why don't you come out and play?" Cort yelled over the music sarcastically.

To her shock and surprise, Spectre did just that. He rounded the corner in his full power armor, her eyes flashed in terror. There was no way her handgun had the firepower to penetrate her target's suit, and she knew it. Before her frightened legs could respond, Gideon raised his right arm and fired once. The bullet blew threw the drugged-out woman's head, killing her instantly.

"5:45."

More patrons to the bar ran every which way, but the music man was entirely unaware. He had given himself over to the rhythm and was oblivious to the carnage around him.

Charlie remained behind her table while Spectre checked for more targets. Three more men stood up slowly. Each wearing their own unique colored body armor. Their helmets flipped and formed around their heads while they raised their weapons.

The dingy green one on the right fired his laser rifle, hitting the ex-bounty hunter in the chest, cutting the clock by thirty seconds. Gideon ducked down, avoiding the other two men's attacks. He fired his pistol, hitting the one on the far right in the hand. While the yellow armored one was relatively protected, his hand was only covered with a glove. Blood shot out, and he screamed in pain as his gun fell to the floor.

Before Spectre could get a clean killing shot, the injured bounty hunter ducked down. Gideon fired over his head and moved for cover. While his power armor was enough to deal with most attacks, every successful injury he took lowered his timer as the suit repaired itself.

"5:03."

The green hunter stood again and flung several more bolts Gideon's way while his orange-colored comrade moved up with his laser SMG on the left. Spectre popped up and fired three times into the primary attacker. Each hit, but none dropped him.

Dammit, he's got some thick armor...

Spectre's HUD highlighted the orange bounty hunter in time for him to fire several shots into him as well. One of the bullets successfully pierced through between the armored plates of the shoulder and chest, causing the man to lower his gun long enough for Gideon to close with him. The man was able to shoot a stream of red bolts from his SMG into the advancing ex-bounty hunter.

The intense damage did not cause serious harm, but the timer did drop considerably.

"3:27."

Gideon slammed his shoulder into the attacker, knocking him back. Using his left hand, he wrapped his arm around the eager bounty hunter's helmet. He jammed his Magnum up under the other man's chin and fired twice. The bullets did not penetrate through the top of the helmet, but the man's body went limp.

The green hunter popped up again in the corner of Spectre's eye. Using his enhanced strength, Gideon whipped his arm out, sending the dead assassin flying through the air. Before he was hit by the flailing corpse, the green hunter ducked down again.

"3:04."

Spectre connected the pistol to his hip magnetically. In a flash, he drew his commando rifle, and it switched into active mode. A bright bolt darted across the space between the two men just as the green hunter rushed back up. His own laser rifle was hit, and a puff of smoke rose out from it. In that exact second he knew he was dead. He stood there in amazement before the next bolt burned through his white faceplate.

Gideon rechecked the area for threats, but this time found none. Those that were still in the bar cowered behind whatever cover they could find. While it wasn't uncommon for a brawl to break out in the Last Shot, it had been a long time since such a coordinated strike occurred quite like this.

"2:49."

The sound of deep steps and clanking drew closer to the last surviving bounty hunter that took part in the ambush.

"Poosh!" he whispered angrily while he held his bleeding right hand.

Spectre loomed over the man like a predator cornering his prey. The injured bounty hunter's helmet flipped back and collapsed at the base of his neck. He looked terrified, but it did not deter the angered fugitive.

"Who hired you?" Gideon asked, figuring he already knew the answer.

While it wasn't standard for a hitman to give out information on his employer, in this case, the injured man didn't want to die for what he knew.

"It uh… it was Frank Corbo."

Inwardly a chill ran through Gideon's body. He was surrounded by others that could be looking for a chance to get a shot in on him. However, it was unlikely after they just witnessed him single-handedly dispatch a group of attackers that they would make a move just yet.

He needed them all to get the message clearly that he wasn't messing around.

"No, no, no!" the man cried out as Spectre raised his rifle and fired.

"2:26."

Victoriously, he stomped back to where he had left his bags. Everyone alive stared in fear, including Charlie. His armor withdrew to the amulet in a swirl of particles. The pistol on his hip dropped to the ground. He scooped it up, reloaded it with a fresh magazine from his bag. After the rifle was switched back to storage mode, he stowed it away. He slung the duffle bag and gripped the other bag in his left hand, being sure to keep the loaded magnum easily seen in his right.

No one dared move as they watched the deadliest man in the room exit the bar.

Chapter 15

Cycle: 412 Month: 9 Rotation: 14
Corre Republic Space
Prefecture: Expansive
Planet: Benedictus
Location: Downtown Avalon

Hours had passed since one of the gunmen escaped the Last Shot bar. At least, that was the official patrolman report. Multiple dead, more wounded, and the media were everywhere, wanting to be the first to get a story.

Lights from several nearby officers' cruisers strobed in the darkness that was setting in. The dead and injured had already been transported out of the gruesome scene. However, several eyewitnesses were still being interviewed in the area.

Knowledge had discovered the incident when he was scanning through the planet's stream. His personal shuttle, a retrofitted *Sparrow*, flew in and began to hover over the parking lot. Several officers pointed upward at the spacecraft.

Special Agent Daykers had been on the scene for hours by now and was still feeling the exhaustion from dealing with Gideon Adama at the precinct. She covered her eyes as dust blew around from the thrusters. The *Sparrow* eased itself into a clearing, and the rear ramp lowered.

Most of the time, spacecraft like this one was reserved for tactical teams in the Republic Armed Forces. This one, though, looked modified and was dark blue.

"Ah, frag!" Daykers cursed under her breath.

"Who's that, ma'am?" a male officer inquired.

"Trouble."

The Keeper exited his ship. His helmet instantly began scanning the area and the citizens' personal ID chips, feeding him even more information than the typical human eye could possibly process. Many green icons displayed on his HUD representing each patrolman in the immediate area, along with their last names. Catherine began also showing the citizens nearby with an orange icon.

Knowledge's steps echoed as he made his way down to the stonecrete. A handful of the officers reached for the pistol on their hips, but the Special Agent held her arm out.

"Stand down."

"I thought I told you to contact me when you located him?!" Knowledge growled loudly for all to hear.

Daykers looked away and blushed angrily. She twisted her head back and spat, "I was trying to confirm the details first."

Now within arms distance, the large armored man came to a halt. "Perhaps I didn't make myself clear previously. This suspect is way outside of your possible capabilities. If he is located, you are specifically to notify me immediately. You are not to engage him under any circumstance."

The female officer pursed her lips and lowered her gaze. She nodded, upset with herself in the situation.

"What do you know?" the Keeper asked coldly.

"It looks like Gideon was here to purchase firearms."

That caught Knowledge's attention. "Did he mention why?"

"That… we don't know." Daykers jutted her thumb over her shoulder and back to the bar. "We know that this establishment is used to arm some of the more dangerous folks in Avalon, but we haven't been able to locate how they do it?"

The armored man tilted his head curiously.

She hated to admit it openly, but Daykers didn't see any point in holding anything back. After taking a breath, she continued. "I can't tell you how many raids we have conducted here…"

"Twelve," Knowledge said plainly as he read the report from his AI.

Both the male officer and the Special Agent were shocked.

"Ho… how did you…" the woman began.

"It is my job to know things, child. I could already tell from the description of the main shooter that this was him. However, what I need to know is why he was here to buy weapons. Why go here and not someplace else?"

"I… I don't know," Daykers said hesitatingly.

Knowledge grew irritated with the entire situation. "I need to speak with the owner of this business."

"She is inside, being questioned."

The Keeper stormed off and headed for the front door. He knew what needed to be done. The Special Agent, though, would certainly not approve.

An officer guarding the door saw the tall armored man making a straight line toward him. He gulped, but thankfully saw Daykers waving him through. The patrolman stood aside, and Knowledge briskly walked in.

The sight of the shot up bar was similar to plenty of other bullet-riddled places he had been to before. Unlike some of the other Keepers, Knowledge was more of a follow-up rather than the one doing the majority of the smashing. He was certainly skilled to take care of himself, he simply preferred non-violence when possible. His line of work, though, brought many instances when a gun was the only solution.

Deep down, he knew that finding Gideon would probably end up in a showdown of sorts. The last time they had been together hadn't gone over so smoothly. It didn't change that they needed the amulet back. If he could help it, Knowledge was going to be the voice of reason. That was an awfully large if.

Shattered glass crunched beneath his heavy boot as he entered. Several crime scene officers were taking photographs of the enormous mess. Hologram projectors hovered in place over where those that had died breathed their last. They filled in a more complete picture of the scene while the corpses were taken to the morgue for processing.

Knowledge spotted two officers in the corner with a woman in ordinary clothing. His helmet invisibly scanned her face and pulled up her profile from the Keeper's database. He wasn't surprised at the length of her criminal record, he had seen it all before. Very little shocked him anymore. It was the curse of knowing so much. However, it was necessary for his role in the order. Someone had to do it.

One of the officers spotted the trio and patted his companion's shoulder. The other man saw the Keeper but didn't know what to make of the sight.

"Can we help you?" one of them asked.

"I need to speak with Ms. Kenner... privately."

Both of the men glanced at one another then looked back at Knowledge. Meanwhile, the keeper was simultaneously scanning the report they had filled into their tablet that transmitted back to the station's archive.

"What jurisdiction do you have?"

Knowledge took a breath, and his helmet pulled up the two officers' profiles. Neither had led a particularly strong career in the force. Frylone Drake, for example, on the left, had been given a leave of absence while there was an internal investigation to the shooting of a suspect that was linked to a local gang.

"Officer Drake, I was not asking for permission. Speak with your superior if you have an issue."

Frylone's eye twitched for a second then he pursed his lips. "Maybe I will."

The two officers walked off, both appeared annoyed by the interruption to their interview.

Charlie looked the Keeper up and down. There was something about the armor that was captivating to behold. Her demeanor was utterly calm despite the bullets and lasers that had zipped through her business just a short time ago. She couldn't even begin to count how many times someone drew a firearm since she owned the bar. Undoubtedly many more occurrences than the authorities had been called about.

"I need you to tell me what happened here," Knowledge said plainly.

"Why don't you go talk to those two officers you blew off? I already told them everything." Her defiance wasn't as much aggressive as it was deflecting. "But, if you'd like, I could get you a drink when you're off duty."

The woman reached out and caressed the Keeper's chest. She bit her lip as her mind slipped into imagining what the armored man must look like beneath.

Knowledge, however, was entirely unaffected by her charm. "I need you to tell me what happened here immediately. I already read their report. It lacked… details. Why was Gideon Adama here?"

"Well, I don't know what to tell you," Charlie said before she bit her lip sensually.

The Keeper was again becoming very irritated. "Alright, then let's try this. Your establishment has been raided on multiple occasions."

While he spoke, he began reviewing the building plans that had been submitted to the city hall along with the corroborating reports from the patrolman's searches.

"So?" the woman shrugged.

She was stunned to see Knowledge stroll off and walk right through the crime scene that the investigators were still photographing. Several of them looked up in confusion.

Unsure of what to do, Charlie remained in place. That is until she saw the Keeper turn the corner to the hallway. Something nagged at the back of her mind that this was no ordinary government goon. She rushed after him and nearly slipped on a piece of debris in doing so.

Her heart began to beat faster when she saw the basement door wide open. In a flash, she ran down the hall and discovered Knowledge standing right in front of her secret entrance.

"Can I help you with something?" she asked, trying to hide her nervousness.

The Keeper's suit alerted him to her elevated heart rate, and he knew why. His HUD clearly displayed an illuminated icon as soon as he entered the room. An electronic signature from the tiny hole in the wall.

"Interesting," he said as he raised his finger up to the entry point.

Charlie smoothly came down the staircase. She scoffed under her breath. There simply was no way the armored finger of this strange man could possibly fit into that hole. To her amazement, a small bright orange cloud of particles swirled around the Keeper's finger and extender to a thinner form. He inserted his digit into the gap and pressed.

Internal fear gripped the bartender just as the hidden doorway illuminated. Knowledge withdrew his fingertip, and it returned back to the standard shape. He nudged the door, and it abruptly swung open.

Even though his face was covered, the woman could sense the cynicism beneath his wide pitch black faceplate.

"Look what I found," he said bitterly.

Charlie pointed her finger and spoke conclusively. "Tha... that elevator isn't safe. You step on there, and your heavy suit is gonna fall straight through the floor."

Knowledge chuckled. "I'm sure I will be just fine. Would you care to accompany me?"

"I'm not getting in there with you!" she hissed fearfully.

A gun formed in the Keeper's hand, and she suddenly located her cooperation. Disdain poured from her pouty lips, but the bartender sternly walked through the doorway and stepped onto the lift. Knowledge followed behind her. He moved methodically. There was no pride in him for discovering what the local authorities had failed to do. Uncovering secrets was what he did.

The ride to the lower level was quiet. Charlie was the first one off, and Knowledge made sure to keep his eye on her while his helmet scanned and surveyed the hidden product display room. While he wasn't afraid of whatever weaponry she could possibly be hiding down here, it was more so that she didn't end up killing herself.

Sometimes when apprehended, suspects and fugitives alike sought ways to escape being interrogated by someone as intimidating as the Keeper. In the past, life and the preservation of it had been held with high esteem in the Corre Republic. That time had long since expired. Now it was more about happiness and worldly joy. It was almost culturally permissible to escape hardship by taking one's own life.

Knowledge had personally witnessed many atrocities in his lifetime. He remembered a time when life meant something. Nowadays, the importance of his role was what kept him going.

"Kay, I have identified a turret concealed in the ceiling just up ahead," Catherine said while she simultaneously displayed a silhouette of the defensive weapon on his HUD.

Charlie's heart continued to beat faster as she entered the next room and turned to face the keeper. She honestly had no idea if the weapon would be able to pierce his armor or not, but getting caught with this many firearms would have her locked away in prison for life.

"This is quite the collection of firearms," Knowledge said condescendingly as he slowly approached the doorway. "All of which, no doubt, is illegal."

His suspicion was confirmed when his suit alerted him it had located a "Class 5" hacking device. Typically such pieces of equipment were utilized in cracking a WarMech's systems and overriding its fail-safe. It was one of the only ways such an expensive part of military power could be stolen.

The woman tucked her arms behind her back, defiantly.

"Do you know what the sentence will be for distributing these items?"

Plenty of patrolmen had tried to intimidate her before. Knowledge wasn't any different just because he wore power armor.

"No, what?"

The Keeper tilted his head and spoke cruelly. "Death."

Charlie smiled devilishly. "As if."

Knowledge's pistol morphed into a much larger rifle. He aimed it at the hidden turret and fired repeatedly. After the tenth bolt blasted it apart, the secret hatch hung limp, and sparks shot out from what was left of the automatic weapon system.

Charlie's eyes were wide in fear. She rushed to the wall and ripped one of the military-grade rifles off and loaded in a powercell. Before she could even swing the weapon toward the keeper, Knowledge shot her in the shoulder.

The arms-dealer dropped the ground, screaming in pain as her arm hung there motionless. Her right hand trembled as she tried to tenderly clutch her wound.

Knowledge knew he could not count on the arms-dealer to be honest with him about what happened with Gideon. Thankfully, he had other means of learning what he needed to know.

He began walking toward the woman and released his own gun that he had been holding. It dissolved into an orange vapor, adding to the dramatic effect of his menacing approach. "Per the Essential Peace Act signed by Prefect Major Talion Caedis, the illegal selling of firearms within the Inner worlds is punishable by death."

Charlie's eyes bulged, and she pushed herself up against the wall behind her.

"I'll… I'll tell you whatever you want to know."

The Keeper's fingertips began to glow. He raised his hands up toward the sides of her head. "The time for questions is over."

No one up above could hear the screams from the woman as she wailed in agony as her mind was scanned vigorously by the Keeper's onboard system. She finally sank to the floor, dead. Trails of faint smoke lifted up from the burn marks on her scalp.

Knowledge turned back to the lift. "Catherine, once her memories are processed, pull up the footage of when she first saw Gideon today."

Knowledge felt no remorse for what he had done. Getting information was his job, and he would do what he must. All that mattered was getting the amulet back.

Chapter 16

Cycle: 412 Month: 9 Rotation: 14
Corre Republic Space
Prefecture: Expansive
Planet: Benedictus
Location: The Corbo's Estate – Outside of Avalon

The cover of darkness of night had fallen on Avalon and her citizens. Gideon had finally made his way outside of the city and drew near to the crime lord's massive mansion. After changing his bandages and tending to his wounds, he used the commando rifle to scan the area.

Multiple men patrolled the outside of the estate while several more stood to watch on top of the structure. It truly was a beautiful home, but it looked much more like a compound with the high walls and extreme level of security overlooking it.

During his time in the military, Gideon had taken on more armed fighters than this at once. However, he usually was accompanied by a team. The solo life of a bounty hunter forced him to rethink many of his strategies that had been hammered into his head through his veteran experience.

Storming the mansion would not be a simple task. His blood boiled, knowing that his wife's murderer was safely protected within.

I'm coming for you, Saul…

No matter the challenge, there wasn't anything that was going to prevent him from getting to the little bastard. His time was nearly up.

Due to his physical injuries, Gideon forced himself to calm down and mentally go over his plan one more time.

Okay... push through, locate Saul, kill him. Escape before the beacon goes off.

It wasn't much of a plan, but it was better than nothing. He knew that he was going to have to alter strategies after the shooting started. Once he was in a safe but nearby position, Gideon set his duffle bag down. He reached up with his right hand and activated the amulet, his suit formed tightly around his body. While it appeared to be heavy and possibly cumbersome, it was quite maneuverable from him. While it was very durable and incredibly resilient to damage, it still allowed the wearer to physically be able to respond to threats without being overly cumbersome.

The same exhausting timer appeared on his heads-up-display.

"12:00."

Then the same message as before also repeated.

"Commencing healing process."

Again, due to its owner being injured, the power armor diverted energy from its defensive durability to begin healing Gideon's body. The timer immediately dropped to "6:00."

I gotta do this quickly...

In a flurry, he connected his pistols to his thighs and attached the sword to his back magnetically.

Then he hurriedly joined his spare magazines and power cells around his waist.

"5:48."

With the laser rifle in hand, it flipped into active mode. He aimed it at one of the men on top of the expensive home and fired. The bright crimson beam lanced straight through the unsuspecting criminal, melting his brain in a wisp. Before the first man's body even dropped off the roof to the bushes below, Spectre fired twice more, killing two additional guards.

By now, the men protecting the entrance spotted the radiant bolts and ran over to the protective wall. Gideon took the chance and sprinted inhumanly fast around the thick barrier to the other side. The voices of the men grew as more and more were drawn out to deal with the situation.

Using his suit's jumper pack, the ex-bounty hunter lifted up and over the wall and landed in a roll.

"5:12."

"What's happening? Is it him?!" Frank Corbo exclaimed.

The crime lord had steeled himself for this very moment. However, he still wasn't entirely convinced deep within that they had much of a chance against the famed killer. Still, he wasn't about to let any of his people know that.

"Sir, we have multiple deaths confirmed. The other exterior guards are moving to locate the shooter," Jin, Frank's head of security, said with his eyes fixed to the surveillance screen.

"That fragger has to be here somewhere. Tell them to be on alert. He may be trying to split us up."

Jin nodded briskly. "Yes, sir." Using his earpiece, the security supervisor issued orders to his team leaders.

Bringing his rifle up, Gideon checked the area. His HUD showed no other threats outside other than the ones congregated together, thinking they were protecting the border from danger. He attached his rifle and drew his left magnum while also unsheathing the sword.

The suit began scanning the structure as Spectre closed the distance. Two silhouettes of other guards could be seen running toward the front door. Gideon darted forward and pressed himself up against the wall before they saw him. Both men burst out of the door and ran to assist the others.

"4:47."

Need to move faster.

Spectre quietly entered the building and paid no attention to the illustrious interior. He was a man focused on one thing right then, revenge.

Just then, his suit alerted him to a new heartbeat approaching him from behind. He spun on his heel and aimed his pistol. Before the man even realized what was waiting for him around the corner, he was shot twice. Without even so much as a groan, he flipped over a chair and lost consciousness as he bled out.

With a masterful stride, the ex-bounty hunter navigated through the expensive estate, heading toward the only room that had a group of heartbeats.

"4:02."

Frank leaned over Jin's shoulder and searched over the wall of camera feeds.

"Something's wrong... he must be here!" he frantically searched over the extensive collection of screens but couldn't spot the fugitive.

"Why can't we see him?!"

One of the cameras on the lower left of the large display showed a muzzle flash and one of his guards ducking behind cover.

"There he is!" he shouted. "He's already inside!"

Jin's heart skipped as he realized the massive mistake his people had made. "All units, Spectre is inside the main building. I repeat, all units return to the main building."

After a quick exchange of bullets within the lounge with one of the defenders, Gideon slashed the stubborn man across his chest. Blood sprayed out before the ex-bounty hunter again brought the sword down and mercilessly killed the guard.

"3:34."

This is taking too long.

He was only two rooms away from his destination when an alert chirped in his ear. His mini-map showed fourteen heartbeats heading straight for him.

I can't allow them to box me in.

Gideon flicked the bladed weapon, sending what little blood was on it to be flipped off for the most part. He sheathed the sword then reloaded the magnum. The first guard was just on the other side of the wall when Gideon drew his right pistol and brought both handguns on target. He fired once from each of his weapons, hitting the man twice in the chest.

Bullets began blasting through the walls as the other thugs realized what happened. None of them wanted to be the one to enter the lounge first, and they had been given the order to do what they needed to. Even still, Frank cursed while he watched his beautiful home be shot up by his own people. The alternative, though, of Spectre getting to him could not happen.

Despite having hired Gideon on several occasions himself, Frank had never witnessed the experienced assassin at work. There were stories galore of his exploits, but not many lived after seeing him in action.

The ex-bounty hunter ducked for cover. Laser bolts scorched through the walls and burned into the opposite side. Machine gun fire tore up the North wall, absolutely shredding a piece of artwork that had ordained it.

"2:58."

Gideon connected his handguns to his thigh armor and again drew his laser rifle. His HUD displayed perfect silhouettes of his attackers through the wall, giving him fantastic vantage to know where to shoot. Three guards were killed before one of the team leaders figured out what happened. The others dispersed in different directions, all seeking better shelter from the commando rifle's bolts.

The crime boss was furious. Being attacked in his own home was unfathomable. He had climbed from the lowest levels of the crime world to be at the top. Too many of his people had already been killed by Spectre. It needed to be brought to a halt.

"Sir, I'm getting reports that their scanners can't see him," Jin said nervously.

He had spent good money on equipping his people with bullet-resistant armor beneath their suits and advanced glasses that had some integrated military imaging equipment. While he would have preferred his guards to be fitted with a more tactical loadout, he still had to remain mindful of the planet's government getting nosey. As it was, he had to consistently send hush money to the Governor himself to keep him off his back.

Enough was enough, though. Gideon had to die. Frank spun around and pointed at his own armored team that was stationed within the room. Previously they had been a crew of freelance hitmen. Now they were more of a personal guard.

"Tak!" the crime lord said, shouting to the squad leader.

"Sir," the camouflaged colored armored man said through his suit's external speakers.

"Deal with this," Frank hissed.

Tak glanced at the rest of his team, who racked their weapons. The sharp sounds of their rifle's bolts and laser weapons charging filled the room for a few seconds.

"Of course. This is why you pay us the big bucks. Alright, boys, if he's inviz, then we use the ole mark one optics," Tak said to his team.

"2:21."

Many of the other men had backed off, but Gideon was still no closer to his target. Even though his rifle was at "43%" charge, he popped out the powercell. It clanked on the tiled floor, and he slid a fresh one in place.

Just then he heard a heavy sound, similar to footsteps, coming from up above him. Before the attacker could respond, a barrage of bullets obliterated the ceiling and rained down into the lounge. Spectre narrowly dodged out of the way as a large shape fell through the floor from above. It landed hard in the room and stood up straight.

Gideon glared beneath his faceplate at the sight of the Centurion power armor that stood before him. Unlike his own suit, the Republic designed power armor was much larger and more visually impressive. It was a standard model of power armor used in the Republic Armed Forces, and they were not enjoyable to go up against.

"2:06."

The green and brown Centurion slowly spun around and brought its arm-mounted chain-gun to bear. Gideon opened fire while simultaneously moving to his right, heading for the lounge's entrance. Each hit burned deeply into the thick armor, but none injured the warrior within.

A high-pitched whine shrieked as round after round fired from the rotating barrels of the chain-gun. The stream of bullets missed their target at first, but then the Centurion dragged his arm to follow Spectre until it hit him.

Gideon twisted from the impact and fell behind what remained of a wooden desk. A blue mist of particles appeared around the chest of his armor as the suit fought to repair the damage it just sustained. The timer dropped to "00:31."

Now was no time to stay down, he had to get moving. He expertly flipped to his feet and squatted down while another stream of large caliber rounds shredded through where he would have been standing. Using his jumper pack, Gideon boosted across the floor, grinding against debris and tearing up the tiles beneath him.

The Centurion wasn't prepared for the move, and so was slow to respond. Spectre steadied his aim and expertly fired repeatedly into the knee armor until it weakened and one of the bolts pierced through, disabling the man's leg from the knee down. The heavily armored man growled angrily but his leg gave out, sending him smashing brutally into the floor.

"00:17."

Poosh!

Gideon pushed himself up off the ground and brought his rifle up. Just then, he was hit in the back by an explosive that sent him launching across the room and into a display case. The glass doors shattered as the ex-bounty hunter collided with what remained of the beautiful furniture, completely destroying it.

"Heavy Damage Sustained!" displayed on Gideon's distorted heads up display.

The timer dropped to "00:00," and he cursed.

"Beacon activated," illuminated in place of the previous warning message.

Despite doing all that he could, the combination of his own physical injuries and rushing in unprepared had cost him dearly. Now warriors much worse than these goons were going to be notified of his location and come looking for him.

He coughed but was able to get to one knee. His rifle had been mangled in the blast.

"You ain't so tough," a voice called out from outside of the room.

Gideon's helmet restored itself, and his HUD normalized. However, he still couldn't see who was speaking. The silhouettes of the cowering thug guards were still there, but not whoever had shot him in the back.

Inhibitors...

Each of the walls on either side of him burst inward, and armored men stepped through. Gideon drew his pistols and opened fire. The bullets hit but were not strong enough to penetrate. Both stood absolutely still as a small rocket boost through the main entrance of the war-torn lounge and hit the ex-bounty square in the chest.

Again, he flew back, and this time slammed into the wall. His suit warned him of taking the critical damage, but there wasn't much else he could do. Other than being even more pissed off than he already was. For cycles, he was the most feared bounty hunter in the region. Now here he was getting floored by some new hunters.

Everything ached as the suit had to draw away power from healing him to attempt to repair itself, but Gideon knew that his wounds under his suit were getting worse. Its power source was dangerously low, and a new flashing icon appeared in the corner of his HUD.

I'm dead if the suit loses power completely.

The hunter in the Centurion armor managed to get into a sitting position. No doubt, he also was in a tremendous amount of pain. Both of the other warriors stood there, guns lowered. A crunching sound came from outside of the room.

Gideon finally saw the green and brown armored man step into the room. He held a modified dart launcher tightly in his gloved hands. It had the classic tactical look with added sights, custom stock, and a mini scattergun attached to the bottom. His armor, along with the other two mercenaries, was a newer model of Bruticus power armor made by the Union of Stars. They were much sleeker than the Centurion, but a bit less durable.

"I imagined it would have been much harder to pin you down, Spectre. Frankly, it's a bit disappointing," Tak said sarcastically.

The ex-bounty hunter managed to get to his knees. His helmet showed him where the damage was to his armor on its display. His suit displayed a new message, "Unable to Repair Damage. Power Low."

Not… good…

"I'm not done… yet," he stammered.

Tak squatted down and peered into Spectre's faceplate. "You don't get it, do you? You're about to die, and I will have made my name greater by killing you."

"I'm not… dying here…"

Tak looked up at one of his men and nodded his head. The other mercenary strolled over to Spectre and punted him in the head with his armored boot. Gideon's head shot back. He was struck that he flipped onto his back and dropped both of his pistols.

New alerts appeared on his helmet's screen. His vision blurred for a moment then returned to normal.

In cycles past, he would have cleared the entire mansion of enemies without breaking much of a sweat. His mind had been so distracted from the loss of his wife that his decision making was adversely affected. Not to mention, it had been a very long time since his own suit was operating at full capacity. Things would have played out very differently if his suit was powered up.

The mercenary leader scoffed and connected the dart thrower to his back magnetically. He spoke very animatedly with his hands. "This is pathetic. I was expecting something... I don't know... more epic. You are the most famous bounty hunter that has ever lived. And here you are... a husk of your former self."

He motioned with his hand, and the other two mercs rushed forward and pinned Spectre down. The wounded mercenary remained slumped up against the wall, profoundly wishing he could be the one to finish off the ex-bounty hunter.

Gideon tried to resist the two men, but he was too injured to push them away with their own enhanced strength.

Tak yanked out the knife sheathed on his chest armor. He gripped it tightly in his hand. The edge of the blade began to glow red. "Oh well, guess I'll just have to mourn for you with my newly earned fortune."

Under his helmet, Gideon's eyes burned angrily. *I'm not dying here!*

The men that had taken cover during the earlier shooting had now moved up and watched in disbelief as Tak toyed with Spectre. Suddenly an intense explosion rocked the building. The thugs and other guards rushed toward the origin of the damage to investigate what just happened.

The mercenaries were distracted for just a moment, but it was more than enough time for the ex-bounty hunter. With all of his might, Gideon yanked his right arm free in one swift motion and used his fist to strike the armored man on his left side. Tak spun back in surprise to watch Spectre punch the merc on his left with such force that he lost consciousness.

"No you don't!" the leader exclaimed.

Gideon wrestled with the other merc that was trying to subdue him while Tak brought the knife up and was trying to go in for the kill.

Spectre used his legs to shove the warrior off of him and sent him bashing into the wall. In one smooth motion, Gideon flipped up to his feet. He instantly deflected the heated knife from stabbing straight through his suit. Tak responded with a knee attack to Spectre's stomach, sending shooting pain up his side.

"Gah!" Gideon bellowed, stepping back to avoid another hit.

Another explosion rang out, sending streams of debris to crash into the lounge. The maimed Centurion mercenary tried to aim his mini focus beam mounted onto his right arm because he couldn't get a good shot on Spectre.

"So, you still have a bit of a fight left in you?" Tak mocked. "Good."

By now, the merc that had been temporarily knocked out and the other armored man stood up. They surrounded Spectre, and the other two drew their own knives. Gideon knew full well that any one of them could potentially kill him with the heated weapons.

The gunshots finally came to an end, and the sound of someone walking filled the emptiness. Each step was distinct though, just like whoever was heading toward the showdown was wearing power armor too.

"Hello, Gideon," a voice said from the next room.

Of all the men in the room, only the ex-bounty hunter recognized the speaker. His HUD confirming it by displaying the silhouette of the new arrival. Unfortunately, the hired warriors had no idea what challenge had just joined in the fight.

Great. It had to be you...

The crime lord enlarged the footage of one of his surviving surveillance cameras. Its angle wasn't the greatest, but he could make out that whoever just killed most of the men he had left stopped short of what remained of his once lovely lounge.

"Who in the void is that?!"

None of his men watching could answer him adequately.

"Are they here to kill him too? Or..." Frank stood back up straight. "Maybe I should get out of here just in case."

The crime lord snapped his fingers, and the other men with him jumped to their feet.

"We're leaving!"

They quickly began to file out of the room.

Tak stepped to the side, giving him a way to see toward the opening of the ravaged lounge and still keep an eye on Spectre. He motioned with his hand, and the Centurion aimed his chain gun at the entrance.

"Who's there?" the mercenary leader shouted loudly. "This is my kill. Back off!"

The sound of the steps finally came to a stop. "He is coming with me. Lower your weapons, and you can leave with your lives."

Gideon happened to notice on his mini-map that the only other cluster of heartbeats that he had been heading for were now on the move. Knowing his chance at killing any of the Corbo's that was here was running out, he tried to come up with a plan.

One of the other mercs sneered at the forceful suggestion from the newcomer. "Yeah, okay. You want a bowtie with that too…" the man was interrupted by a burst of orange bolts that burned through his neck plating.

He dropped to his knees and gasped for air as blood poured out of his body. The Centurion unleashed a wave of bullets that tore through what remained of the wall with his chain gun. Gideon used his jumper pack to launch himself up through the second floor. Tak drew the firearm on his right hip. It quickly transformed into an SMG with a holographic sight that hovered over the weapon.

A series of green laser bolts etched into the ceiling, but Spectre dodged to the right and avoided them.

"Frag!"

The other two mercenaries continued firing into the opening and doorway until their weapons emptied. Tak spun back around and steadied his SMG.

Gideon bolted down the hallway. With no firearms left, he was going to have to make up a new plan as he went.

Meanwhile, Tak and his other two bounty hunters remained motionless. The other man in the Bruticus armor reloaded his rifle while the Centurion tried to crawl backward some more.

"Did we get him?" the mercenary leader inquired.

Just then, a dark blue shape jumped through one of the busted walls and rolled to the side. The Keeper of Knowledge spun his heated swords in a flurry and sliced through the standing merc as Tak dove for cover.

The Centurion warrior pointed his focus beam and fired before he aimed adequately at the keeper. A bright purple beam lanced through the wall and burned toward Knowledge, who quickly ducked and dodged to the right.

Boosting backward, Knowledge released his short swords, and they evaporated into a mist of bright orange particles. A massive cannon type weapon formed in his hands, and he planted his feet in place. He lowered it on his shoulders and fired a ball of energy at his target. The crippled merc screamed just before his upper half was disintegrated.

Tak crawled out of the room on all fours. He stood up and sprinted as fast as his legs would carry him.

The Keeper's helmet surveyed the area while Knowledge tracked Spectre's footsteps running away from the battle. Even without being able to track him directly, Catherine had many ways she could follow a target.

Knowledge released his cannon and ran out of the lounge, attempting to cut off his target's supposed escape.

"Frank Corbo and his men are heading for an exit ahead of Gideon," Catherine pointed out.

Knowledge ran faster when his AI showed him the likely location they would head out from.

Gideon leaped through a closed window and dropped down to the pristine yard as glass and debris sprinkled the area around him. He rolled into a crouch, and his helmet identified the group of escaping thugs up ahead. They were quickly heading straight for a parked black vehicle. While this portion of the property appeared still in good condition, several nearby trees had a red glow about them from the fire burning intensely from the other side of the structure. The sound of approaching sirens grew louder and louder.

Saul isn't here… but Frank is.

211

The crime lord turned around and spotted the ex-bounty hunter charging toward him. He pointed at the pursuing man, "Kill him!"

Jin opened the door to the awaiting hover vehicle while three men broke off and took cover. They began opening fire, one of the bullets hitting Gideon in the shoulder. He dodged left then right, trying to avoid being shot since his suit wasn't repairing itself currently.

Spectre gripped the handle of his sword and launched himself into the air with his jumper pack. Jin ducked inside the vehicle, and its engine roared. Each of the guards fired upward as the ex-bounty hunter descended in his arc. The top of the hovercar crunched down, the roof narrowly avoiding the crime lord within.

Gideon's helmet drew a silhouette of where Frank was sitting, and using his enhanced strength, drove the sword through the roof. A loud shriek filled the vehicle's cabin from the bladed weapon slicing the metal overhead, but the edge of the sword stopped just short of the crime lord.

"Fragger!" Frank exclaimed angrily back at his attacker.

Terror gripped Jin's face. He pressed himself up tightly against the door and shouted to the driver. "Get us the void out of here!"

Spectre yanked the sword free to strike again, but the bullets hitting his armor were damaging his suit further.

The driver threw the vehicle into reverse, accidentally running over one of the guards outside.

Not being prepared for the sudden momentum shift, Gideon tumbled from the roof and flopped to the grass. Seconds later, the crime lord's SUV was peeling out down the driveway and was evacuated safely.

Both of the other guards continued firing their handguns at the downed warrior. Some of the rounds bounced off the injured ex-bounty hunter, but still inflicting some minor damage. Gideon forced himself to stand.

The sensation of failure washed over him. He was unsuccessfully able to kill either Frank or Saul. And now the Keeper of Knowledge had located him. Everything was falling apart.

"Power Low," flashed again on his HUD.

Gideon wished that his suit's phasing ability would work. It would undoubtedly help him to have avoided the unnecessary damage he sustained.

While he gripped the sword in his right hand, he yanked a knife free with his left. Using all of his might, he threw it at one of the men, the blade dug deep into his forehead. The remaining guard saw what happened to his friend and cowered. Two laser bolts burned into his back, severing his spine.

Spectre looked to his left to see Knowledge approaching. The two armored men stared at each other for several moments, both prepared for reacting to the other.

"I guess you were in the area?" Gideon finally asked boldly, disturbing the relative peace.

"It's over, Gideon," Knowledge said plainly. "Hand over the amulet, and I will let you live."

The sirens continued to grow in volume. Time was short before they had additional company of prying eyes.

Pain from his previous bullet wounds tugged on Gideon's body. His heart raced within his chest, and he was breathing heavily. His last knife and sword were no match for the Keeper's limitless arsenal. But he wasn't about to surrender right now. Not until he exacted his revenge.

Knowledge didn't raise his laser rifle but was ready to in a moment's notice. "Hand it over. You've already suffered enough. There's no sense in giving up your life too."

Gideon smirked angrily beneath his helmet. "I guess you know about Joan? Of course, you do… you're the "steward of all knowledge in the 'verse" after all."

The Keeper tilted his head. "I didn't want it to be like this."

"Yeah, neither did I!" the ex-bounty hunter snarled. "You put me in this position!"

"You abandoned us."

Knowledge's tone was cold and decisive. Gideon took a deep breath and forced himself to calm down. He would need his head to be clear if he was going to get out of this situation.

Going toe-to-toe against one of the keepers that guarded the Republic was a foolish idea most of the time. Spectre had evaded their search for longer than he cared to count, but the danger of his suit being low on power added to the list of negatives.

The Keeper was growing annoyed. "Give me your suit, Gideon."

Spectre shook his head slowly. "I can't. Not right now."

"You've been hanging onto it for over fifteen cycles. Peace has been locked up in a chamber ever since what you did to him."

"Good," Gideon spat.

Knowledge tilted his head. "You understand what his role is to the Republic, right?"

Spectre shook his head angrily. "Of course I do, Kay. But he is a monster. I'm not about to hand over the amulet and let him escape that prison!"

The keeper and the fugitive stared each other down for another moment.

"I won't ask again," Knowledge finally said. "It's over."

Gideon's body tensed. "Is that a threat?"

"No… it is a warning. I don't want to have to resort to killing you to take the amulet back."

The ex-bounty hunter smacked his lips. "That's not going to happen. I have taken on much deadlier opponents than you."

Knowledge looked him up and down. "True, but you are severely injured, and your suit is nearly depleted of power."

A stream of water shot up above the mansion then was angled back behind it. The fire crews fought to contain the flames that continued to spread.

Knowing that his own threats were nearly meaningless in his condition, Gideon decided to be honest. "Kay, look. I need it to avenge my wife. I can't give it back… not yet."

"Oh, I'm not here to stop you from your rampage to kill some inconsequential criminals. I came for the armor, and that's all," Knowledge said, angling his foot in a ready position.

Gideon spotted the change in the other man's stance and knew that the conversation was about to abruptly end. He was at a significant disadvantage being caught out in the open like he was.

Seeing as how the ex-bounty hunter was refusing to give up easily, Knowledge was left with no other option.

"I don't want to hurt you, but you leave me no choice."

The Keeper tossed his rifle aside. Before it even touched the sod, it disappeared in a puff. Two short swords formed in his armored hands. Each began to glow orange along the blade.

Gideon gripped his own sword tightly. "I will do what I have to, my old friend."

Using his mind, a cable formed out of his suit and connected to the bottom of the melee weapon. The powercell began charging and energizing the blade with power drawn from his armor. His own sword blade began to glow red.

"I do have one other question," Knowledge said plainly. "What is in that bracelet you wear that allows you to be hidden from cameras?"

Gideon clenched his jaw. "You wouldn't probably believe me if I told you."

"Is it experimental inhibitor technology?"

216

"Nope. It was a gift."

Knowledge's head perked up. "From whom?"

"Are we gonna fight or what?" Gideon asked, frustrated by the situation.

Both warriors got into their preferred stances and remained motionless. Several firefighters rounded the building and froze in place when they saw the two armored figures staring one another down.

Knowledge darted forward and swung wide with his right sword, then followed it quickly with a slash from his left. Spectre blocked both strikes and sliced with his own. The Keeper used both of his swords to shield his body.

"I still don't understand why you left everything behind," Knowledge said calmly. "You were a protector of the Republic."

Gideon jumped backward, the swords making an electronic interference sound as he pushed off. "I tried to tell you. But instead, you sided with the others."

"I stuck to the oath we all made." The Keeper pointed one of his swords at his adversary. "The same one you took."

"I didn't join to prop up a country as evil as this one!" Gideon growled. "You of all people know what is going on in the shadows."

Emotions that he had long ago buried began to well up deep inside.

I can't lose myself to my past...

Knowledge walked forward slowly. "How can you be so deluded. The Republic is far from perfect, but it is the only beacon of hope against the Synthetics returning and extinguishing all of humanity."

"You're the one that's delusional, Kay!" Spectre shouted before charging forward.

Both men exchanged strikes once more. Neither was able to touch the other. Despite their armor being incredibly durable to most damage, heated blades could inflict serious harm.

I can't fight him off much longer. I got to get out of here.

Spectre deflected another slice attack from the Keeper. He used his own left arm to pin Knowledge's right forearm to his side. Before the dark blue armored keeper could respond, Gideon headbutted him with all that he had, cracking his own faceplate. Knowledge staggered backward, then regained himself and charged forward.

The ex-bounty hunter ducked beneath the Keeper's right sword, narrowly avoiding being beheaded. He leaned forward and used his jumper pack to launch himself into the other man, sending them both flying into the mansion's East outer wall.

They blew through a second wall within the building before their momentum came to a halt. Debris crashed down all around them, and smoke was everywhere from the fire consuming the crime lord's personal residence.

At some point during the crashing through everything, Knowledge had released his swords. He remained within the crater of the hardened interior wall, obviously dazed by the impact. Not wanting to miss his opportunity, the ex-bounty hunter kicked as hard as he could with his right heel into the keeper's chest. His adversary's body sank a little deeper into the wall, and a framed piece of artwork that survived all of the destruction fell to the ground and broke.

The fugitive then lashed out with a brutal kick straight to the side of Knowledge's left knee. The Keeper let out a visceral scream of pain and agony.

Gideon knew he needed to be quick because it wouldn't be long before the other man's suit would heal the injury, and he would be right back at it. He pointed his heated sword square with the Keeper's faceplate. Parts of his armor had begun to crumble and disintegrate, revealing the civilian clothing he wore beneath.

I could kill him right here and now. I should… but why am I hesitating? I know he won't ever stop pursuing me until he has the suit.

Knowledge lifted his head and glared at his old friend. "I trusted you," he said with a massive amount of tired disdain in his voice.

"I never meant to betray you, Kay. You chose Peace instead of listening to me. I won't be giving back the armor," Gideon replied with contempt.

"Wh… why? Tell me why you left."

I don't have time for this.

"You know why!" Spectre growled.

Knowledge leaned his head forward, then shook it. "Sacrifices have to be made…"

The ex-bounty hunter irately cut in. "Don't give me that! Don't you give me that lie!" he breathed angrily. His suit further began to crumble. "No. I won't protect a nation that does such evil in the shadows. Never again."

"So instead you will abandon it to further evil?" the keeper asked brutally.

"Listen to me clearly, Kay. Don't. Follow. Me." Gideon then turned to walk away.

"I can't just ignore the fact that I found you," Knowledge called out. "I have to hunt you until I get the suit back. It's protocol. We must have Peace back. Everything is starting to fall apart across the Republic."

Spectre glanced over his shoulder, "Your rules are what stopped you from listening to me all of those cycles ago. Do what you have to. Next time though... I might not hold back from killing you."

With that, Gideon quickly walked out back through the carnage. His boots crunched debris beneath him.

Knowledge began to struggle to pull himself out of the wall. While his suit continued to repair itself, Catherine tried to track the fugitive.

"I've lost him," she said reluctantly.

"Dammit..." he grumbled.

It didn't concern him though, now that he knew he was in the area, it would only be a matter of time before he located the traitor again. Yanking the rest of his body free from the grip of the ruined interior wall, the keeper stormed out of the building to again search for Gideon

I'm not about to lose you again. We must get the suit back!

Revelations: Spectre

Chapter 17

Cycle: 412 Month: 9 Rotation: 14
Corre Republic Space
Prefecture: Expansive
Planet: Benedictus
Location: Outside of Avalon

Frank's black armored SUV sped down the street. The roads were illuminated by the bright lights of the businesses and other establishments lining the road on either side. The driver had maintained the same frantic speed ever since they left Spectre and the other mysterious warrior behind at the estate.

With part of the roof caved in, the crime lord's mind was working overtime to try and process everything going on. He retrieved his personal communicator from his suit jacket pocket and pressed the contact button for his right-hand man, Deni Moore.

There were two rings before he answered. "Boss, is everything alright?"

"Things didn't quite go as planned. We are heading toward you now. How's Saul?" Frank's asked with a low rumble to his voice.

One thing that had been proven clear to him in the last engagement was that he hadn't estimated on Spectre being able to get as close to him as he did. Tak and his mercenaries were supposed to be the trump card, but they had less than stellar results. As far as he knew, they were all killed.

"He's secure. Do you need me to make any special arrangements?" Deni asked neutrally.

Both of the men were experienced enough in this line of work to know that their calls had a chance of being bugged or intercepted. They, along with their associates, had to speak in a type of code to avoid being clearly understood by any Republic officers.

Frank took a deep breath and thought about what he needed to do. There was already an expensive contract out for anyone that could kill the ex-bounty hunter, but those that tried had already gotten shot in the process. He knew that there would be other trained killers that were interested, but that probably wouldn't get themselves involved without a significant enough bounty.

While the crime lord loved his fortune, he had to be alive to spend it. He swallowed hard and nodded his head to himself. "Yeah... order some flowers for my wife."

Deni interpreted the code to be that his boss wanted to up the contract already out on Gideon. "Yes, sir. How many bouquets are you thinking of getting her?"

The senior Corbo pursed his lips while he weighed his options one last time. Outside he spotted a red light, but the driver drove right threw it.

"Make it a dozen."

"A dozen, sir?"

Deni had personally seen to the dispatch of many contracts for hits over the cycles, but never one so high for someone that wasn't a government official or some other type of authority figure.

"You heard me. Get it done." Frank ended the call, and carelessly tossed the device onto the empty seat beside him.

Jin glanced at his employer from the corner of his eye. He knew better than to speak at that moment.

Internally, Frank felt a sensation of rage wash over him. "That fragger is going to get what's coming to him. I swear it. He's a dead man walking."

Chapter 18

Cycle: 412 Month: 9 Rotation: 14
Corre Republic Space
Prefecture: Expansive
Planet: Benedictus
Location: Downtown Avalon

Gideon did his best to limp along the sidewalk of the busy street. People passed him without so much as acknowledging his presence. It was better this way, no sense having more eyes drawn to him than he needed.

This is the furthest I've ever pushed the suit. I hope it can recharge enough for me to do what I need to.

Everything in his body seemed to ache. He knew that his bandages were in desperate need of being changed. Still, he needed more distance between himself and Knowledge. While he was invisible to any electronic optical equipment, it didn't stop patrolmen or hired guns on the streets of Avalon from spotting him.

After retrieving his duffle bag, he headed away from the Corbo's mansion as fast as he could. His primary focus was on getting patched up. If he bled out, then everything would be a waste. His mind wandered to his three children.

How can I tell them that Joan died? What am I going to do without her?

He clutched his side and found that to was beginning to bleed through his older bandages.

225

Gideon licked his lips while he thought about his options. Without a doubt, getting off the streets was his most significant need at the moment. The problem was he couldn't just go and get a room in some hotel. They would absolutely check him for an ID chip. Seeing as how he didn't have one, they would have to go through other means that would flag him in any of the systems or databases. Which of course, Knowledge would then easily track him down.

Hannibal! I can go see Hannibal.

He wasn't sure if his fellow hunter still lived at his previous residence. But it was the only option he could think of in his wounded mental state.

The journey to the bounty hunter's apartment took much longer than it should've, but Avalon was a vast city. After hours of traveling on foot, Gideon was nearly there.

It was the darkest part of the night by now, and he felt this weird sensation of aching numbness. Not many people were out and about now. A canine barked loudly down the street, but Spectre ignored it. His vision began to blur, and he forced himself to continue onward.

I can't pass out here… gotta keep… moving.

The blood loss was wearing on his body. While his suit had done what it could to repair him, it simply wasn't enough for the trauma to be successfully dealt with. Each step was becoming more and more tiring. To make matters worse, it was getting more difficult to focus.

He spotted the apartment complex Hannibal lived at. Desperation was beginning to well up within him.

This is bad.

Memories of his wife came back to him. One, in particular, replayed more vividly than the others. A gentle breeze caressed a wide-open field of tall blue-ish grass. Joan wore a lovely white dress with red polka dots. Her hair fluttered gently as the wind grazed her cheeks. It was that moment on Antioch that Gideon's painful past was temporarily non-existent. All the memories of the wars he fought in, the people he had killed, that horrific moment that made him turn away from being a Keeper of the Republic, it all faded away as he admired her beauty.

Joan slowly turned to face her husband. A smile spread over her face, and she reached out for him.

"Gideon, wake up."

The ex-bounty hunter extended his hand, but his wife brushed it aside. In a flash, she appeared right in front of his face, her eyes wide.

"Wake up!"

Spectre awoke on the steps of the large residential building. Its exterior was crusty and worn looking. Gideon grunted as he forced himself up off the stonecrete steps and stood up.

Gripping his side tightly, he walked up to the door and found a panel to his right. With a trembling hand, he pressed the screen, and it displayed a welcome message. It then faded to a list of names and he agonizingly scrolled through to find his old friend.

He paused when he read, "Fronnt Ilk," one of Hannibal's aliases. Relief started to wash over him, then his side throbbed again from the pain.

"Uuuuk…"

Gideon doubled over then paused to make himself breathe. He stood back up and pressed the bounty hunter's fake name on the screen, leaving behind a bloody thumbprint.

The screen transformed into a different display then a ringing sound chirped from the speaker box. It rang several more times before Hannibal answered.

"Hello?" he asked grumpily. "Who is it?!"

Gideon finally noticed the black bulb covering a small camera on top of the electronic panel. He was tempted to remove his bracelet but then thought better of it.

"It's me," the ex-bounty hunter stammered.

"Who? Gideon?!" Hannibal exclaimed. "Gideon, is that you?"

"Yeah, yeah, it is. Could… could you let me in?"

"Oh yeah, sorry." A moment later, Spectre heard the audible sound of the front door unlocking.

He thrust it open and entered the apartment. The inside air was cool but stuffy. Loose leaves lay about the foyer in the corners, and a lone potted plant sat nearby. Its branches were barren, and the soil was dry.

Lovely…

228

The ex-bounty hunter shuffled his feet toward the elevator straight ahead. He pressed the button with his fist and waited as it descended to the first level.

In his physical condition, time felt like it was stretching on and on while he waited. A slight *ding* alerted him that the lift had finally arrived. The doors slid open quietly, and he stepped inside.

Gideon pressed the button for the fourth floor and leaned his head against the wall behind him. The ride to the upper level was quick enough, but his body urged him to lie down right where he was. He felt about as exhausted as he could remember ever being. His eyelids were heavy, his legs could hardly support his weight, and then he began to feel cold.

I'm not... dying... yet...

With great determination, he walked out of the elevator and down the long hallway. Just before he reached the bounty hunter's unit, Spectre heard Hannibal unlocking multiple locks from within. The door opened inward, and his old friend had concern shown all over his face. Gideon spotted the pistol holstered on his hip and figured another one was in his hand behind the door. In their line of work, you always had to be cautious. It wasn't unheard of to use bait to lure someone into a trap.

The bounty hunter could tell that his friend was in genuine agony. "Come in, come in," he said quickly.

Gideon shambled inside. The apartment didn't look much better than the foyer. For the most part, it was devoid of any significant appeal with sparse furniture and random empty bottles scattered about. Overall, it resembled a bachelor pad more than anything.

Old gray carpet laid about on the floors as far as he could see. A weary-looking wooden table was positioned to his right with two chairs, none of which matched one another. Straight ahead was the entryway to the kitchen, which didn't look any better than the front room did.

Hannibal briefly looked him over as he shut the door behind him.

"Holy poosh. You look terrible. Are you hurt?"

"Yeah… just a bit," the ex-bounty hunter said groggily.

"What the frag happened?" Hannibal asked. He turned back to the door to begin locking it.

Meanwhile, Gideon sauntered over to a chair at the table and carefully sat down. The little bit of comfort from being off his feet didn't quite replace the sensation of overwhelming pain that shot up his spine.

He held back a harsh groan. It certainly wasn't the first time he had been seriously injured throughout his life. His mind grew even foggier, and it became furthermore challenging to focus.

Once he was finished securing the entrance, Hannibal rushed through the room and disappeared around the corner in the hallway. Spectre could hear some sort of rustling sound. Despite his injuries, Gideon's trained senses scanned the room for potential danger. While he was basically at the other man's mercy, he still wasn't confident how much he could trust him.

I need to knock it off… if he was gonna shoot me… he'd have done it already…

He leaned back in the chair and allowed himself to try to relax.

"So, what in the blazes happened?!" the bounty hunter shouted from wherever he was.

"I went to Frank's place," Gideon shouted then grit his teeth in agony.

"You what?!" Something heavy fell and sounded like it busted open. "Ow!" Hannibal bellowed. He reappeared a few seconds later, carrying a small plastic box and multiple towels. "Sorry, I'm in the process of moving, so I've started packing certain things away."

The bounty hunter handed one of the towels to Spectre then set the box on the small table beside his friend's seat. Gideon attempted to unbutton his shirt, but his left hand was trembling too much. Instead, he took the towel and firmly held it against where he was bleeding from his abdomen.

Hannibal genuinely showed a small amount of concern, which, of course, didn't make the ex-bounty hunter feel any better about his situation. His own skin had started to become pale from all of the blood loss.

"Just… sit back," Hannibal said sternly. He retrieved a pair of orange synthetic gloves from the box and slid one over each hand. Then he lifted out a bottle and popped the cap off. He dumped several red tablets into his gloved palm. "Here, take these. They're chewable."

Gideon accepted the small pain killers and tossed them into his mouth and ground them up. They tasted both vibrantly sweet and bitter at the same time. His left eye twitched momentarily from the sensation of the flavors as he swallowed the quick-acting medicine.

The bounty hunter set the bottle back down and took out a small black pouch. He unzipped it and laid it flat on the floor. Various medical tools were neatly organized within it, along with several vials. Hannibal pulled one of the cylinders out before he then forcefully yanked the injured man's shirt wide open.

"Gah!" Gideon growled.

Hannibal didn't even bother looking up. He slid the shirt down his left arm and pressed the vial against it. Spectre faintly felt a prick and figured that the bottle contained medication for fighting off infection. There had been plenty of moments throughout his career as a soldier that he administered medical aid to his squadmates.

"Fancy necklace you got there," the bounty hunter remarked as he got back to work treating the wounds.

It was strange, suddenly the amulet and its chain felt heavy around Gideon's neck. His mind started to wander to his duel against his old friend, Knowledge. He shook his head to bring him back to the here and now. It was getting harder and harder to focus himself. Suddenly, everything started to get dark.

I... I can't... pass out. I... don't know if I can trust him...

Before he could resist any further, Gideon began to slump to his right. His eyes also started to shut.

Hannibal noticed the change in the ex-bounty hunter's demeanor. "Gideon?" He shook his leg. "Gideon? Gideon?!"

The bounty hunter cursed and then dug around in the medical box. The last thing Spectre heard was the sound of Hannibal's voice trailing off.

"Don't you die yet you bastard. You're not dying here..."

Chapter 19

Cycle: 412 Month: 9 Rotation: 14
Corre Republic Space
Prefecture: Expansive
Planet: Benedictus
Location: Downtown Avalon

The coolness of the evening spread its way through the bustling city. Hovercars navigated the busy streets while citizens of the area headed for restaurants and other evening luxuries. One elderly woman walked into the road, and a wheeled truck slammed on its brakes. The woman screamed furiously at the large vehicle and its driver while the man stuck his head out of the window and shook his fist at her. She gave the man a rude hand gesture and continued on her way.

Way up above all the commotion, the Keeper of Knowledge sat on the roof of one of the skyscrapers. His suit was wirelessly connected to the stream and was downloading vast amounts of data while simultaneously processing any possible information on the location of Gideon.

With both of his arms raised, he used his hands to sift through the info. Despite in the natural, there appeared to be nothing, his gloves were connected to his helmet, and the movements of his fingers allowed him to navigate through the data seamlessly.

Knowledge's eyes scanned back and forth as he read the lines that scrolled across his heads-up display. He had accessed every sort of readout, scanner, camera, and any other source of information that came out of the area surrounding the crime lord's estate. There was literally no sign of Gideon ever being there. If it wasn't for him seeing the fugitive with his very own eyes, he might not even have believed it himself.

"How am I going to locate a man that is hidden from cameras?" he muttered to himself.

"Can I be of assistance?" the artificial intelligence asked kindly.

The keeper shook his head. "No. My brain just keeps wracking over, trying to figure out just what kind of device allows Gideon to conceal himself from every sort of scanner there is."

Catherine pondered for a fraction of a second while her enhanced mind played out a multitude of scenarios in an instant. "What if he has a piece of technology from one of the other nations?"

Knowledge scoffed. "No, it can't be that. I've infiltrated the top levels of research and development for every nation except for Vena. No one has anything like this, even in the beta phase. He literally has something that shouldn't exist. This is how he has been able to avoid me for all of these cycles."

"What of the Lotus Imperium, though? They have many technological advancements the other nations lack."

"No. I would have heard about it if they did."

Suddenly the AI recognized two newcomers that were approaching. "We have visitors," she remarked neutrally. An alert of two individuals approaching the keeper from behind showed on his HUD.

"Took them long enough," Knowledge mumbled. "Glad you both could finally make it," he said coldly to his comrades.

He didn't need to turn around to know who they were since he already knew. The Keepers of Life and Death stopped several steps short of their ally. Even in the dim light from this high up above the city, Life's armor was clearly seen as being bright white with a light blue glow. Her armor appeared feminine, but Knowledge knew her suit was just as deadly as his own. Death was the larger of the three. He stood easily a head taller than Life, and his power armor was tailored to resemble the nightmares of the embodiment of Death itself. A cloaked hood covered the sinister-looking helmet beneath it. Only the glowing red eyes could be seen easily in the darkness.

Wanting to move past the less than stellar greeting, Life crossed her arms. "We got the signal that his beacon was activated. Were you able to locate the traitor?"

"I did. We fought, but he managed to escape," the dark blue keeper said solemnly. Of all the keepers, he would never equate himself to being as skilled as a warrior as the others. He could certainly hold his own, but those like Death and War were in a different league unto themselves.

"Has he been able to get his suit back to full power?" Death asked with a hiss in his voice.

Knowledge shook his head. He returned to scanning through information.

Life glanced up at Death, who just stared back at her. After several moments the darkened figure shrugged then walked away. The female keeper sighed then turned back to Knowledge.

"How confident are you that we can capture him this time?" she asked as calmly as she could.

Knowledge didn't bother looking back toward her. "I'm confident this time we will succeed."

"How can you know that?" Death growled. "I've heard that before."

"Because he is after the people who killed his wife," the dark blue keeper said plainly. "He won't be going anywhere until they are dead."

Life motioned with her hands. "How can you know that?"

Knowledge stopped scanning through the lines of data and twisted around. He just stared at his fellow keeper for several heartbeats.

The female warrior looked down and shook her head. "Of course, you know, you're Knowledge!" She clapped her left hand against her thigh armor.

"I've known Gideon for a very long time…"

"That bastard doesn't deserve to have a name!" Life screamed.

Death stared strangely at his companion while Knowledge seemed totally unfazed by the outburst.

With her fury boiling up within herself, Life pointed an angry finger at the blue keeper. "This has gone on for long enough! He abandoned his post, and now we are paying the price."

The two men shared a moment of silence and glanced at one another. Knowledge looked back to the infuriated woman and tilted his head.

"And what would you have me do?"

Placing her hands on her armored hips, Life cocked her head upward. "Your suit gives you unprecedented abilities to infiltrate and hack almost anything. And yet here we are uncertain of where the traitor is hiding." She turned her head and gazed at the cityscape. "You know what I think?"

"What's that?" Knowledge asked plainly.

"I think that you are still holding onto some kind of friendship for a man who left you behind... and it's interfering with your job."

The blue keeper turned away from the heated conversation. Life, knowing that she had hit a soft spot, began to walk away.

"He has some sort of device that hides him from cameras," Knowledge said coldly.

The female keeper stopped in her tracks but did not bother to face her ally. "What do you mean? Is he camouflaged or something?"

"No. He has a bracelet that makes him entirely invisible to the optics of our camera and scanning equipment. But when I faced him, I could see him perfectly fine, but my helmet could not locate his suit despite being right in front of me."

Life turned her head back away. "Regardless, we have to wrap this up and get Peace out of that damned chamber he's been trapped in. Every single rotation that bastard is loose on the streets is another rotation that Peace could be doing his job."

Without another word, Life continued on her way and stormed off. Death stared at Knowledge for several more moments before he too left the rooftop leaving the remaining keeper to dwell on his thoughts.

I miss when things were simpler. When the keepers were preoccupied with protecting our country and not furthering Peace's plans.

Knowledge turned back to the city below and watched as the traffic negotiated the overburdened streets. He had served the Corre Republic for a very long time. Various key moments replayed in his mind, many of which were working alongside the now ex-bounty hunter.

He lowered his head and fought back any emotion from attempting to overtake him. It was not often that he felt this way. Witnessing the number of atrocities humans had committed over a long career had made him see the true capacity for the horror that mankind could commit.

"The many outweigh the few"… I have to find him and do what I must.

Knowledge lifted his head and redetermined himself. He again accessed his search and got to work to locate the fugitive.

Chapter 20

Cycle: 412 Month: 9 Rotation: 15
Corre Republic Space
Prefecture: Expansive
Planet: Benedictus
Location: Downtown Avalon

Hannibal toyed with the handle of a long knife in his hand. In his other, he held his sleek silver communicator. He glanced over at Gideon Adama as he lay fast asleep on his couch. After he had passed out from the massive blood loss, the bounty hunter got to work applying fresh bandages and treated the other man's injuries as best he could.

He sighed heavily and set the device screen down on his reclining chair's arm. His right hand absentmindedly continued to play with the bladed weapon while the other massaged his weary face. Beneath his large beard were multiple old scars from when his jaw was fractured in a bar fight. His aging body was covered in permanent memories of his struggles as a hunter and hitman.

His nostrils flared widely, and he exhaled abruptly. "Dammit!" he whispered to himself.

Reaching back over, he angrily yanked the communicator up and reread the text message for what felt like the hundredth time.

"12,000,000 Cuso bounty for the death of Spectre."

The short sentence felt like a hurricane in his mind. Here Hannibal had one of the most dangerous warriors in all of the Corre Republic passed out on his sofa. A small fortune was within his grasp and had been for almost eighteen hours. A part of him hated the idea of killing one of the only fellow bounty hunters on Benedictus that had previously helped him. It wasn't often in their line of work to find someone that wouldn't shoot you in the back for a bounty. His list of friends was very short, but the temptation was there to make it one person shorter.

Another part of him, though, dreamed of what he could do with so much money. While Spectre still looked just the same as ever, Hannibal knew that he was getting older and that his own time to be a capable hunter was drawing to an end. His last two bounties were already hard for him to wrangle. In fact, his left artificial leg still had a limp from when he fell out of a two-story window onto a parked car. He needed to get it checked out by a tech, but it wouldn't be cheap if he needed to replace his entire leg.

The pistol on his right hip hidden beneath his shirt tugged at him in his mind as he remembered he was carrying the weapon. He bounced his right knee while he thought some more, stuck on the fence of indecision.

Uncertain of what he was about to do, he began to stand up when Gideon violently awoke from a nightmare. He reached up and pressed his hand against the amulet around his neck. Hannibal jumped to his feet as the power armor formed around his friend's body.

"What the frag?!"

A makeshift IV that was in Spectre's arm was severed as the armor took shape, and it began spilling fluid everywhere. That was the least of Hannibal's concerns. The sudden startle caused him to flip up and over his chair, sending the communicator he was holding to go flying across the room.

The ex-bounty hunter breathed heavily as he began to recall where he was.

"11:54," appeared in the corner of his helmet's HUD along with the text as his injuries were assessed.

A new warning message appeared before his eyes.

"Power source is critically low. The healing process is disabled."

Seeing the other man's eyes severely widened made him realize how this all must look. "Oh, right."

He deactivated the suit, and it vanished in a cloud of particles. Hannibal observed them as they disintegrated.

"I had heard the rumors, but never did I truly suspect they were real," he remarked in disbelief.

Gideon suddenly felt the aches of his body. He carefully lowered himself back down onto the couch and sighed quietly. A thought of terror gripped him, and he quickly searched for his bracelet, but it was missing.

Hannibal stood up from behind the chair. "How the… but… how does…"

"Look, it isn't important," the ex-bounty hunter said, trying to move past what just happened.

"Nah, you have to tell me how that thing works!"

"It uh… I'm not totally sure. It just does."

The bounty hunter appeared stunned and dismayed while Spectre searched around him for where the jewelry was.

"You don't know how your own suit works?"

Gideon tried to feign that he wasn't sure. "Well, I kinda… stole it," he said, telling a half-truth.

"Huh? From who? Who has that sorta tech? That's like golden age level stuff!" Hannibal was totally beside himself as he tried to wrap his mind around what he just saw. "They don't make stuff like that anymore."

"No… I guess they don't. Hey, uh… dc you have the bracelet I was wearing?"

Still, in amazement, the bounty hunter ran his hand through his short dark hair. "Well, that beats what I've been wearin' by a long shot."Hannibal blinked strangely then his brain processed the question. "Oh… yeah, here," he said as he removed the item from his pocket and tossed it over.

Gideon caught it in the air but felt in a sharp pain at his sudden movement. He grunted then slid the bracelet on. A sigh of relief washed over him as he felt more at ease.

"Look, it isn't a big deal," Gideon started to say while he tried to sit back up. A sharp twinge kept him lying back, though.

"Yes, it is!" Hannibal moved out from behind the chair and motioned widely with his arms. "Who'd you steal it from?"

Spectre eased himself onto his back. He clenched his jaw from the pain as he lowered down then let out the breath he had been holding.

"It doesn't matter now. Anyway, what've I missed?"

The bounty hunter suddenly remembered his communicator. He anxiously looked around for a split second before he caught himself.

I can't let him know...

"Uh, nothing really." He spotted the device across the room on the floor over by the couch, right beside his friend. Its screen was pointed upward, and his stomach dropped.

Gideon closed his eyes for a moment to adjust himself on the couch so that hopefully the soreness would subside. Trying his best to act casually, Hannibal strode over and scooped up his electronic device. He thumbed the home button and slid the communicator into his pocket and turned back to head for the kitchen.

"Are you hungry?"

Without looking over at him, Gideon asked, "Have you heard anything from Frank?"

Hannibal froze in place then glanced back to his guest. He knew there was no point in lying to the other man. Both were very experienced bounty hunters and understood the inner workings of the criminal underworld.

"He raised the bounty."

An awkward silence fell on the room.

Hannibal had made certain to check if the ex-bounty hunter had any weapons on him when he was treating his injuries. It had been odd to him that he found only the old sword. At this moment, though, his body tensed. He knew the apartment and where all of his hidden firearms were, not to mention the concealed pistol on his hip.

Gideon also had figured that the bounty hunter had checked him for weapons. He needed to know what the other man's intention was, though. Sitting in a viper's nest wouldn't bring him any peace.

"How much is it?" Spectre asked neutrally.

Hannibal hesitated for a second. "Twelve-mill."

Bracing himself to respond quickly if needed, Gideon added, "That's quite a bit of money."

Both men were unsure of what the other must have been thinking, although they each had a pretty good guess.

Could I shoot him before he reaches for that necklace? What am I thinking?!

Reluctantly the bounty hunter forced himself to calm down. Even from beneath his clothing, Gideon could see that the other man's muscles relaxed.

Hannibal turned around and held his hands open. "I'm not going to take it, Gideon."

"Why not?"

"I told you. It isn't enough money for me to shoot an old friend," the bounty hunter said with a devilish grin.

Spectre couldn't discern if he were just joking around or if he was serious. Either way, he too eased himself and relaxed some.

"Thank you for helping me," he said ashamed.

Hannibal waved away the pleasantry and scoffed. "You helped me back with bringing down Edmon Gray. It's the least I could do."

Gideon nodded and took a deep breath while the bounty hunter went to the kitchen to grab something to eat. Plates clanged, and some indistinguishable noises emanated from the other room while Spectre's mind wandered.

What am I going to do about my suit? I have to get a replacement power source. But where could I even find one? I wish I had spent more time learning how these damned things worked when I was a keeper.

He continued to ponder on his next course of action when Hannibal returned with two dishes in his hands. Gideon carefully sat up and accepted his plate then the bounty hunter sat down in his recliner.

"It isn't much. I normally eat out," Hannibal said before he took a bite of his own sandwich.

Gideon's stomach growled when the smell of the food entered his nose. He gobbled down the sandwich and scarfed up the included fried chips within minutes.

The bounty hunter watched his guest essentially attack his food. "Woah now. There's no need to rush."

The injured man swallowed hard then smirked. "Sorry. Force of habit."

Hannibal took a large bite and spoke with only half of his mouth. "You're sure you have no idea how your suit works? It is some crazy tech."

Spectre just shrugged in response. He winced as he set the plate down then tried to settle himself to a more comfortable position.

"You've been wearing that for however many cycles, and you don't understand how the blasted thing works?!" the bounty hunter asked in disbelief.

"Yeah…"

"It is power armor, though, right?"

He's asking an awful lot of questions…

Gideon thought to himself as he nodded. "It is. But it's much lighter."

Hannibal shook his head. "That's incredible."

"It really is. The bad thing is that it is kind of broken."

"How so?" the bounty hunter inquired before taking another large bite of his own food.

"Its powercell is almost entirely fried. Without that, pretty soon, it will be useless," Gideon answered before setting his plate down on the small table in the center of the room.

Leaning over made him ache, so he slowly eased himself back to the couch cushion. He reached up and placed his right hand behind his head.

"What sort of powercell does it need?" the hunter asked while he chewed his food.

Spectre shrugged. "I don't know."

Hannibal chuckled to himself. He set his plate down and reached over to grab a bottle of liquor in an amber-colored bottle. There was a loud *porp* sound as he flipped the lid then took a long pull from the drink. Once again, he laughed all the while, Gideon just stared at him curiously.

"You mean to tell me, the deadly Spectre that has killed dozens of men doesn't even know how his own fraggin' suit works?" the bounty hunter asked sarcastically, before losing himself to the humor of the realization. "These are strange times."

Gideon's cheeks turned a shade of red, and he pursed his lips at the irony.

Finally, Hannibal decided to stop nagging his old friend. He wiped a tear that had formed at the corner of his eye from his intense laughter. "Aaaah… Gideon, you are quite the hunter." Retrieving his plate and the last of his sandwich, Hannibal asked, "What are you gonna do now?"

"I'm not leaving Benedictus until I kill the Corbo's," Spectre said coldly.

"Is that smart to try in your condition?"

"They killed my wife. I will return the act without remorse."

The bounty hunter nodded emphatically while he vigorously chewed his food. "Alright… but how do you plan to do that exactly?"

Gideon smacked his lips, then lowered his arm. "I think I have enough power for one more go at him."

"What are you gonna do for weapons?"

"Guess I'll have to find another dealer."

Hannibal shook his head. "Not with that little bit of cash you got left."

Gideon's eyes got incredibly serious. "You went through my bag?"

"Look, a shot up bounty hunter comes to your door for help, you gotta check things out. Plus, if you died, then I should at least get a little something for disposing of your body," Hannibal said with a toothy grin from beneath his burly beard.

The ex-bounty hunter scoffed but couldn't help but smile. "Fair enough. But it will have to do. I can't stay on the planet long."

"Someone else coming to look for you?"

"Something like that…" Gideon said as his voice trailed off. "Anyway, I can't be a bother to you any longer."

Hannibal devoured the last of his meal and held his hand up. He chewed as quick as he could so that he could again speak. "I can help you out with some weapons."

"Hannibal, I couldn't ask…"

The bounty hunter quickly interrupted the injured man. "Just give me the cuso you do have, and don't worry about it. I've got more damned guns then I have fingers and toes. It'll help me to have a little less for when I move."

Gideon reluctantly shrugged and gave the other man a tired smile. "I appreciate that."

Hannibal set his plate down again and pulled out his communicator. He rapidly sent a text message then hopped up to his feet before walking toward the hallway. "So, the Corbo's will likely be at their hideout."

"And where's that?" the ex-bounty hunter asked as he followed behind.

"I don't know one hundred percent, but I know it is roughly somewhere outside of the city. I think it is in the residential district of Rind."

Gideon recalled Rind being nearby Avalon. He had been there a couple of times over the cycles that he lived on the planet. It was a wealthy town that businessmen, doctors, and crime lords all poured money into to develop for the upper members of society. Mainly it was there so that the more fortunate didn't have to live within the swarmed streets of the older city, and they could just commute in for their professions.

A small *ding* sound came from Hannibal's communicator.

"What makes you think they would head there?" Spectre asked.

The bounty hunter checked his device then grinned cruelly. "Because one of Frank's people just gave me their address." Hannibal held the communicator up so that Gideon could read the text for himself.

"What did you tell them?"

"Well, don't be mad, but when you blacked out, I went ahead and took a picture of you with your shirt off."

Spectre's eyebrow raised confusedly.

Hannibal shrugged. "I figured if you died, I could collect the bounty anyhow. Regardless, it was a pretty convincing picture, wasn't it?" he asked before scrolling up to show the image.

It was strange to him, for all intents and purposes, the photo did make Gideon appear that he had been killed. Blood trailed out of his wounds, and his body looked very banged up.

"I got to give it to you. You definitely do play all the angles."

The bounty hunter smirked then continued on his way. He strolled into an open room and went for the closet. Gideon noticed the stacks of boxes to his right. Many were labeled while others didn't appear to be.

"Where are you moving, again?" he asked, then caught up to the other man.

Hannibal opened the closet door and reached inside to place his hand on a hidden palm scanner. A red light went up and down, then turned bright green.

"I'll be headin' to Marie once I get approval from the Department of Transportation."

"Marie? What's there?" Gideon asked curiously.

"A calm and quiet life. This bounty hunter business is behind me now. Time for me to get away from worrying about someone shooting me for some old grudge."

Gideon nodded. "I can appreciate that."

A clicking sound came from the closet, and Hannibal smiled. He reached back into the storage space but maintained eye contact with the ex-bounty hunter. The secret door that was hidden swung open, and Gideon nodded at the sight.

The bounty hunter had at least twice the assortment of firearms as did Charlie back at the bar. Everything from sub-machine guns to portable laser repeaters, all very illegal to possess on an inner world like Benedictus.

"You like it?" Hannibal asked, knowing the answer.

Spectre shook his head in disbelief. "Wow… this is an impressive collection."

"Well, that's not everything. But I'm willing to sell you anything in here, except for the torch laser up there," he replied and pointed at a custom painted green weapon above the others. "That one's coming with me."

Gideon nodded then tried to consider his options. Suddenly, a thought of hesitation set in. Meanwhile, Hannibal's communicator chirped.

"I don't know what sort of situation I'm going to be walking into," the ex-bounty hunter said regretfully.

The bounty hunter held up his handheld device. "Someone that works for Frank just told me where to meet them with your head."

Spectre leaned forward to read the text for himself. A strange feeling emanated from around the base of his neck. Immediately he was happy to still be alive and relatively intact.

A plan began to form in Gideon's mind, and the intense desire for revenge again boiled up within him. He scanned over the assorted weapons and nodded once more. His suit was nearly depleted of power, and his body was beaten up badly. However, he wasn't about to let them off without shedding their blood for Joan's.

"I need a way to move about the city without being recognized. Do you have a blank pay card and a Mask Projector?"

Hannibal again smirked devilishly. "I do. That will help disguise you to get in close, but what about your injuries? You aren't going to be very spry in your condition. Are you sure you want to do this?"

Without a split second of thought, Gideon found himself nodding enthusiastically. "Yes. They think that they are safe, but I won't stop until they are dead."

Chapter 21

Cycle: 412 Month: 9 Rotation: 15
Corre Republic Space
Prefecture: Expansive
Planet: Benedictus
Location: Rind – Frank Corbo's Hideout

Frank Corbo sat in his dark brown leather chair in the living room of his luxurious backup home. Typically, he used this residence as a place for visitors that came from other planets to stay. It allowed him to monitor his guest and to keep them out of Avalon near any prying eyes of authorities. Similar to his primary residence, he had not held back from furnishing his property with the very best money could purchase.

It was a barely hidden secret that Rind was established as a crime lord getaway. Being near to the major city granted anyone of significant power to operate their business yet be within a different judicial district. The local government oversight was filled with plenty of individuals who either sold out their beliefs for cash or were literally criminal hirelings.

Over the cycles, Frank positioned himself as a powerful force within the black-market underworld, and he made sure that his affairs were not tampered with by anyone. More than once he had ordered the murders of either an investigator from Avalon or one of their families. His message was loud and clear.

The irony that he was now hiding in his own hideout was not lost on him. He held a glass with a measure of alcohol in it. While his gaze was fixated on the head of an Azrael beast from Canopy mounted to his wall, he swirled the liquid in his imported cup.

Deni tapped on the archway opening that led into the room. The noise caught Frank's attention, and he sat up straighter.

"Have you found the bastard?"

"Better," the well-dressed thug said with a smirk. "I just got notified that a bounty hunter killed him."

The idea of the man who attacked the crime lord in his own home being dead made him feel elated. But he resisted getting too excited. "Do you have proof?"

Deni handed over the slender communicator. Frank set down his drink to accept it and then stared at the image for several seconds. He finally nodded approvingly and gave back the device.

"It looks convincing. But I need more than that to feel satisfied. I want to see his severed head myself!"

Saul happened to be walking down the hall when he overheard parts of the conversation. He stuck his head in the room.

"Pa, what's up? Did someone find him?" he asked with an air of annoyance in his voice.

The father nodded to his son, solemnly. Deni glanced at Saul then back to his employer.

"I told the hunter that you would need proof that he is, in fact, dead."

"I want his head!" Frank growled.

"Already requested."

Saul wasn't entirely convinced. "Where is this hunter meeting you at?"

Deni again turned back to the younger man. "He didn't want to meet up in Avalon. I gave him the address here."

The crime lord gave his right-hand man a side glare.

"Relax, it's Hannibal. He's worked for us plenty of times. We can trust him," Deni said, trying to ease his boss' concerns.

Frank steepled his fingers and leaned back in his seat. "I want an increase in security just in case something is going on."

Deni cocked his head to the side. "Are you worried?"

"I don't trust anyone enough to take the chance that the infamous Spectre is actually dead."

Saul wasn't bothered by the remark, but Deni was slightly insulted. He did his best to hide his internal conflict with the statement, and thankfully, neither of the Corbo's noticed.

"Tak contacted me last night wanting to meet. I haven't responded. Would you like me to bring him in?" the thug asked the crime lord.

Frank's face looked like he had tasted something bitter. "Oh, gods no. That man is a pathetic excuse for a hitman and bodyguard. Tell him to frag off!"

Saul chuckled and then wiped his nose with his finger.

Deni nodded and left the room, leaving the father and son all alone. Frank's eyes met his son's.

"You are going to owe me for all of the trouble you've caused."

The son's face sobered considerably, and he looked at the tiled floor. "Look, Pa…"

"I don't want to hear it!" Frank spat angrily. His right eye twitched, and he smashed the arm of his chair with his fist.

Saul jumped then attempted to regain his appearance. "If you would have given me a chance, I would've finished this for you."

Frank rolled his eyes and crossed his legs. "Son, you can barely dress yourself. How in the damned void would you stand an insect's chance up against one of the deadliest men who's ever lived?"

Feeling the need to defend himself, Saul puffed out his chest. "I got pretty close the first time," he said, referencing the incident in the alley.

"Yes, and simultaneously opened the door for a multitude of investigations and government probes into my business in Avalon." Frank pointed his thumb at his own chest to emphasize his point. "And yet you seem content to aggravate me further. Get the frag out of my sight!"

Being scolded by his father brought the son back to when he was younger. His shoulders sank, and he shuffled out of the room. Frank, as pissed as ever, retrieved his glass and downed the drink in one gulp. He toyed the cup in his hand for a second to gaze upon its craftmanship. Then, he chucked it in disgust against the wall.

Chapter 22

Cycle: 412 Month: 9 Rotation: 15
Corre Republic Space
Prefecture: Expansive
Planet: Benedictus
Location: Downtown Avalon

Knowledge had worked for hours poring over enough data and information to make a room full of intelligence officers' heads spin wildly. Despite not locating his old friend, the keeper did formulate a new idea.

He stood up from the spot on the skyscraper roof that he had sat at for the entire previous evening and most of today.

"Catherine."

"Yes, Kay?" the synthetic program responded immediately after he spoke.

"Contact Death and Life for me, please."

"Right away."

Knowledge held out his gloved hand and admired the sunlight illuminating his armor.

I wish I could feel it…

"Have you located him?" Life asked grumpily.

The voice of the female keeper shook Knowledge out of his inner dialogue and back to the here and now. He tightened his hand and lowered his arm back down.

"No, but I do have a plan. I know Gideon, he isn't going to stop until he kills his targets. I did a quick search and located the man that he had been after when I encountered him. He was on the move, but he stopped at a residence located outside of Avalon in a small town called Rind. Meet me there."

"You really think the traitor would be stupid enough to stick around knowing you are in the area?"

Knowledge pressed a button on his gauntlet and summoned his personal spacecraft. "I do. Notify me when you arrive."

The sleek dark blue *Sparrow* swooshed in overhead. Its shadow grew over the skyscraper until it consumed most of the area. Knowledge stepped up to the ledge of the building while his ship got into position. Its bay door lowered, and the keeper comfortably stepped on without any fear of falling from such a height.

By the time the ramp was shut, he was already halfway to the bridge, and the *Sparrow* was beginning to lift off. Knowledge sat in his chair, and Catherine automatically began syncing the data received on the ship to his power armor's database nodules.

The keeper pressed a button on the holoscreen that appeared on his left, and he entered the coordinates to Rind. He leaned his helmet on the headrest of his modified chair. It wouldn't be long before he arrived in the small town. He knew that it was wise to pull up any necessary data on the location, but instead, he couldn't get Gideon and the memories they shared out of his head.

I'm letting my friendship get in the way of my job. I should have shot him when I had the chance. I need to rewatch again why Gideon must be stopped.

Since his artificial intelligence was preoccupied, Knowledge pulled up the hologram projector in his left gauntlet. He accessed his personal saved files and pulled up the rotation that Gideon abandoned the Keepers of the Republic.

Setting the footage to replay on his HUD, Knowledge got in a relaxed position and used his right hand to press play. The footage began from the literal beginning of that rotation's morning. Forming his right hand into a circle as if he was reaching for a doorknob, he twisted to the right to fast forward. He resumed normal speed after a few hours scrolled past.

It was as if he was there again, reliving that exact moment. The Keeper of Peace, War, and himself had headed to the last known location for Gideon, or then as he was known as the Keeper of Truth.

Building up to that specific rotation, Truth had been investigating a deep conspiracy, or at least that was the best that Knowledge could put together after it all played out. He had known hints about it from previous conversations with Truth. Still, his comrade had informed him of some sort of plot that went all the way to the Prefect Major, Talion Caedis, himself. Before Knowledge could get firm details, Truth told him that he was heading to Ash to gather together the information he needed to blow the plot way open. Afterward, Knowledge had reached out to Peace, the de facto leader of the keepers, to inform him that something was wrong with Truth. Peace quickly agreed and brought War along with him.

Ordinarily, the keepers operated on solo missions. The Corre Republic was so vast that it was challenging for more than one of them to perform their duties without working alone. Every now and then, something important enough would come up that another keeper would offer their assistance.

After the death of the previous Keeper of Liberty, Peace didn't want to take any chances that Truth may also get himself killed while conducting an investigation. There was concern that the keepers might be being targeted by a rogue element within the government.

Knowledge transmitted HOP coordinates that were just outside of the planet Ash's atmosphere, giving them a significant reduction in the time it would take to land. Ash was used as a prison world for the worst known criminals and fugitives. They were sentenced to work the mines for Hydrol, fuel used in the HOP drives that allowed spacecraft to travel the stars in an instant.

Being sent to the scorched resource-rich world was a death sentence, as each prisoner was to work until their bodies gave out in the intense heat, or they died from other living conditions. It was peculiar that Truth would have gone to Ash in the first place.

After arriving at the HOP point, Knowledge detected that Truth's emergency beacon had been activated. The other keepers met up together on the surface, not wanting to waste any more time. Knowledge had pulled up all the maps he could find about the spot where the other keeper vanished and shared them with the group. Peace led the way through some abandoned caverns leading to Truth's last known location.

The audio from the video clip played through his helmet's internal speakers.

Unlike the others, Peace had chosen his armor's helmet to resemble that of an emotionless face. Two large golden horns stuck out above his emerald shaded faceplate then sloped backward. "There's no sign of him," the green-colored keeper said.

Several guards in their pressure suits lay sprawled out in the dirt of the surrounding area. Knowledge stepped forward and knelt down. He rolled one of them over and surveyed the damage.

Two burned entry marks from a laser weapon had pierced the man's plastic faceplate. His lifeless eyes were staring unnaturally upward.

After standing back up, Knowledge used his suit to begin to scan the tunnel for any residues or traces of what could have happened.

War inspected the rounded wall of the passageway. He was much larger in size than the other two keepers were. In fact, he was the biggest of any of the others in their order. His suit was a deep bronze color, and in every way, seemed to embody his namesake. Similar to Peace, his helmet had horns that grew out of his helmet, but his were smaller and angled forward. Teeth lined above and below his faceplate, giving him the appearance of some sort of monster.

"It looks like he was here," Knowledge said as the results from his scan came back positive. "But, there is a trace that he powered down."

Peace and War glanced at one another curiously, then both looked to the other keeper.

"Why would he deactivate his armor here of all places?" War asked with his deep voice. "The air here is poisonous."

Peace touched his chin in thought. "Perhaps someone overpowered him? Maybe they captured him?"

Knowledge shook his head. "I don't think so." He pointed at the center of where a scuffle took place.

Multiple sets of boot marks that matched the guards' suits were in the soil. Another set also was present. It matched Truth's footprints.

"This is odd…" the dark blue keeper muttered aloud.

"What is?" Peace asked before stepping forward.

"Truth was here," Knowledge pointed out by motioning to the footprints.

The three men followed the prints until they suddenly changed into what appeared to be tracks from a barefoot human.

Peace stated the obvious. "This must have been when he deactivated."

The new style of tracks headed away from the scuffle, and they followed all the way to where another dead guard laid further inside the tunnel. Unlike his fellow peers, this guard had been stripped of his protective suit. His skin had an orangish tint to it from the condition of the extended exposure to the toxic air.

"Why would he take his suit?" War asked confusedly.

Knowledge, too, was perplexed. "I don't understand. This doesn't make any logical sense."

Peace knelt down to look over the dead guard. "I don't see any entry points from a weapon." He stood back up and slowly looked to the other two. "Either way, we need to find him quickly. We can't take the chance that someone may be after him. I won't lose another one of us."

With time drawing near in the here and now for his arrival at Rind, Knowledge decided to fast forward again to a more appropriate spot. The footage fluttered on his heads-up display inside his helmet. He slowed down the accelerated speed, but he realized he had gone too far. Rotating his hand to the left, rewound the footage to where he wanted to resume normal play speed.

They had tracked Truth through the dirt tunnels to a thick blast door. Knowledge strolled up to the panel situated to the right of the doorway and held his hand over it. Instantly his hacking program wirelessly connected to the terminal and ran through a series of attempts to hack it until it succeeded. Within seconds the door opened slowly without a peep to show a small room with another door further inside. The keepers stepped in, and the first door shut. Knowledge again hacked into the next terminal to gain entrance to what was waiting for them on the other side.

Each of the keepers' helmets began scanning the moment the door opened to form a map for them to follow.

"I don't like this. Someone has gone through a great deal of effort to keep all of this concealed," the dark blue keeper murmured.

War scoffed. "You worry too much, glasses."

Peace was the first to enter the next tunnel. He motioned with his head to the others. "Come on."

They followed the tunnel to a large opening that revealed several structures that were built in a wide-open cavern.

"This facility isn't on any of the known maps for Ash," Knowledge remarked in disbelief.

"Why does that matter?" War asked harshly.

"Because, if I don't know about it, then that means it isn't even deemed classified. This place is being operated on a government-controlled planet by someone that desperately doesn't want this operation to be discovered. I find that to be disturbing."

There were multiple large buildings with a series of paved roads between them. Strangely though, there wasn't any sign of anyone in the area. Various vehicles were parked here and there, which added to the weirdness of it all. Thick black smoke rose up from behind the cluster of buildings.

Peace didn't seem like he was concerned about who the buildings belonged to. He brushed past the other two, and a cloud of gold particles appeared around his right hand and formed into an exquisite laser rifle. He hoisted it upward and motioned to the left.

"Kay, you take the left. War, the right. I'll move up the middle road. We need to find him."

War swaggered forward, and a brutal looking firearm formed in his left hand. It was a tremendously large weapon, much too big for an average man to hold, but seemed adequate based on his overall height and size. Beneath the triangular barrel were two fierce blades that looked almost like tusks.

Knowledge had personally witnessed his fellow keeper slice a man in two in a brawl that broke out aboard a pirate vessel.

Without another word, the keepers split off and quickly entered the secretive compound. Knowledge formed two laser pistols in his hands, his personal favorite choice, and pressed himself up against a wall facing where they came from.

The dark blue keeper cut his outer speakers so that he could speak freely within his helmet. "Catherine, do a search on the area. Scan for any life signs then hack any network that you can locate. I want to know who owns this facility."

"Right away, Kay."

While his artificial intelligence gathered precious intel, Knowledge carefully leaned around the corner of the structure. His helmet began to scan what he could see. A silhouette formed around something lying across the road. The object was zoomed in on, and the keeper realized it was someone's boot.

He kept low and moved up to an armored truck that was parked nearby. Not seeing any movement on his motion sensor or with his own eyes, the keeper crossed the rest of the distance to discover the shoe was worn by someone wearing combat fatigues. A standard issue rifle lay beside him, soaked in blood from the deceased person.

Knowledge released his left pistol, and it evaporated. He rolled the deceased body over to see that it was a young male. What was truly odd was the patch on his arm. Using his database, he ran a quick scan for a match, but it came back negative.

"What the...?"

Finding a place such as this under Ash's surface was already annoying him enough because he didn't know whom it belonged to. Now he found a guard, or possibly a soldier, that had designations he had never encountered before.

"Catherine," he said with a frustrated tone.

"Yes?"

"Run a search on this patch and cross-reference it to any known database in other nations."

"Do you suspect he is employed by another country?"

Knowledge let go of the dead man's shoulder, and his body slumped back over to the ground where he was found.

"This whole situation is bothering me. There's no telling what is going on at this point."

"By the way, my scan is complete."

The keeper stood up and tapped his helmet's chin while he thought. "What did you find?"

"There are several dozen life signs spread about through each of the structures. Many seem congregated together, and they have heightened heart rates. However, I did not locate any wireless network to tap into."

That last bit caught the keeper off guard. His eye twitched as he processed what that could possibly mean.

"How in the void could this place exist with our modern technology, but they don't use... they must be using wired connections."

The looks of the situation were getting more suspicious. Whoever owned this place truly did not want to be found.

"Oh, and I have not been able to confirm a match to the insignia on the patch."

"Fantastic..." the keeper muttered when a violent explosion erupted further up ahead.

"What in the void was that?!" War barked over their shared radio network.

"That sounded like a *Sierra's* 14D cannon," Knowledge answered casually.

More gunfire could be heard starting out of sight. Knowledge moved deeper into the compound and noticed Peace's silhouette hop onto one of the taller buildings.

"What do you see, Peace?"

"There's a *Sierra*, one *Enforcer*, and looks like maybe two fireteams of infantry advancing toward some sort of wreckage. But I don't... wait, I see him!"

Knowledge leaped onto a short nearby building. From his new vantage point, he watched while Truth stepped out from cover. He raised a rifle and opened fire, killing two of the other men instantly. The rest of the infantry fired back. Instead of being hit, the deep red colored keeper phased to the left, entirely avoiding all the bullets meant for him.

The *Sierra* targeted Truth's new position and opened fire with its machine guns. As the stream of anti-personnel rounds headed his way, the keeper again phased to the side just in time. The bullets tore through the now empty space and dug deeply into the road, sending debris up into the air.

To avoid being stuck out in the open, the keeper dropped his rifle, and an elegant sword took shape in his grip. He phased two more times to close the distance to several of the soldiers. They were surprised to see him so close in such a short moment. One of them tried to use his rifle's stock to strike the armored assailant, but he was gutted by the heated blade.

His screams were unheard over the sound of the rest of the infantry trying to use their rifles to ward off the keeper. Several backed up but couldn't get away in time before they were killed by the rapid slice attacks from Truth.

While the *Sierra* seemed hesitant to fire on his comrades, the *Enforcer* had no such reservations. Unlike the primary configuration, which carried a Phase III Focus Beam for a right arm, this one was outfitted with dual Heavy Scatterguns for each arm's armament.

The pilot triggered a round of scatterfire from each weapon. Truth narrowly hopped above the carnage as the pellets peppered the area, shredding apart many of the other infantry.

Knowledge broke out into a full sprint for the fighting. Several more loud shrills from the WarMechs attempting to kill the keeper echoed off the cavern's walls.

He rounded the last building between him and the battle just in time to see Truth carving a hole into the *Enforcer's* torso with his sword. The pilot tried to thrash his machine back and forth, but the keeper's boots magnetized to the outer hull. Knowledge spotted a cylinder-shaped item digitize into the red keeper's left hand. He dropped it into the opening in the *Enforcer* then jumped to safety.

Before the pilot could successfully react, an eruption blasted out of the gap in the armor, and the machine stumbled over to the side.

"Can we engage?!" War snarled.

"We don't even know who these people are," Knowledge pointed out.

"Doesn't matter, we need to back him up!" Peace shouted.

The green keeper formed a longer rifle in his hands and opened fire. A bright gold beam lanced through one of the remaining soldier's helmets. Peace fired several more times as Truth dodged the *Sierra's* cannon and machine gun rounds.

Knowledge watched while War rushed forward, screaming.

"Raaaaaaaaah!"

He fired a burst of laser bolts into one soldier's back and used the blades of his weapon to dissect another.

"Truth. Truth, what is the meaning of this?!" Knowledge barked.

"We cannot establish radio communication with Truth," Catherine pointed out calmly.

The blue keeper was confused by the statement. "What?"

Seeing War barrel into the brawl, Truth phased out of the area.

Knowledge chased after him while War pounced onto the *Sierra*. His fingertips became bright red, and he began clawing at the WarMech's thick armor like an animal.

The pilot watched in horror as the hatch on top of his machine was ripped clean off. His eyes widened with extreme fear at the sight of the keeper's daemonic appearance of his helmet. Unable to do anything except scream, War chuckled when the short-barreled bladed weapon again formed in his left hand. He aimed it at the pilot and fired madly.

Chapter 23

Cycle: 412 Month: 9 Rotation: 15
Corre Republic Space
Prefecture: Expansive
Planet: Benedictus
Location: Downtown Avalon

"Truth! Truth!" Knowledge called out after losing track of where his fellow keeper had vanished. The tunnels all visually looked basically the same, so it made it difficult to know where one was.

"Did you know about it?" Truth roared through his speakers from out of sight.

"Know about what?"

"Don't lie to me!"

Knowledge used his suit to triangulate where Truth's voice was coming from. Before the search was complete, the red keeper stepped out from behind a bullet-ridden vehicle that took up most of the tunnel.

"What is this all about?" Knowledge asked, motioning back to the battle.

Truth took a step forward. "I need to know, Kay… did you know about what they were doing here?"

Knowledge shrugged. "I didn't even know this place existed until a few moments ago."

"Don't fraggin' lie to me! You know everything."

"I swear to you, I didn't know about this. This looks like some sort of top-secret compound. Who are these people? Why are you attacking them?"

Truth was about to share his reasoning when he spotted Peace and War approach. The green keeper dragged one of the deceased soldiers, his boots bobbed back and forth.

"Yes, Truth, why were you attacking these men?" Peace asked accusatorily.

"What they are doing is beyond despicable. It's cruel. It's... it's..." the red keeper stammered.

Knowledge had never seen his friend act so frantically. He held out his hand to ease the other keeper. "Woah now, slow down. Explain it in detail."

Peace shook his horned head. "Why not instead tell us why you attacked a government facility?!"

The blue keeper quickly turned to face Peace.

"What do you mean?"

In disgust, Peace tossed the dead man in the middle of the gathering. War grumbled to himself like a wild animal. Truth, though, just stared back at the glowing eyes of Peace's human-like facemask.

"Turns out these are Republic soldiers. This must be a secret compound. Probably R&D."

Knowledge shook his head enthusiastically. "Impossible. I would have known about such a place. It isn't in any of my records."

Peace tilted his head defiantly. "Perhaps you don't know as much as you thought you did."

The gold keeper chuckled at his own friend's comment to the blue keeper.

"I'm only going to ask one more time. Why did you attack a Republic base?!" Peace growled.

Knowledge looked at Peace confusedly. "How do you know they are with the government?"

"I've seen this patch before. These soldiers are part of a level three classified organization that reports directly to the Prefect Major."

"That can't be…" the blue keeper stammered. "I would have known…"

The green keeper glared at his companion. "This was on a need to know basis. You weren't cleared to be informed."

"Being "informed" is literally my purpose. How can I do my job with missing information out there?"

"Regardless, this doesn't change why you would open fire on this facility," Peace said, turning his attention back to their target.

Truth was undeterred. He stood still for several heartbeats. The tension between the keepers was mounting, and Knowledge was shocked that an official government location could have been kept hidden from him.

"I was on a case that began to unravel back on Vault. I followed the trail out to Ash. That's when I learned what they are doing here."

"What in the void are they doing?!" Knowledge shouted, losing his temper.

"They are using prisoners to create a kind of artificial intelligence by scanning their minds to download a version of them. Then they use inhibitors to block the memories of the false human and use them to enhance the WarMechs they are installed into. However, the process to make these smart AIs kills the human they come from."

Knowledge felt his stomach drop as he slowly turned to the green keeper. "Is he talking about making Hollows? How would they have that technology?!" he asked meekly.

Truth's fury boiled up within his power armor. "So, you did know!"

Peace ignored his comrade's question and pointed aggressively back toward the smoldering wreckage behind him. "And that meant you drew your weapon on Republic soldiers?! We have a duty to protect her people."

"Oh, don't talk down to me, Peace. You have killed far more than your share of citizens. We all have!"

War started to protest, but the green keeper held his hand out. Peace slowly tilted his head back to Truth.

"We only kill when we absolutely must. Our mission is to protect the Republic from enemies both within and out. But there is no reason to kill soldiers."

Truth visibly disagreed. "There is when you discover the Creator's honest truth. What they were doing here was evil. And I won't allow it to continue." A handheld explosives trigger digitized in his hand.

At the sight of the trigger, Peace formed a sword while War's handgun shaped from red dust. Knowledge jumped forward in the middle, nearly stepping on the lifeless body of the soldier. He put his hands up between everyone.

Their advanced power armor was able to form virtually any weapon they could possibly think of, in any style they wanted out of particles of energy that emitted from their suits. However, when the keeper would let go of the item, it would vanish as it lost the connection of energy from the power source in the armor.

A digitized item was one that was a small object that the keeper's suit disintegrated and was stored in their armor. It could be digitized at any point. Still, it again became a physical item they could hand to someone else as it wasn't composed of energy particles from their suit.

"Woah, woah, woah! Peace, what are you doing?!"

The green keeper remained motionless, but they all knew that could change within a split second. "You've been acting strangely since Liberty died. I'm starting to wonder if you weren't behind his death after all."

Truth's demeanor stiffened. "Yeah, I was there. But I did everything I could to save him. You wouldn't understand, there was some kind of monster that attacked us. It was after the amulet."

"Why is now the first time you've mentioned this?" Knowledge asked dumbfounded by the revelation.

"I… didn't think anyone would believe me," the red keeper admitted.

"You have that right. So, you hid evidence from us, now this? I can't allow you to destroy this compound. Its research is too important for the war effort," the green keeper said confidently.

"What war? There is no war going on. The Republic already lost the 2nd Reunification War. And right now, there is peace on the borders. Isn't that what your job is? To make peace? You literally should be thrilled!"

The Keeper of Peace tilted his sword ever so slightly, then the blade began to glow bright orange. "I can't allow you to press that button, Truth."

The red keeper looked offended by his body movement. "Are… are you threatening me?"

"I will do what I must to protect the Republic, from *all* dangers."

Truth clenched his left fist but otherwise remained motionless. "So be it. I wondered how high up this scheme went, now it's clear."

Knowledge looked back and forth between the two locked in the staredown. "Now hold up. Nobody do anything stupid! We are on the same side!"

War rolled his shoulder in anticipation for the signal to strike. "I've been waiting for this."

"Yeah, I know you have," Truth remarked sarcastically.

"Guys, we don't have to do this. Let's talk this through rationally and…"

Peace abruptly interrupted Knowledge's plea. "It's too late for that. Press that button, Truth, and realize that you are turning your back on all of us. On the Republic."

The red keeper prepared himself for what was about to happen. He formed his own sword, and the blade too began to glow.

Knowledge fought within himself for what was the right choice to make. They all knew the code that they swore an oath to.

Seeing the defiant keeper not relenting in his decision and knowing there would be no time to stop him before he pressed the button, Peace verbally pushed forward. "You leave me with no alternative. For your betrayal against the code, and against the Corre Republic, you are henceforth stripped of your role as the Keeper of Truth and are now labeled as Erravi. Traitor to the Republic."

"No…" Knowledge muttered soberly; his spirit crushed.

Gideon glared back at his fellow keeper.

Peace stared right back angrily. "Relinquish your armor."

"That's not gonna happen."

The tension in the area instantly shot up. They each knew the code. If a keeper ever betrayed or abandoned the order, they were to hand over their power armor immediately as they were no longer fit to wear it. Refusal was a death sentence.

"Truth, think this through," Knowledge cautioned.

A long few seconds hung in the air before the traitor responded. "I have. I can't turn away from what is being done here. It must be stopped."

"Kill him!" Peace roared.

War fired several laser bolts at the Erravi while Peace burst forward on the left. Gideon easily phased out of harm's way from his attackers further up in the tunnel. Growling in anger, the gold keeper darted straight ahead just as the traitor slammed the remote trigger.

Multiple violent explosions rocked the tunnel they were in along with the entire cavern system nearby. Knowledge saw one of the building's crumple as smoke billowed out of several windows. It dropped straight down and blew out away from the destruction. Each of the other structures also fell, sending even more ash and debris into the air.

A wave of dust entered the tunnel and restricted visibility in addition to the lights flickering in and out. Each of the keepers' HUDs displayed one another with a bright silhouette matching the glow of their armor.

Gideon tried to escape the battle, but Peace flipped over in front of him. The traitor overheard War stomping up to him and was just barely able to deflect the crushing blow from his battle-ax. The weight of pressure from the strike was so incredible that his boots sank somewhat into the dirt floor, leaving cracked fragments below him.

"I'm not your enemy!" Gideon shouted to his old comrades.

"It's too late for that," War snarled.

Still unsure of what to do, Knowledge remained on the sidelines as the other three attacked and parried one another's strikes. The traitor phased out of the fight, but Peace was ready for him.

With all of his might, the green keeper chucked a fragmentation grenade at the traitor. Its explosion sent Gideon careening into the tunnel wall. The impact was so significant that he lost the grip of his sword, and it vanished into particle dust before his body hit the ground.

"Ergh..." he exhaled, fighting to push himself back up. With one extreme shove, he launched himself back to his feet, and he sprinted away from the decimated compound.

The four armored warriors ran through the network of tunnels and passageways beneath the hellish landscape of Ash above. It seemed as though there was no end to the number of halls. Peace fired his laser rifle, and Gideon phased back and forth to evade the shots. One glanced his shoulder, but the suit repaired itself immediately.

They eventually entered a large open area with a massive door at the other end. A rail system was installed at the top and bottom of the entryway, with boulders aligned around it. War, Peace, and the traitor again engaged in melee combat.

"Catherine, where are we?" Knowledge asked, looking all around.

Something felt off, but it was difficult to focus with the others fighting.

"We appear to be on the other side of one of the work camps mining zones."

"Then why have a door installed?"

"Maybe to keep the prisoners from wandering around unsupervised," the AI pointed out.

"No, that can't be it."

Off to the left was a strange object built of stone. Despite the incredible show of heated weapons swinging and blocking attacks of the other three, Knowledge couldn't shake the strangeness of the scene. His mind raced to figure out what could have driven Gideon, one of his only friends, to betray the order and the Corre Republic at the same time. It just didn't make sense.

Knowledge glanced back at the traitor who narrowly avoided being sliced in two by an expert move of swordsmanship from Peace. The green keeper's energized sword hit a large boulder behind Gideon, leaving behind a glowing scorch mark.

The nagging sensation in his mind brought the blue keeper back to his thoughts. He brought up the scans Catherine made of the room and quickly read it over. One line caught his immediate attention and made him pause.

"Catherine, what do you mean by this?"

"By what, Kay?" the program inquired.

"There is a mound of bodies?"

Due to the artificial intelligence working with her owner for a very long time, Catherine knew that Knowledge would want to see her findings. She illuminated the discovery on his mini-map, and the keeper headed for it.

The sound of the bladed weapons hitting one another shrieked through the cave and echoed off the walls. It wasn't enough though to divert the blue keeper from what he saw.

Now to his right was the odd object crafted out of stone. Beside it was a pile of bodies and dried bones. Knowledge had personally witnessed plenty of death in his time as a keeper that corpses on their own no longer bothered him. However, it was more for the carelessness of which the men had been organized together as if they had simply been tossed into a heap. Some appeared to have been chewed on or missing body parts.

Criminals that had been sent to Ash were known to not return. The conditions of the prison world were beyond harsh, and the life expectancy upon arrival wasn't very long.

He knelt down next to the pile of the castaway men and noticed that they all wore the typical orange uniform for the prisoners. They each were dingy, which wasn't a surprise because of all the dust that they probably worked in. However, what did stick out was that they all appeared to have a laceration along their necks.

Knowledge used his helmet to enhance the image in front of his eyes.

"It appears that each of these prisoners has been murdered," Catherine said plainly.

"No, this looks like something else. If it were a murder, then they wouldn't just be tossed together like this. Plus, it looks like they have been chewed on by something."

Knowledge stood up and decided to turn his attention to the stone construct. The area around the design, except for the bodies, was covered in all kinds of boot prints. One set of prints caught his attention, and he knelt to get a better view.

"Catherine, what creature made these tracks?"

"Unknown."

Knowledge figured it was linked to whatever had nibbled on the deceased men and focus on the sculpture. A full circle with a man-sized "t" at the center appeared to all be chiseled out of the same stone. There was a dark red spattered stain on the floor of the circle, and leather straps were wrapped around the arms. To add to the oddity, the tall object in the middle looked as though it was hewn with modern equipment, but something much more basic.

"This looks rough, like it was done with a chisel and hammer..." the keeper muttered to himself. "Run a comparison of it through the database. Specifically of known occult or ancient practices."

"Do you think these men were sacrificed in a ritual?" the AI asked nervously.

The keeper nodded. "I do."

He ran his gloved hand along one of the raised arms until the sound of the fierce battle interrupted his thoughts. Knowledge looked back over to the others, his mind though still trying to figure out what was going on here.

Gideon grunted after taking a severe blow to the chest from War's shoulder. He tumbled to the ground and rolled into a crouch, while still managing to hold onto his primary sword. A second sword formed in his other hand, and he stood up slowly.

"I can't believe you have known about this operation and didn't bring it up to the rest of us," he growled to his pursuers.

Peace paced aggressively while maintaining steady eye contact with the traitor. War breathed heavily, a mist puffing out from around his helmet, adding to the appearance of him being some kind of monster.

The green keeper aimed his sword at the Erravi. "We are on the precipice of a great war with the other nations to unite all of humanity under the Corre Republic again. The work these scientists were doing here would advance our WarMech efforts beyond anything anyone else has."

Truth shook his head. "No, this is wrong."

"You do not get to be the judge of what is necessary for this nation to survive," the green keeper snarled.

"Yes, yes, I do. That is my job. It is my burden!" the traitor shouted passionately. "Magnus would never have gone along with this."

Peace scoffed and laughed to himself. "He brought us together to pull the Republic out of the ashes of the war against the Synthetics, but he was a fool. Technology is not to be feared, it is to be embraced."

Truth became angrier. "This isn't technology like a HOP drive or a new computer chip. This is evil. It's… it's daemonic."

"Enough talk, traitor!" Peace lunged forward and spun his sword around.

Gideon dodged the attack and phased away as War leaped up and crashed his battle-ax down where he had just been standing.

"I get why you're with him, War, but Knowledge, are you with them too?" the traitor called out.

The blue keeper looked at Peace, who didn't pay him any attention. Using the pause in the fight, the green keeper charged up energy in his left hand and unleashed a blast wave that smashed Gideon and threw him into the wall behind him.

Once again, War rushed in and swung his ax down, coming within a second of ending the Erravi's life. Thankfully, Gideon managed to roll to the side, dodging the deadly attack. He swept with his leg and knocked the large gold keeper off balance. A loud thud emanated from his impact onto the dusty floor.

"My scans confirm that this red stain is dried blood. It is likely it came from the prisoners here," Catherine said, jarring the blue keeper from the distraction of the battle. "And I only have one confirmation of a time when a stone object was shaped just like this one."

"And where was that?"

"On Prime."

Knowledge's eyebrow furrowed. "Prime?"

"Yes. It is suspected to be thousands of cycles old."

"Which group was it used by?" the keeper asked as he inspected the stone sculpture once again and found that there were no other markings on it.

"Unknown. Archeologists have never been able to determine its purpose or who constructed it. If I may be so bold in asking, why are you not assisting Peace and War in apprehending the traitor?"

Knowledge continued to examine the object and then walked back over to the pile of bodies.

"Because I'm not much of a fighter."

"I disagree. I have personally witnessed you dispatch of many enemies of the state in our time together," Catherine said with a twinge of sarcasm.

"That's true, but those three right there far surpass any of my skills. Besides..." he paused for a moment to glance back at the brawl.

Peace jabbed his sword forward. Gideon deflected the attack and spun away. War swung his ax wide, and the traitor bent backward as the double-sided weapon swooshed over him.

"...besides, I need to understand what in the void is going on here."

With his battle-ax in his left hand, War opened his huge right glove. Fire formed and began to swirl around in his hand.

"Raaaah!" the gold keeper growled as he swung his arm wide, and a wave of fire formed.

Gideon raised his left arm and a shield wall formed to protect him. The surge of flames aimed at him was blocked, while the rest pushed past him and kept going until it hit the wall of the cave.

The ground all around the red armored warrior was severely burned. Gideon lowered his arm and also released the sword he was holding. He put his hands together, then drew them apart slowly. Blue streaks of energy sparked and seemed to shape into a glowing sphere that floated above his right hand.

Peace jumped backward while War stood there defiantly. He pounded his chest twice with his left arm while a tall shield formed around his right forearm.

Gideon shoved his hand forward, and the ball of energy shot out at lightning-fast speed. The gold keeper managed to raise his shield in time to block the devastating attack, but his protection was shattered. Its particles went in every direction, some bouncing off the ground before they entirely disintegrated.

While being distracted, Peace darted behind the traitor and slashed upward with his sword, then spun around and stabbed him through. A loud scream from Gideon shook the inquisitive keeper from his concentration. Knowledge twisted around to see his friend crawling on the ground with Peace standing over him.

The green keeper elevated his sword while Gideon raised himself up onto his knees. Blood poured out from his injury, but his suit closed itself up. From here, Knowledge could see the traitor brace himself.

"Any last words?" Peace asked, gloating over the Erravi.

"Yeah... how long did you know? Did you help them set this facility up?"

War stomped over to the pair while the blue keeper looked on from the sidelines.

Peace scoffed then slashed down with his sword. Gideon phased to the left, but the green keeper anticipated some sort of evasive maneuver and quickly swung his sword. He, however, wasn't prepared for the traitor to phase again so soon, but this time behind him.

Before he could react, a dagger digitized in Gideon's left hand. The red armored warrior wrapped his right arm around Peace's head and bent it sideways. War charged forward but wasn't able to prevent Gideon from stabbing Peace in the neck, straight through his protective armor.

The gold keeper hit the traitor square in the back with his ax, and Gideon screamed in pain. Sparks and energy particles shot out, and he released Peace, who staggered forward. The traitor fell again to his knees as War yanked his weapon out.

Fumes puffed up from Gideon's back, and Knowledge rushed over, his armor clanking with every hurried step. War brought his weapon up, and the valiant Erravi just stared at Peace.

The green keeper stumbled several more steps with a wisp of gold particles pouring out from the bladed weapon still stuck in his body. With great painful effort, Peace managed to face Gideon. He reached up, his arm struggling to comply, and gripped the handle of the dagger.

Without so much as a whimper, the green keeper yanked the blade out. He inspected the dagger and its handle for a moment as his suit prioritized healing his wound. It was a very exquisite weapon, covered in what appeared to be people being tortured by creatures of darkness.

Peace cast the blade away, and it clanked against the dirt floor. He staggered forward, then realized his armor was not repairing quite right. A mist of particles emanated from the gap in his neck but continued to float upward until they vaporized.

"Peace, are you alright?" Knowledge inquired nervously.

"I uh… don't… something's wrong…" the green keeper mumbled before he collapsed to his knees.

With ax still raised, War looked to his wounded friend. Gideon mustered enough strength to see Peace staring right back at him.

"Truth… my suit can't heal me… I need… need you to recharge my amulet," the green keeper pleaded shyly.

Seeing that this all was becoming very dire, Knowledge rushed over and inspected the injury. "I've never seen anything like this happen to our suits before, what kind of weapon was that, Truth?"

"Peace, I will not heal you. If I'm to die, then you will die with me."

The green keeper's breathing became heavy and labored. War's eyes burned with rage beneath his helmet. He looked down at the traitor and tightened his grip on his weapon's handle. Gideon remained on his knees, wisps of particles working fervently to repair the damage done to his back and armor.

"I will rip the amulet from your body!" the gold keeper growled before bringing down the melee weapon.

Without even looking, Gideon sensed the incoming attack and managed to phase far off to the left, easily avoiding the ax. A burst of dirt was shot into the air as the heated edge of the weapon scorched the soil.

In a blur, the traitor scooped up the discarded knife and threw it. The blade perfectly hit War in the chest, right in his heart.

Knowledge extended his arm to warn his comrade. "Don't pull it out!"

In his defiance, War ripped the knife out and chucked it away from the fight. Gideon stayed motionless, unsure if the blade was able to penetrate deep enough into the armor to harm the large keeper or not.

War took a step forward then lost his balance, crashing into the floor. Knowledge rushed over to aid him while Peace carefully turned his head to face the traitor.

"What have you done?" he asked, his voice coarse.

Despite being in pain, Gideon stood up to his full height. "I don't know who to trust anymore. I'm sorry it came to this."

Knowledge's hand began to glow as he held it over War's chest wound.

"No, help Peace," the gold keeper growled meekly.

"Don't be foolish. I'm not leaving you here to die. I can't heal him, but you can help me get him back to my ship."

Gideon headed toward the massive door. He reached the panel and extended his finger to press the open button.

"I don't understand," Knowledge called out.

The traitor turned back to face his friend. "Don't come looking for me, Kay. I can't give the suit back. Not to him," he said, motioning his head toward Peace.

"We… we will never stop hunting you. You know that we must… have the suit returned to us. We need it in case… they ever return."

The wound over War's chest began to close as did the damage to his armor. Something was still wrong with his own breathing, though.

"Please, Truth, don't end things like this. You can still help, Peace," Knowledge said neutrally.

While there wasn't a great deal of visible emotion in the blue keeper's voice, Gideon had worked with him long enough to know that inside, he must be hurting.

Without another word, the traitor hit the button and stepped through once the door opened. The three other keepers watched as the man who betrayed their order faced them one last time. A long moment past between them before Gideon smashed the terminal on his side with his fist, shutting the door behind him and sealing his fate as a traitor forever.

Chapter 24

Cycle: 412 Month: 9 Rotation: 15
Corre Republic Space
Prefecture: Expansive
Planet: Benedictus
Location: Rind

Aboard his *Sparrow* spacecraft, Knowledge recalled the rest of the events that played out once Gideon abandoned them there in that tunnel. After healing War, the two evacuated the area with Peace.

At one-point, Knowledge attempted to return to the rubble of the secretive compound to discover it had been removed. There wasn't any sign that buildings had been there at all, except for the obnoxiously large opening in the tunnel that they had been located in.

A short *chirp* alerted him that he had arrived in Rind. He deactivated the replay that had been paused on his heads-up display within his helmet.

I wish that moment would have played out differently, Gideon. I really do.

An icon on his ship's cockpit holo-projector highlighted where the Keeper of Life was waiting in the middle of a field. Knowledge's *Sparrow* slowed to a halt. The blue keeper strode to the back of his spacecraft just as the door lowered.

A gust of wind rushed inside, but Knowledge could not feel the sensation through his suit. He nonchalantly stepped onto the ramp and leaped down. The *Sparrow* sped off while his suit automatically activated a burst from small jets built into his suit, slowing his descent at the last second.

Life nodded to her comrade just when Death's ship sped overhead. The black-armored keeper jumped from his speeding spacecraft. He landed in a crouch then stood up to his full height.

"Glad you could make it," the female keeper quipped to Death.

"You know I hate to miss the fun," he replied sarcastically.

Citizens in the area saw the spectacle and began to gather round to watch, most very nervous of why three armored warriors would just appear in broad sunlight. Life paid no attention to them, but Knowledge couldn't help checking on the ID confirmations of those around them that his suit brought up for him to review.

"I know this isn't exactly protocol, but I think it is best if I take point on this one. I want to resolve this as calmly as we can," Knowledge said plainly.

"No way," Life said rudely. "You've had your chance. We're going in guns blazing."

The dark blue keeper could easily sense her resistance, but he couldn't relent just yet. "I don't think either of you really understands this man's lethality."

"I've seen him in action," Death remarked.

"True, but things were different then. And Life, you weren't even a keeper at the time."

The white keeper rolled her head and placed her left hand on her hip. "What does that matter?"

I don't have time to get into all of this child…

"Before Gideon was brought into the order, he was one of the finest soldiers there ever had been. He was instrumental in defeating the Synthetics rand he is never to be underestimated."

The last statement caught Death's attention. "Wait, you don't mean to say…"

"Yes, Gideon was the original Truth."

Life's demeanor lightened somewhat. "So, you're saying that he's as old as you?"

An interesting way to put it.

"Yes."

Death and Life shared a glance at one another. The black keeper shrugged. "If he's as good as he's saying, then maybe it's worth a try."

Knowledge thought he had finally won them both over, but Life still had a bit of defiant spunk in her.

"Isn't he injured, though? There's no way his suit can heal him by now. It's amazing it even works anymore since he hasn't been able to charge it for all these cycles."

"Suit or not, Gideon is dangerous. I've seen him in action on numerous occasions, and we need to exercise extreme caution."

The female keeper finally gave in and surrendered. "Fine. What's your plan to get him to return the amulet?"

Knowledge looked away from the conversation for a second, then faced Life head-on. "I was able to locate his family. I can use that as leverage."

Death shook his head in disappointment while Life was intrigued.

"How do you know he'll go along with it?" she asked.

"He will. Or we'll have no choice but to kill him to get the amulet back."

Life crossed her arms. "Alright. What's first?"

"Simple. We head for Frank Corbo's property and wait for Gideon to make his move."

Chapter 25

Cycle: 412 Month: 9 Rotation: 15
Corre Republic Space
Prefecture: Expansive
Planet: Benedictus
Location: Rind

The local sun was high in the sky, and the weekend's activities were in full swing in the small town. Several vehicles drove through the intersection just before the traffic light changed.

A dingy white cab came to a stop behind a freshly waxed, and costly, silver hover truck. After he wrapped things up with Hannibal, Spectre had gathered his weapons and headed straight for Rind. The bounty hunter had elected to stay behind rather than get involved. He gave his friend the burner communicator he used to message Deni Moore with.

I can't blame him for wanting to stay out of this. I'm not exactly in great shape to even go about this.

Gideon had ridden in the taxi for over an hour now. Weekend traffic was heavy and had no sign of letting up. He happened to glance up from the backseat and spotted himself in the rearview mirror. The only problem was he didn't see his own face. Instead, it was that of a middle-aged man with numerous different features than his, including a significantly larger nose.

The digital face mask that the ex-bounty hunter wore created the believable illusion that he was a totally different person from his beard up to his forehead. It was strange to not see his actual appearance, but it made him feel much more relaxed despite being in the vehicle with the scruffy-looking driver. Despite his best efforts, the driver continued to insist on speaking to him.

"Man, what a town. What a town! You don't get better than this," the driver said, half-twisting his head back to speak to his passenger.

"Yeah," Gideon said disdainfully.

Freaking just get the hint and leave me alone.

"This is the best place to wind up… that is if you could afford it!" the scroungy man laughed wildly at his own joke.

The vehicles up ahead began to move as the light changed.

Spectre looked out the window while his right hand absentmindedly toyed with his bracelet. He had elected to leave his duffle bag behind at Hannibal's, only deciding to bring his newly purchased firearms and the bounty hunter's communicator in a dark satchel bag.

I sure hope the suit has enough power for one more go. After this, I need to get off of this rock in a hurry.

Everything in his body ached, including his throbbing headache. With his plethora of external and internal injuries, Hannibal found it to be a miracle he was even able to stand. The truth was, his extended exposure to his power armor had changed him in several ways. One of which was a more rapid natural healing process. It was as if his very DNA was altered somehow.

He never did understand how the suits worked. All that mattered to him was that it allowed him to do his job in service to the Republic.

While the driver went off on some other excited slur of words about how wonderful Rind was, his mind drifted back to memories of his time as a keeper.

So many adventures… so many secrets. But what was the point of it all? To end up a traitor to my country and to chase down back alley rodents?

His thoughts changed from pity to those of his wife, Joan. Just then, his heart hurt more than anything else did.

I still don't know what I am going to tell the kids. How am I going to be able to continue on without her?

A tiny internal voice popped into his head.

You always knew your time with her was short. It was never going to last forever…

Feeling a sense of immense regret and shame at his own internal downward conversation, Gideon's eyes fell to the carpet around his feet.

Joan wouldn't want me chasing down her killers. She would want me to watch over the children. But I… I just can't let this go. I can't.

The widowed husband pursed his lips, then clenched his jaw to fend off the emotions that swirled in his head.

Focus on what's next. That's all that matters right now.

He cleared his throat to refocus himself, which only attracted the attention of the driver. Another pointless conversation continued until the filthy taxi pulled up to the destination.

The driver put the vehicle in "park" and checked his terminal beneath the radio system installed in the dashboard. "Alright, that is going to be..."

Gideon quickly used the pay card he got off of Hannibal on the terminal in the backseat. The price didn't matter, he just needed to escape the cab. Both rear doors unlocked, and Spectre exited on the left side of the vehicle.

Decades ago, it became standard practice for taxis' back doors to automatically lock the occupant inside in case they attempted to ditch without paying. The method had now spread throughout the Corre Republic, even to the less developed inner worlds like Destiny. However, in order to pay, the passenger would have to exchange funds with their paycard, no cash was permitted. This also assisted local authorities in tracking down the movement of released criminals and felons if they needed to be observed. The only downside to this was that each pay card was linked to its owner, but thankfully Hannibal had a fake one set up that Gideon could use without serious concern of raising an alarm to the system.

The warm temperature in the air greeted him while the door for the cab shut slowly on its own. Gideon had chosen to be dropped off at a popular restaurant in town, hoping to not raise suspicion further.

He checked the time on Hannibal's communicator.

Alright, so they are expecting him in a little over two hours. It'll take me about thirty to walk there, and then it's go time.

A mixture of excitement and worry swam within Frank Corbo's stomach. He downed the last of his amber colored alcohol then stood up from his leather chair. It creaked noisily from the sudden change as it expanded back to its empty status.

The crime lord's mind was like a blizzard. Each passing rotation since the attack had left him feeling very uneasy and concerned. Coming so close to death from the deadliest bounty hunter was enough to rattle any man.

Outwardly though, he had to display strength and confidence. None of the other members of his crew could tell what lay beneath, except for Deni Moore.

The boss' right-hand man had added extra security as they waited for their incoming guest. Using some shady connections, he had made cycles ago, Deni had a hacker place a hidden tracking program in Hannibal's communicator by accessing it through the stream. He didn't want to take any unnecessary chances.

The device had been getting closer to the mansion for a while now. Something was wrong. He was going to arrive much too early.

Deni spotted his boss exiting his office. "The guy's on the move."

"Good," Frank said absentmindedly.

He began to turn to head down the hall but was stopped.

"There may be a problem, though."

The way that Frank slowly spun back around clearly displayed his irritation. "Oh?"

Deni had been on the receiving end of his boss' anger on many occasions and had learned ways to ease the situation. A necessary skill that had kept him alive more than once.

"It looks like he is going to arrive early."

"How is that a concern?" the crime lord asked bitterly. "Maybe he doesn't trust us as much as we don't him."

"I don't know, something feels... off about this."

Frank's eyes began to burn. "This was your idea. If you think that my son is in any sort of danger, then I want everyone on high alert."

Deni began to feel like the room was getting hotter. He adjusted his flat black tie. "Yes, sir. I'll see to it."

"If it turns out that Spectre is alive..." Frank stopped himself from saying much more, and instead closed his eyes and shook his hand slightly.

The other man understood what was unspoken. "It's all taken care of, sir. I'll update you if anything else changes."

After exhaling deeply, the crime lord stormed off.

Chapter 26

Cycle: 412 Month: 9 Rotation: 15
Corre Republic Space
Prefecture: Expansive
Planet: Benedictus
Location: Rind

The sky up above the joyous town was a solid light blue. There was no cloud in sight, which was a significant change from the dreary conditions of the past week. While others in Rind were full of excitement and happiness on the outside, Gideon was preparing himself mentally for what was about to happen.

He strolled past a huge white mansion with four thick pillars positioned strategically beneath the overhanging roof. Everything about its yard was pristine and seemed perfect from the view from the street. The homeowner was holding the door to his expensive SUV for one of his children to hop in the back. He happened to glance up and see the passerby staring right back at him.

Gideon instantly recognized the man as one of the rival crime lords that ran operations in Avalon. For his sake, the partial face mask made it impossible from this distance for him to know that it was the ex-bounty hunter. Without waving or any other pleasantry, the criminal climbed into the back and shut the door.

For what felt like the hundredth time, Spectre again checked the time on the borrowed communicator.

I still have plenty of time. Why am I so nervous?

Try as he might, he couldn't shake the sensation that something was waiting for him at the house. Throughout his career, he had charged straight into a wide range of violent and dangerous situations. But none where he was so physically injured.

All that matters is that Saul dies today. Nothing else will stop me. Nothing.

The rest of the walk to Frank Corbo's mansion was as quiet and uneventful as the rest had been. His heart rate accelerated somewhat when he confirmed the street numbers matched the address on the communicator.

Okay, I'll just check things out then figure out what to do next. Maybe I'll get lucky, and they won't be ready.

Spectre elected to walk past the enormous house from across the street, hoping to not gather too much attention. He carefully observed the area as he approached the house for anyone positioned outside. Several guards were posted just out of the sunlight up under the awning in front of the structure. Another one was staged up on a balcony that overlooked the driveway.

"Hmm, that's odd," Deni said aloud to himself while he checked his holo projection emitting from his wrist device.

The location confirmation from the bounty hunter's communicator was passing right by. He stood up from the dark leather couch he was sitting on and strode over to the window. From his vantage point on the second floor, he could see the street below. There was no one except for an older looking man who was walking by.

A nagging feeling prodded him from the back of his mind. Then the hairs on his neck stood up when the man locked eyes with his. In the natural, there was nothing out of the ordinary, but something was wrong.

Before his opportunity was going to possibly vanish, Deni pushed a couple of keys on the touch screen of his own communicator and watched.

Yeah, I see you, Deni. Frank must be here.

Gideon was keeping a steady walking pace when he felt a vibration in his pocket. Hannibal's communicator began to ring loudly, and he started to reach for it then caught himself before he pulled it out.

Well, he probably guessed something's up. Oh well. Might as well scare him.

None of the other guards were paying attention to the stranger, but Deni was intensely focused on him. Spectre slowly lifted his right hand and formed it into a finger gun. He pointed it at Deni and closed one of his eyes and simulated that his finger fired a bullet. A devilish grin spread on his face, and he chuckled to himself.

307

The thug felt a chill run down his spine, and he knew immediately that he made a mistake giving his boss' address away. His eyes widened, and he tracked the man until he disappeared out of view behind the wall. A bright blue flash emanated from behind the barrier then the ex-bounty hunter launcher himself up and over it with a bag in his hand. He had two pistols connected to his thighs, and he yanked a dark square shape out of the sack before he tossed it away.

Deni's hand flew to his ear, and he triggered his mini radio. "He's here! Spectre is here!"

Before any of the men in the front yard had time to react, Spectre's retractable laser repeater transformed into active mode, and he fired a flurry of bolts. A stream of bright red lasers burned through the first man, then a second. The third guard drew a large silver pistol from his coat holster and aimed. Before he was able to get a shot off, he was riddled with bolts, and he dropped to his knees.

The guard on the balcony retrieved the sniper rifle he had hidden just out of view from the road. He ducked for cover when the balcony was hit by a storm of fire from the ex-bounty hunter as he rushed up the lawn and approached the front door.

"He what?!" Frank growled.

Deni was pointing toward the front of the house. "Spectre isn't dead. He'll be here any second!"

Saul's blood drained from his face even though inside, he was trying to locate some courage. A vein bulged on Frank's forehead in his raw anger.

"You did this!"

The right-hand thug's eyes grew, and he backed up. Before he had time to talk any sense into his employer, the crime lord drew a thick black pistol from behind his back and shot twice. Deni slammed into the wall behind him, leaving a trail of blood as he slid to the floor. Frank took a deep breath as the fighting outside continued to rage.

Saul didn't know what to say, but Deni choked on his own blood. Without mercy, Frank again aimed his pistol at the man who had worked closely with him for cycles and fired again and again until his magazine was empty.

The other thugs in the room, along with the crime lord's son, were petrified. Frank licked his lips, then twisted his head to the side.

"Bruce."

"Ye… yes, sir?" the younger man stuttered.

"Get my son out of here. Everyone else, we are going to kill this bastard properly," the crime lord said dryly.

Everyone in the room remained still, but the sound of the gunfire was only getting louder.

"NOW!" Frank screamed so loud that he shook.

Each of the thugs, including Bruce, jumped to their feet and rushed out of the room.

Saul stepped up to his father, unsure of what was appropriate to say. "P… Pa." He dug down deep and nodded his head. "I want to stay. This is my doing. I want to see it through."

Once the others were out, Frank turned to face his only child. Deep pain was in his eyes, and he looked defeated. A sight that the son had never seen before.

"Saul, I can't let him win. You are the most important thing to me."

The younger man was totally caught off guard. His mouth hung open, and he suddenly felt very uncomfortable at his father's vulnerability.

He tried to speak, but his mind went blank on anything substantial to say.

Frank averted his eyes. "Stop. Just get out of here. I... I love you."

Before Saul could respond, a grenade went off and rocked the room. Frank's anger again rushed up, and his eyes grew furious.

"Go! Get out of here!"

The son rushed up to the doorframe while the crime lord reloaded his handgun. Saul poked his head out to see if the hall was clear, then ducked down and ran off.

Taking a very deep breath then exhaling, Frank steeled himself for what needed to be done.

Chapter 27

Cycle: 412 Month: 9 Rotation: 15
Corre Republic Space
Prefecture: Expansive
Planet: Benedictus
Location: Rind

Aboard Life's personal spacecraft, the three keepers sat around waiting for things to change. Death leaned up against the wall in the corner of the storage area while Knowledge was preoccupied surveying the security cameras for Frank Corbo's home.

Life had wandered off to the bridge a short time ago. Knowledge knew she was likely contacting Peace, and of course, he had already tapped into her secure transmission and had both of their feeds on the lower left-hand side of his HUD. Death was totally unaware of any of this and remained silent, possibly he was even asleep. Their hectic life was sometimes filled with the constant need to be on the move. Having downtime like this was rare for any of them.

The room that Peace was in was dim, and it was hard to make out anything else inside of the recovery chamber that had been built for him. Knowledge could barely make out his silhouette, which even seemed a bit off. As if he was leaning up against the wall or something.

His light sensitivity must be getting worse.

311

"According to Knowledge, all of this should be resolved shortly," the female keeper said kindly.

Peace remained still. "Good."

"With any luck, you will be released from that damned prison within the week."

"There will be much work to do even with the amulet back in our hands. A new Truth will need to be chosen. Do you have any potential candidates?" Peace asked.

Knowledge's attention was drawn away from his busy work, and he listened carefully to the conversation.

His voice sounds coarse. Even the chamber isn't able to sustain his stasis. He must be in a considerable amount of pain.

"I have one warrior in mind, but rest assured my top priority after retrieving the amulet will be finding a replacement."

"I knew I could count on you, Life," Peace said affirmingly.

Knowledge recognized the demeanor of the female keeper to alter somewhat.

I'll never understand why she tries to earn his approval.

"Thank you. I… I won't fail you."

The imprisoned keeper's silhouette shifted some. "See that you don't. I have many plans to move forward with. Oh, one last thing."

"Yes?" the female keeper asked neutrally.

There was a moment of silence, and Peace leaned forward, just a tad closer to the camera. "I want you to kill the traitor."

Knowledge watched intently.

"Regardless if he hands the amulet over to you or even begs for his life. I want him killed. He is too dangerous to allow him to live," Peace said with a low growl in his voice.

"It will be done."

Life cut the transmission, and Knowledge licked his lips while he thought.

We need to get the amulet back, but I can't trust it in Life's hands. I need to be the one to get ahold of it.

"Kay, there seem to be multiple shootings that have broken out at Frank Corbo's residence in Rind," Catherine said, breaking up the keeper's internal dialogue.

Knowledge stood up gracefully. "Death, it's time."

The black keeper roused from sleep just as Life strolled back into the room. She spotted both of the keepers stirring and knew something was up.

"Did the traitor make his move?"

"I believe so." Knowledge paused for a moment to look back and forth at the others.

Let's see if Life will be honest with me.

"I can't stress enough that Gideon is a highly trained warrior. He is extremely lethal. However, our goal is getting the amulet back. If he will hand it over, then we grab it and run."

Death nodded, but Life was motionless.

"What if he resists?" she asked, standing still.

"Then we will do our duty. But there is no reason it will have to come to that. I know Gideon, he will do the right thing to save his family."

Life did little to give away her intention, and the blue keeper observed her very closely.

I'm not sure if I can trust you...

"Transfer the coordinates for the location. Let's get this over with," the white keeper said as she stomped off for the bridge.

Chapter 28

Cycle: 412 Month: 9 Rotation: 15
Corre Republic Space
Prefecture: Expansive
Planet: Benedictus
Location: Rind

What was once a gorgeous home with maroon carpets that ran through much of the house, a dark marble kitchen, and other masterful additions resembled more of a warzone now. Several bodies lay in the doorway to Gideon's right while he reloaded his laser repeater. He had paused for a moment in the dining room as it gave him multiple exits to move wherever his target may try to escape from.

He had already disabled the suit from trying to heal his injuries and diverted any energy it had to track heartbeats and scanning the mansion. Nonetheless, it still warned him that its power source was low.

A "6:53," countdown shown in the corner of his HUD.

Got to keep moving. Not much time.

Several clusters of people were spread throughout the building, several of them charging toward him, while others were evacuating. Instead of trying to engage those that were coming for him, he planned to kill enough of the guards that Frank would send him and his son away.

A thug burst through the entrance on his left totally oblivious that he was even there. Spectre fired a burst of red bolts and killed the man before he realized his mistake. His ability to hide from the security cameras and other surveillance feeds made locating the attacker very difficult for Corbo's people.

The man's body crashed into the table and then flipped down to the debris covered floor. Gideon sprang up and raised his weapon. He ducked low, then entered the next room.

On his mini-map, two life signs were pinged, and they were heading away from the conflict while everyone else was converging on his location. Just before he was about to move forward, he heard a familiar *clink, clink, clink*. He turned just in time to see the fragmentation grenade land on the other side of the room. Its detonation filled the room with smoke and shrapnel, but the concussive blast sent Spectre flying into the wall.

A display of his power armor appeared and showed him where the more severe damage had taken place.

Ow... that hurt.

"The time has finally come, Gideon!" Frank Corbo shouted from the other room. "I'm going to enjoy this."

Gotta get up...

The timer dropped exceptionally down to "4:07," as it spent precious energy to mend itself.

The ex-bounty hunter forced himself to stand. Thankfully he had not lost his grip on his weapon in the blast. He brought the firearm up and aimed toward a grouping of thugs behind the wall. Red bolts burned through the partition and skewered one of the men in the chest.

Frank twisted the head of another grenade then lobbed it into the room. Gideon caught the motion of the explosive and dove out into the hall. He landed in a roll then stood back up just as the grenade detonated. Two other thugs popped up from cover and fired their automatic rifles. Spectre managed to kill one before he was able to successfully hit him, while the other hit him all over with bullets.

Again, the time dropped. "3:21."

Dammit!

Gideon ducked down then moved to his right. He fired another burst of lasers, which ripped through his attacker's suit coat like it was paper.

Hearing the ex-bounty hunter on the move, Frank gripped his pistol tightly and signaled for one of his guards to move up. The tall man had been a veteran of the Republic Armed Forces and carried a military-grade scattergun. He checked the corners of the ravaged room where Gideon had been and moved up to the entrance to the hall. Meanwhile, the crime lord navigated through the other hallway in hopes of cutting off the attacker if he could.

Spectre blasted another guard that got too close, but he failed to notice the other man behind him in time. His suit alerted him, and he spun to respond. In a flash, both men fired their weapons at one another. The ex-bounty hunter caught the veteran in the chest and face while the scattergun hit Gideon in the thigh. As the thug slid to the floor, dead, Spectre flopped to the ground from the incredible impact.

His armor left a dent in the hard floor, and he made himself roll to the side.

"1:57."

Ignoring the throbbing pain in his body, Spectre attempted to stand.

"Ahhh," Gideon moaned.

His left hand trembled, but he forced it to respond.

Get... up!

With immense effort, he finally was able to stand. Frank bolted out into the hallway that Gideon was in then he caught himself. Backtracking, he ducked behind the corner and pressed himself up against the wall. His breathing was heavy, and sweat beaded down his forehead. He happened to spot through a window across the way his son and Bruce making for one of the parked cars.

"Saul...," he muttered.

Finding inner courage, he braced himself for what needed to be done. He again turned the corner, this time with gun drawn and ready to go. However, to his surprise, the ex-bounty hunter was gone. Dread filled his heart, and he finally heard the pounding steps of Gideon heading toward Saul.

"No!"

Frank sprinted through his once prestigious home, passing several other bodies. More gunshots rang out up ahead, but he wasn't sure he could make it in time. He tripped over an end table that had been blasted into the middle of the room. The impact sent a surge of pain up his left elbow, and he cried out in agony, but there was no time for his own suffering.

Frantically, the crime lord fought back to his feet and continued on his way.

Bruce reached the car first and threw open the driver's side door. Saul ran around to the other side after slamming into the bumper of the getaway vehicle.

"Frick!" he exclaimed at his own carelessness.

Gideon was just about to reach the back door when one last guard stepped out and sprayed a hail of bullets from a sub-machine gun. Reacting inhumanly fast, Spectre dodged to the right, narrowly avoiding the attack. He aimed and fired the last of his laser repeater bolts, killing the other man.

Spotting his target, Gideon discarded the empty weapon and drew a pistol. He aimed for Saul's head and fired. Before the bullet left the barrel of the gun, Frank stepped in front of it.

Spectre's eyes burned at being so close to killing the man that slaughtered his wife. He fired five more times into Frank. The crime lord fell to his knees and gasped for air. Blood poured out of his injuries, and he momentarily had time to reflect on his life.

Bruce threw the car in reverse and sped back down the rear driveway.

"No!" Gideon blurted out.

He sprinted forward, swatted the dying crime lord to the side. Crossing his arms to shield his helmet, Spectre bashed the reinforced door, ripping it off of its hinges. He fired several more times at the fleeing vehicle, but he was not able to hit either the driver or Saul.

"1:32."

A sense of failure and disappointment flooded Gideon's mind. Everything in him hurt, and he felt utterly exhausted from all that had transpired.

I'm sorry, Joan...

Suddenly, a loud roar overhead shook the neighborhood. Nothing really mattered at the moment, but Gideon happened to glance up to see a light grey *Sparrow* overhead.

Oh no...

Despite there being no markings on the side of the spacecraft, Gideon knew who was likely to be aboard. The ramp at the back of the ship lowered, and the *Sparrow* began to hover in place. Three figures leaped down, and the ex-bounty hunter's HUD identified them.

Life, Death, and Knowledge all landed safely on the bright green lawn. Each stood up and stared at the traitor.

The ship's engine revved, and it flew off to a waiting distance for new orders from Life.

"It's been a long time," Death called out.

Gideon remained silent, his mind racing to figure out how he was going to escape the situation.

Life began to move forward, but Knowledge spoke up.

320

"Gideon, hand over the suit. It's over."

Spectre looked at the dark blue keeper then to Life. The female keeper stopped in place after hearing Knowledge's order to their target.

I don't know if I can win this against all three of them in my condition…

"You know I can't do that, Kay," Gideon responded loudly.

"We all know your suit is low on power and that you are injured. Do you really want to throw away your life?" Life asked angrily.

The fugitive again looked at all three of the keepers, the above sunlight glimmering off their power armor. A warm breeze blew through, and gracefully touched the grass and other plants. None of the warriors could sense any of the life around them, not inside their suits.

…I have to try. I didn't come this far to fail.

The sound of an aircraft could be heard off in the distance. None of them paid any attention to it.

Spectre tightened his grip on the pistol in his gloved hand. Weapons began to form in Life and Death's hands.

"0:48."

Knowledge extended an open hand toward his old friend. "There is no need to die pointlessly. Give us the armor, and I promise you no harm will come to you."

Gideon began figuring what he was about to do when an explosion erupted in the middle of the keepers. The ball of flames engulfed Life while the other two were knocked over from the concussive blast.

Spectre didn't even take time to assess what happened. He used the opportunity to break off into a run and sprinted around the ravaged mansion.

Up above the violence, the bounty hunter Tak brought the *Jasper* aircraft he piloted to begin rotating around the property.

"Spectre is mine!" he shouted over the external speakers.

The smoke from the previous attack faded, and he stared in disbelief when he saw the white armored keeper standing absolutely still in the middle of the crater.

"What the...?" Tak mumbled quietly to himself.

Life tilted her head up to the spacecraft, and the rifle in her hand transformed into a hook-like weapon.

"Get the traitor!" Life barked to her comrades while Death and Knowledge ran after their target.

Tak watched the other two keepers break into a run, and he moved to cut them off. Life jogged toward the *Jasper* then sprinted freakishly fast. She jumped up onto a separate building on the property and then used her jumper pack to hop high into the air. Before the mercenary pilot knew what was going on, he heard a loud thud and grinding sound from somewhere behind him.

"What was that?!" he asked loudly.

The *Jasper* leaned to the left from the added weight of the occupant hanging on the outside of the hull. Tak leaned forward, and his eyes widened considerably at seeing the sleek helmet of the keeper of Life staring back at him.

A mist of sapphire colored particles around the keeper's left hand morphed into a thick handgun. She raised it up to the cockpit and fired madly at the pilot.

Tak ducked beneath the first couple of rounds and slammed his controls to the right, sending the aircraft into a mad spin. Life held on tight to her hooked weapon, which was dug deep into the *Jasper's* internal structure. Multiple loud alarms rang out from the cockpit, and the mercenary bashed the ejection button.

The canopy of the spacecraft blasted apart and the pilot was shot out high above the careening vessel. It continued to spin violently as it fell to the lawn below. Life brought her legs up and jumped off to safety. She landed in a tumble but was otherwise unharmed. The *Jasper* crashed into the mansion, then exploded, sending debris and smoke upward.

Gideon continued running as fast as his legs would carry him. The timer on his helmet was in its final countdown then it would give away his position once again. He jumped over the front wall he had started his assault from.

Knowledge and Death rounded the front of the mansion just as the ship crashed into it. Neither turned back to the eruption behind them. They both were determined to locate the traitor no matter what.

"Where did he go?" Death asked in between his heavy breathing.

"Split up!" Knowledge said as he broke off to the right of the front yard.

The black keeper jumped over the wall and ran left.

"00:15."

Spectre ran down the sidewalk and made a sharp right just in time to avoid being seen by the blue keeper. He burst through the bushes and continued running for several more seconds before he reached the barrier of the back wall of the neighbor's massive yard. Without stopping, he slammed through it and kept running.

"Catherine, access nearby home devices with auditory monitoring. Coordinate any mention of the neighbors at the sight of anything that resembles Gideon."

"Of course," the AI responded kindly.

Knowledge noticed the bushes and that it appeared as though something substantial had just been through them. A laser pistol formed in his hand, and he too ran through them.

"I think I've found him!" he reported back to the other two keepers.

"On my way," Death said resolutely.

Meanwhile, Life stood on the lawn and watched Tak's pilot chair float downward. The dual tan parachutes guided the mercenary down when he spotted the female keeper standing in the yard.

"Uh, oh..."

He unfastened his harness that was tightly connected around his armor. The seat rocked backward then forward before he fell out of the chair. Using his own jumper pack, Tak landed softly. The parachutes caught a gust of wind and blew to the right and landed up against the fence.

Tak stood motionless while Life stared directly at him. He knew she was pissed by her posture.

"Look, it wasn't anything personal, it's just business."

The white keeper held out her hand toward the mercenary, and Tak reached for the collapsed rifle magnetically attached to his back. The weapon flipped into active mode, but he hesitated to fire because the other warrior wasn't moving aggressively.

Life grinned cruelly beneath her helmet as she opened her hand wide, and it began to glow light blue. The soil beneath Tak started to give way, and he sunk to his waist immediately.

"Huh?!"

Try as he might, he could not move his legs. Frantically he used his arms to try and pull him up from sinking into the dirt. Again, he dropped deeper, and panic began to grip him. The female keeper lowered her arm and slowly strode over to the terrified mercenary.

"Help me!" he called out, fear clutching his voice.

Life tilted her head to the side and paused for a moment. "No."

Tak began to scream as the keeper raised her arm again and opened her hand. He activated his jumper pack, and the flames scorched the lawn around him, but it wasn't strong enough to aid him in his escape. The last thing that the hardened mercenary would ever see would be the soil opening up further and him sinking deep beneath it. He sank to the point that his radio could not reach anyone for help.

The keeper scoffed and jogged after the others.

Gideon continued running. He ignored all of the pain in his body, but he could feel a stream of blood around his side. Unfortunately, it wouldn't matter what shape he was in if he was caught.

He spotted a small building behind one of the other mansions in the neighborhood. Due to the onslaught of gunfire and the explosion, many of the people who were at home were stepping outside to see what was going on.

With acrobatic ease, he flipped over the solid stone fence and landed in a crouch. With only a second to spare, he deactivated his suit. Feeling his ribcage, his right hand came back covered in blood.

"Not yet..."

He remained absolutely still while he listened intently to his surroundings. Pressing up against the wall, Gideon glanced up to the right to see a shut window, but the curtains were drawn back. He kept his gaze locked onto that spot while Knowledge stormed on by.

The traitor's heart began to beat faster and faster.

I can't stay here. He'll find me even if he can't see me from any nearby cameras.

With great effort, he limped away from the area and headed for the backyard. He checked around the corner and saw that it was clear. A fancy fountain spraying water up above itself was arranged at the center of a lovely garden of flowers and cobblestone paths.

Not seeing any trail of Gideon, Knowledge paused for a moment to give Catherine time to search the area. Life caught up to the blue keeper from behind.

"Any sign of him?" she asked unhappily.

After struggling to climb the fence, Gideon checked his projected face mask covering his own face to ensure it was still on and active. There wasn't time for him to see that he left a trail of blood behind on the yard divider. What was important was putting as much distance from himself and his pursuers as he could.

Knowledge hated to admit it, but he shook his head. "Whatever device he has that keeps him hidden from cameras is making it difficult to track him."

"How could you lose him?!"

The blue keeper froze in place by his fellow keeper's aggressive demeanor. "I didn't. He escaped."

"He has a powered down suit and has serious injuries. You had a shot, and you allowed him to flee the scene." Life spun around and began to pace in frustration.

Knowledge tilted his head while he observed her behavior breakdown. "We will locate him..."

Life held up her hand to stop the other keeper from speaking. "No, you've had your chance. Now it's my turn."

The keeper of Death finally met up with the others. "What's going on?" he asked, realizing there was incredible tension between them.

"I don't think you understand..." Knowledge began to say.

Again, Life cut him off. But this time, she was shouting. "No, I don't think you understand! We cannot allow him to get off-world with the amulet. Peace needs us to finish this. Enough is enough. I'm taking point now."

The female keeper began to storm off. "Death, come with me."

Both of the male keepers glanced at one another, then Knowledge called out to Life. "What are you planning to do?"

"What I have to," she growled without turning back.

Chapter 29

Cycle: 412 Month: 9 Rotation: 15
Corre Republic Space
Prefecture: Expansive
Planet: Benedictus
Location: Rind

The local sun was heading towards setting for the evening, and the beautiful weekend was long since sullied for young Saul Corbo. His face had been firmly placed in his hands for several blocks as Bruce swerved through traffic.

"Hey, Saul, what should we do?" the driver asked nervously.

The thug leader looked out his window, tears welling up in his eyes. He sniffed sharply then used his forearm to wipe away the sign of him beginning to cry.

Before they had successfully left the property, Saul had looked up in time to see his father take multiple bullets before crumpling to the floor.

Those bullets were meant for me. Dammit! Why didn't I kill Gideon in that fraggin' alley when I had the chance?

Several memories of his Pa replayed through his mind as the streets of Rind passed by. Some were fun and enjoyable, while others were of his father physically teaching him a lesson. It didn't matter that Frank was abusive, he was still his father. The last memory was that of his dad telling him that he loved him. That was certainly not a phrase he had heard more than twice in his entire life.

He's dead because of me...

Bruce glanced over quickly at his leader and friend. "Saul?"

Fury began to boil up within the young man. "I'll kill 'im. I'll be sure of it."

A car up ahead pulled out into their lane at a reasonable speed, but it didn't matter to Bruce. He swung left to avoid a collision and abruptly honked the vehicle's horn multiple times. To which the other driver stuck their hand out the window to express their displeasure with a gesture.

Saul nodded to himself and sniffed again. Doing his best to capture his feelings of remorse and shoving them as deep down as he could.

"We need to go to our hideout. Then we are going to make a few calls."

"What do you mean?" the driver asked anxiously. "Are you seriously going to try and kill Spectre? After all that happened?"

"You're damned right, I am! The bastard killed my father. I won't rest until I crush every ounce of blood from his corpse."

Bruce took a deep breath. He had been in multiple shoot outs in Avalon before, but never had he gone up against such a determined person as the ex-bounty hunter.

While Saul sat there brooding, an idea finally hit him.

"With Pa dead, I inherit the gang, right? All of his contacts and all his money. I'm going to use it all to make things right."

The driver clenched the steering wheel a bit tighter than he even had been. Going back up against Spectre terrified every bit of him to his core. The new crime lord, though, was exceptionally determined by his new life focus.

He pulled his communicator out of his suit pocket and dialed the first member of his gang that he could remember was alive.

"Hey, Ren… yeah, I'm alright. Listen, meet me at my hideout in two hours. Get everyone together that you can."

Bruce ran his left hand through his hair, and he took a deep breath.

"…that's right. Everyone. I… I know he's gone. I'm in charge now. The first order of business is dealing with the piece of poosh that got 'im. Money is no object. All I want is him dealt with."

A little over two hours later, Bruce and Saul arrived at their destination. Both men slammed their doors shut and checked around them. The hideout was located in the slums of Avalon, fairly far from most prying eyes of the local authorities.

Saul had been silent for most of the trip, spending his time mainly focusing on how to lure Spectre into a trap. He was confident that his plan was going to work, now all that was needed was to convince the surviving members of what used to be his father's operation to fall in line behind him.

Without Deni, it would take some time to get all of their accounts in order, but Saul believed it was doable. He had already called and set a meeting with the man in charge of his father's finances to begin transitioning everything into his name. But first, he needed to squelch any fears in his people. He needed to be strong so that they would obey and follow him.

The thug leader took a deep breath and grinned. He knew what waited for him upstairs was the chance of a lifetime.

"Yo, Bruce."

"Yeah?" the driver said, looking over the car's roof to his boss.

"This is my chance to take things over. I need you to back me up on this."

Bruce half-smiled. "You know, I will."

Saul, though, got very serious. "No, for real. This is a crucial point in all of this. If we don't convince them that following me is the best course of action, we might not be walking out of there."

The driver's eyes grew considerably. He had been so preoccupied with all that had happened that he didn't even think about what could be coming up next with their own people.

Frank Corbo had employed a slew of less than savory personnel. Many of them had, of course, died in the recent engagements with Spectre. Those that were left were undoubtedly going to be less than pleased with the situation.

"Uh, yeah... whatever you need," Bruce stammered.

Saul nodded then looked back up to the decrepit apartment complex. Its old stonecrete exterior had been painted over multiple times but had since begun to peel in some places. The air around the parking lot was stale and was a mixture of old discarded food. Not exactly the scenario Saul would have preferred, but he had to make do with what he had. If nothing else, the hideout was likely as safe a place as any at the moment.

The pair made it up the elevator to the fourth floor. They stepped off the lift to find a scrawny looking man in the lobby.

"Lester Rok," the thug leader said, sternly recognizing the other criminal.

"Hey, Saul. Everyone's inside," the thin criminal said, jerking his head toward the hall.

All three of the men walked to the unit. Lester stood to the side, and Saul noticed his position.

Well, if I'm gonna die, then so be it. Otherwise, these boys need to fall in line!

The young man used his keycard to unlock the door then pushed it open. He wasn't certain of how many would attend the meeting, but to his surprise, the entire room was full. About thirteen men and women packed themselves into the living room. Many didn't look too thrilled to be there, but others were emotionless.

Saul stepped inside, then Lester followed, with Bruce being the last one in and the one to shut the door. The scrawny man squeezed past a rather rotund man with an artificial eye and disappeared out of sight only to return with a heavy metal box. He set the box down on the table in the middle of the room and unfastened four thick clips. Without trying to lean over and see the full contents, the thug leader could already tell there were several comm pads, communicators, and other devices inside.

"Please, put your communicators in the box," Lester said dryly.

Bruce tried to show he was at ease, but no one in the room believed him. He pulled out his device and dropped it in. Saul's eyebrow arched as he looked around the room at the other occupants before he too complied.

Lester set the lid back in place then locked it down with the clips. He then stepped away and found a wall to lean against.

Taking a moment to again survey the room, Saul considered the best way to break the silence. Every eye was on him.

"Alright, so I'm sure you all know that my father is dead." He checked around the room, but no one gave any indication that the news was a shock.

"Who was it?" asked one of three heavily muscular men standing in the kitchen that was adjacent to the living room.

"It was Spectre."

A subtle murmur broke out through the room.

Saul held up his hand, and the thugs and criminals got quiet again. "With my father's death, I'm now in charge of this operation."

Lester remained quiet along with Bruce, but several others appeared less than pleased. One sultry dressed woman pursed her lips at the thought.

"Do you even have what it takes?"

The others all looked at the woman and listened closely.

"I mean, your father was a man's man. You, you're just a boy," she said before scoffing.

Her face was full of contempt, and she was clearly challenging his authority.

What would my father do?

Without so much as a moment of hesitation, Saul drew his pistol and shot the woman twice in the chest, one round hitting her in the heart. The others near her barely had time to step aside. Her body tumbled over the wooden chair she was sitting in and fell to the dingy floor where she bled out. The twin bullet casings clanked against the hard floor and rolled away from the shooter.

Everyone in the room stood motionless while the wisp of smoke from the barrel drifted up and dissipated. Several of them had gotten sprayed by some of the blood, while others were absolutely ready to draw and return fire if things were to escalate.

Bruce found his own hand was inside of his jacket, resting on the grip of his firearm. No one else, however, budged.

Saul glared at the gathering of criminals and fugitives. "Listen carefully. I'm in charge now. You either follow my lead, or you can get the frag out. But I won't allow instigators."

Lester smirked at the situation and chuckled. "I'm in."

The muscular men in the kitchen began to relax somewhat as others nodded or chimed in with their agreement.

Saul allowed himself an internal moment of feeling a small triumph.

"Alright, so we are gonna be making some changes around here, but first, we are going to rid the 'verse of the filth who killed my father. Bruce, I want you to spread the word. We are raising the contract on his head to two dozen."

Bruce couldn't help himself. "You want to raise the hit to twenty-four million?!"

Saul glared at his friend, who quickly got the hint.

The driver cleared his throat. "I'll take care of it."

"Next order of business..." the new crime lord began to say when he was interrupted by a knock at the door.

One of the men nearby wanted to show his worth to his new boss. He held up a hand to the room, then drew his pistol. With great care, he stepped up to the door and pushed the screen that showed who was on the other side. Two large metal figures blocked most of the view of the camera.

Before the man could react, the black figure kicked the door in, ripping it from its hinges. The impact slammed into the thug, and the door fell on top of him. Everyone else in the room pulled out their weapons and aimed at the door.

The keeper of Life stepped in as if she was entirely invulnerable for the potential danger and located the leader. "Hello Saul, I think we can help each other."

No one dared move. Several sets of eyes checked over with Saul. He was busy trying not to wet himself.

Saul swallowed nervously and attempted to regain his composure. "Who are you?" he said with a touch of stuttering.

"All that matters is that both you and I want the same thing, to see Spectre killed. He has something that I need to be returned to me. We will assist you in killing him, permitted we receive it in exchange."

Confused, the crime lord's face contorted while he processed the statement. "Wha... what is it that he has?"

Life lifted her chin and placed her hands on her hips. "He has possession of a necklace. We get that in return. Deal?"

Saul could barely believe what he was hearing. Something so minuscule in exchange for two power armor warriors aiding him. Easy deal.

Without wanting to ask too many prying questions, the crime lord was eager to enlist the help from the mysterious duo.

He nodded in agreement, and the others in the room began to relax.

Bruce, though, was still not convinced. "How are we going to be able to even hurt him? He has power armor. I doubt any of us are packing much that can deal with that."

The white armored keeper looked around the room while her helmet confirmed the driver's statement. Without them knowing, Life's HUD displayed each of the weapons they had concealed beneath their clothing and in their hands.

"Spectre's suit is more like an armored skin. It isn't impenetrable. More that it heals itself after taking damage."

"Then how can we possibly stop something like that?" Lester asked, confusedly.

"His suit is low on power and can't heal him very effectively. Simply put, if you can do enough damage to him fast enough… then he can be killed like any other man."

Saul glanced over at Bruce, and the two shared a confident smile.

One of the big muscular men tilted his head up like he was addressing an officer of the law. "How do you know so much about his suit?"

Life put her hands on her hips, giving off the sense that she was immediately annoyed by the question. "I'm not here to be berated by your petty questions. All you need to know is that Spectre can be killed."

Upon a nearby apartment building, Knowledge listened to the conversation between the thugs and Life through the microphone installed in one of the occupant's wrist pads they had forgotten to throw in the box. The blue keeper could gain access to anything that the government could, and that was mainly any electronic device that was being manufactured today.

So, I guess she is prepared to make a deal with criminals now…

"Catherine."

"Yes, Kay," the AI replied kindly.

The keeper stood up from his perch and headed toward the opposite side of the building to wait for his *Sparrow*.

"I want you to constantly search for anything that could match up to Gideon. We need to locate him before Life does."

"Right away."

I can't allow her to get her hands on the amulet. I must find Gideon first.

Chapter 30

Cycle: 412 Month: 9 Rotation: 15
Corre Republic Space
Prefecture: Expansive
Planet: Benedictus
Location: Downtown Avalon

It had taken Gideon hours to escape Rind and make his way back to Hannibal's apartment. The plan had been that after he was finished dealing with Saul that the ex-bounty hunter would return to get his belongings then get off the planet. Now things had yet again changed. Killing Frank would undoubtedly help in destabilizing the criminal organization that Saul would now be in charge of.

The question was, would the young Corbo look to take the fight to Spectre, or would he go into hiding. Right now, it didn't matter. Stopping his loss of blood or subsequently dying on the filthy streets of Avalon was a much more pressing issue.

Nightfall was beginning to set in once again on the bustling city. Lights began to turn on for businesses and shops below the far-reaching skyscrapers. The sky was a brilliant mixture of purple and pink.

The stench of the area attacked Gideon's nostrils. His mind had already begun to get fuzzy, and focusing was getting increasingly more difficult.

Two men leaned up against a corner store. The one of which eyeballed Gideon from about a block away. With each approaching step, he plotted his mischievous scheme.

The ex-bounty hunter couldn't help but dwell on his children.

I wonder how the kids are doing. Oh, Creator… what… what am I going to tell them?

A deep pain gripped his chest, and tears began to swell at his collection of failures that had amassed since they left the hospital.

While locked in a struggle against his inner turmoil, Gideon had failed to recognize the two men or listened that they approached him from behind.

"Lost, pal?" one of them called out mockingly.

Spectre stopped in his tracks and looked up to the sky. A couple was walking toward Gideon and the two men and could sense that something was wrong. Rather than get involved, the man led his female date away from the scene by crossing the street in between traffic.

The slums of Avalon were no place for a lone wanderer, unless they were prepared to fight when the time presented itself.

"Hey, you!" the other man said boisterously.

Both of the tough guys laughed as they stepped up behind what they thought was an old man due to the projected disguise.

Gideon lowered his hands to his side and slowly turned around. His expression was that of exhaustion and annoyance.

"A little far from the old folk's home, eh?" the lead mugger said with a grin.

The ex-bounty hunter allowed them both to get in close before he acted. In a flash, he reached up and grabbed the leader by the back of the head and threw him to the ground. Not being at all prepared for what was about to happen to him, the thug's face smashed into the stonecrete sidewalk, breaking several teeth. The other punk pulled out a knife and lashed out with a stab. However, he was clearly not trained and left himself way too exposed. Gideon grabbed the arm with both of his hands and bent down until the elbow cracked. The man fell to his knees and cried out in agony.

Spectre swatted him across the face, knocking him unconscious. He happened to look to his left across the street to see the couple staring at him as he walked off.

The rest of the journey to Hannibal's had been uneventful, but each step was getting harder and harder. His left hand brushed the arm rail for the small staircase, and he found that he needed to lean on it to make the arduous trip up the three steps.

Just before he reached the terminal to call Hannibal, Gideon nearly tripped over the unlevel pavement. Thankfully, just before his balance was totally lost, he caught himself. The sudden jarring motion sent a shock of pain up his side.

"Gah…"

With labored breathing, he managed to scroll through to find the bounty hunter's alias once again.

"Hello?" Hannibal asked through the speaker. "Gideon?"

Spectre's lips were parched, but he managed to get his response out. "Y... yeah."

The bounty hunter quickly pressed the entry sequence, and the front door of the foyer unlocked. Gideon entered the apartment's first floor and shuffled his feet over to the elevator. He pressed the button with his right hand, and it illuminated.

"Poosh!" the ex-bounty hunter exclaimed meekly when he saw that he left a smudge of blood behind on the button.

Using his shirt, he wiped it off as best he could just as the lift arrived. He limped inside, and the door slid shut. After he pressed the button for the bounty hunter's floor, Gideon leaned his body up against the wall. A wave of nausea washed over him while the lift raised higher and higher at its accelerated speed. He was barely able to contain himself, but he was successful.

Can't... pass out yet...

The severely wounded ex-bounty hunter shuffled down the hallway for what felt like an eternity. Using every ounce of strength left to him, Gideon took step after agonizing step.

Once more, Hannibal did not wait for his visitor to arrive at his door. He quickly unlocked his ensemble of protective mechanisms and stuck his head out.

"Oh frag!" the bounty hunter quietly exclaimed.

To his shock and surprise, Gideon looked worse than he did the first time he came to him. He rushed out the door and helped his friend back into his unit.

343

"What in the void happened? Did... did you get him?" Hannibal asked as he set his friend down on the couch.

Gideon began to lean back but felt something hard pressing into his spine. He meekly reached behind him and yanked out an empty liquor bottle.

Hannibal reached over and took the brown glass bottle from him. "Oh, sorry 'bout that." He carelessly tossed it away, and it bounced off the carpeted floor.

The pain from lying down nearly took Spectre's breath away. His stomach muscles flexed from the sensation, which then caused his gunshot wounds to send shooting pain up his side.

"So, how'd it go?" the bounty hunter again inquired.

"It went... well, Frank's dead." The ex-bounty hunter removed the mask from his face and gently tossed the projector on the floor.

Even though that was part of the plan, Hannibal was still a bit impressed that the heavily injured ex-bounty hunter managed to pull it off.

"What about Saul?"

Gideon could barely keep his composure together. He grit his teeth from the pain and could only shake his head at the question.

Hannibal realized that he had quite a bit of blood on his hands. He wiped them on his pants several times and leaned over his wounded guest.

"I'll be right back."

"Oh, don't worry. I'll be here..." Gideon groaned.

The bounty hunter quickly left Spectre's view. Meanwhile, Gideon just focused on trying to breathe calmly.

I… really wish my suit was working about now…

Hannibal finally returned after several long minutes. He had a syringe inserted into a tiny glass cylinder. After filling it with the clear liquid, he set the vial of medicine to the side and held the needle up as to not accidentally smack it on something.

"What's… what's that?" the ex-bounty hunter asked in between squeezing the couch with his hands from the agony.

"This should take off some of the pain. Help you sleep so you can get some damned rest."

Gideon shook his head. "No. I need to stay awake."

The bounty hunter, though, wasn't asking for permission. He reached over and gripped his friend's right forearm to give him a better angle to insert the needle into his vein. Gideon tried to yank his arm free but was too weak.

"Look, I can't help you if you bleed out. Stop bein' a fool and let me help you."

Spectre's nostrils flared in irritation at his predicament, but he relented. He eased his arm down, and Hannibal inserted the needle.

A cool sensation began to course through the parts of Gideon's body, not in extreme discomfort. He stared up at the slightly discolored white ceiling and breathed angrily.

"I was so close. So close to getting him."

The bounty hunter set the syringe on the side table and pulled the medical kit he had left on the floor from the last time over to him. He threw open its lid and pulled out thick, sealed sterile pads.

Spectre's eyelids began to feel heavy as the cooling sensation spread more and more throughout his body. He realized that most of the pain was subsiding. What was strange to him though was that Hannibal didn't tear open any of the pads, instead he was just holding them and staring back at him.

Wh... why is he staring at me?

That was when he realized he couldn't move his fingertips.

Huh? What did he stick me with? Why can't I move? Wait... why can't I speak?!

The bounty hunter took a deep breath then set the medical supplies down. He slowly stood up to his full height.

"I'm sorry, my friend. This isn't anything personal. I bet everything on you, and I can't risk it anymore."

Gideon fought to speak, but he could barely move his lips. Rage burned in his eyes just before everything went dark.

Hannibal's voice was the last he heard before he lost consciousness. "I'm sorry..."

Chapter 31

Cycle: 412 Month: 9 Rotation: 15
Corre Republic Space
Prefecture: Expansive
Planet: Benedictus
Location: Downtown Avalon

A stillness had fallen over the apartment. Hannibal stood over Gideon's body for several minutes, contemplating his decision.

He looked around at the dingy pieces of furniture he had collected over his time as a bounty hunter. On more than one occasion, he had earned a fortune for himself. Heavy drinking, a gambling addiction, and his affinity for women made sure to drain him of everything he had amassed for himself. All except for his possessions that were contained in this tiny dank apartment unit.

"I have to do this…" the bounty hunter muttered to himself.

Gideon's injuries were most likely fatal if he didn't receive treatment. Despite his friend's condition, Hannibal went to the kitchen and opened his refrigerator. It was devoid of food and was almost entirely empty except for a bottle of citrus juice and a bottle of ale he had opened the night before.

The bottom of the glass bottle raked along the metal grate shelf as the bounty hunter pulled it out. Feelings of remorse and regret tried to well up within him. He stared at the bottle for a long moment before glancing back at his most recent bounty.

"Bottom's up..." Hannibal downed the rest of the ale with several gulps.

Normally this was his favorite drink on all of Benedictus. Right now, it didn't contain any satisfaction for him. He had made many decisions in his life that would have been considered selfish or cruel by others. Growing up in the slums of Avalon had taught him the lesson that he had to look out for number one.

He firmly set the bottle down on the countertop beside him then retrieved a secondary communicator he had in his pocket. The device felt extra heavy in his hand, and again, the feelings of pity tried to overtake him.

It's too late to turn back now...

The contents of the syringe were not meant to kill Gideon, only to knock him out. Hannibal knew that while he was willing to sell out his old friend, he couldn't go through shooting him.

He strolled over to the unconscious man and removed his necklace and bracelet. Sliding both into his own pocket, he then checked Gideon for any other weapons or items. The only other thing he found was the throwaway communicator he had given him, covered in blood.

The bounty hunter walked back over to the kitchen counter. His legs felt like pacing, but he knew what needed to be done.

He took a picture of Gideon and sent it to Saul. Within seconds his communicator's screen lit up, and it began ringing.

Hannibal held the device up to his right ear. "Hey…" he said, answering the call. "Yeah, it's really him. I'll give you the address, but I want the two-dozen transferred to my account."

He couldn't help looking over to Spectre and the trail of blood that now was spilling down onto his carpet.

"No, he's still alive. Barely though. Yeah, I can keep him breathing 'til you get here… Okay. Sounds good." The bounty hunter hung up the call and then rapidly typed in his apartment's location.

A *swoosh* sound from his device signaled the message had been sent. Now all that was left was to wait.

Hannibal went back to the kitchen and opened a drawer beside his stove. A few random items rattled around, but he wanted the small bottle of potent alcohol that he had placed there.

Long ago, he told himself that the next time he came into a big payday, he would open the flask of strong booze from off-world. He walked over and plopped down in his recliner. His eyes were locked on Gideon's helpless body.

Poor bastard…

After breaking the seal on the bottle and removing the cap, the bounty hunter took a swig of the room temperature liquid and swallowed it. Immediately his throat warmed as it traveled down to his stomach. However, what was missing was the

349

sense of accomplishment that should have come with it.

I'm a frag head to do this… but I need the money…

Not wanting to further risk his cruel scheme from getting away from him, Hannibal took out the pistol he had hidden in his waistband and set it on the chair's dark green arm.

Something firm was digging into his thigh. Reaching into his pocket, he realized it was the amulet. He held it up to the light to admire the ruby-like color of it. The silver chain dangled in the air while the charm glimmered.

Wonder how much I can get for this?

In the darkness of his mind, a voice called out to the dying man.

"Gideon, wake up!"

The ex-bounty hunter's weary eyes opened slowly, but he couldn't remember where he was. His head felt like a thick soup, and it was difficult for him to see straight at first.

"Gladriel? Is… is that you?" he asked aloud, meekly.

Looking over to his right, Gideon found Hannibal staring back at him. However, his eyes were like the size of disks.

The bounty hunter slowly stood up in disbelief. "Ho… how are you awake?"

Spectre was totally out of it and didn't fully understand the question. "Huh?"

"I gave you enough sedative to knock you out for two rotations…"

Then the memories for Gideon began to return to him. His eyes changed from confusion to again bitter fury as his memories came back to him. He instantly spotted the necklace and intuitively forced his left arm to feel around for his amulet only to confirm the bounty hunter did have it. That was when he realized his bracelet was absent as well.

Not… good…

Hannibal held the necklace tightly in his left hand while he used his right to carefully pick up the pistol beside him. There was no real present threat of danger, so the bounty hunter kept the weapon by his side.

"Why… did you drug me?" the wounded man growled. "How could you?"

Seeing no point in further lying, Hannibal shrugged. "I told you I wouldn't kill you. But the money is too good to pass up now. It's not anything personal. It's just business."

The ex-bounty hunter's mind was having difficulty processing the plain statement. "But… you helped me. I don't understand."

"I felt bad before. And there was still a slim chance you might actually get revenge. But you came up short and now the contract has doubled. I'll be able to retire for the rest of my life on money like that."

Gideon struggled, but he was finally able to get up on his elbow to better glare at the traitorous man he once called a friend.

Hannibal didn't like the feeling in the pit of his stomach at the ex-bounty hunter's eyes. "Don't give me that look. You would have done the exact same thing in my place."

With immense exhaustion tugging at his psyche, Spectre didn't have the energy to rebut the claim. He shook his head deliberately slowly. The message was crystal clear to the other man.

"No matter. Saul and his people are on the way. This will all be over soon. Might as well lay back and relax while you can."

Saul's face lit up like a child receiving a huge wrapped gift. He patted the communicator against his empty palm and grinned widely.

"We found him," he announced to the room.

Life and Death looked at one another.

"All we are waiting for now is... and there's the address. Alright, people, we're moving," the crime lord said confidently.

All the thugs and criminals in the room got to their feet while Lester unlatched the crate with all of their personal devices inside. The two keepers began leaving the apartment when Saul took notice.

"Whoa, where are you two going?" he asked with outstretched arms.

The white keeper half-turned her head back to the new crime lord. "Don't worry, we'll be there. Just make sure you don't hesitate to kill him if you have a shot."

Saul grinned again, impishly. "Don't worry about that, lady. Spectre's time has finally run out. Tonight, he's a dead man."

Gideon's body was partially numb from the sedative while the rest hurt so much that he could barely move. He lowered himself back down onto the couch, and he did his best to come up with a plan. Unfortunately, his mind was so groggy that he couldn't really think straight.

The sound of heavy footsteps came from down the hall. Hearing the noise caught the ex-bounty hunter's attention as well as Hannibal's. Both men looked to one another, but the bounty hunter's face betrayed his internal thoughts.

"How could they be here already?" Hannibal asked, his voice just above a whisper.

Gideon, of course, remained perfectly still like a statue.

If this is my time to die, then so be it. I won't go out crying for mercy. I've killed my share of men, and I know where I'm going…

The bounty hunter kept his pistol close as he quietly made his way to the door. Just before he pressed the door camera, the door rocked madly from something powerful bashing into it from the other side. Fortunately for the now terrified bounty hunter, the locking mechanisms and his investment in a heavy-duty door looked to be paying off.

Gideon stretched out his hand, and the amulet tore out of Hannibal's clutches. Before he could react, the ex-bounty hunter gripped the necklace in his hand, and the armor formed around his body.

Another loud boom shook the door, and Hannibal spun back around to respond to whatever it was that was breaking into his home. His heart rate jumped as he realized his mistake.

The third time the heavy reinforced door was successfully kicked open and revealed a dark blue armored figure. Hannibal raised his gun to take a quick shot while he began to sidestep. A pistol formed in Knowledge's left hand, and he fired in rapid succession.

Four of the bolts burned through the bounty hunter's body, and he tumbled to the floor. The pistol bounced and landed near Gideon.

Fearing what was about to come next, the bounty hunter attempted to use his left arm to drag him away from the doorway.

"No, don't do this. You can claim the bounty. Just don't kill me!" he begged with his coarse voice.

Knowledge stepped forward and assessed the room while his artificial intelligence relayed him mass amounts of data and information.

Spectre weakly stretched out his hand to scoop up the black ballistic pistol. Both he and the keeper knew that the weapon was not a caliber that would significantly harm Knowledge. But the keeper wasn't his target.

Hannibal had not yet turned around. He crawled as fast as he could manage. "Gah…" he winced in pain from his dragging right leg.

The sound of a power suit moving from the other side of the room caught his attention.

"No… no…" the bounty hunter whined to himself. "I was so close…"

Knowledge did nothing to prevent Gideon from limping over to the wounded hitman.

"Hannibal, I want you to know that I never would have taken a contract to have you killed."

Realizing his time was about at an end, the injured man rolled himself over. Once again, he winced from the pain lancing through him. He propped himself up on his left elbow and stared back at Gideon's armored helmet. The blue glowing lights on the side of his head gave him an inhumane appearance.

"Well… guess you're just a better man than me then," he said dryly.

"No…" Gideon said as he raised the pistol at Hannibal's face. "… I'm just the one with the gun."

The ear-piercing shot that killed the bounty hunter rang out through the room. Spectre lowered his arm gracefully then looked over to the blue keeper.

"You know why I'm here," Knowledge said as if a man didn't just die right in front of him.

Gideon nodded. He did his best to ignore all the flashing warning reports displayed on his HUD. His armor was nearly totally out of power, and the amulet was about to fall into dormant mode.

I've got nothing left to fight him with. Should I just give him the amulet? Is it worth dying for?

The blue keeper released the pistol from his hand, and it disintegrated into a cloud of fine orange particles. Gideon's head tilted in confusion.

"Life, along with Death, has teamed up with Saul. They are on their way here right now to kill you. She intends to take the amulet to present it to Peace herself."

"What a kiss-up," Spectre snarled.

Knowledge straightened. "Indeed."

The keeper stepped over to the kitchen counter with Gideon's gaze locked onto his every move.

"I can't allow you to leave Benedictus with the suit again. However, I have come to negotiate with you." Knowledge spun around and tucked his arms behind his back. "In exchange for Saul Corbo's life, you will hand over the amulet… willingly."

Gideon took a deep breath.

I can't very well argue with him in my condition.

"Looks like I'm kinda backed into a corner on this one."

Again, Knowledge agreed plainly. "Indeed."

With nothing left to negotiate with other than the suit itself, Gideon relented. "The bad thing is… in my condition, I can't exactly put up much of a fight."

"I know that. However, I will recharge your suit, which will obviously take care of your injuries."

"You'd trust me? Just like that?" the ex-bounty hunter asked in surprise.

Knowledge nodded his bulky helmet. "We once were friends, Gideon. I see it as a personal courtesy."

Spectre looked away while he processed the offered deal. He faced the keeper and nodded only once.

"Okay, I'll do it. But I need you to promise me that you hold onto the amulet. Life or War can't get their hands on it. You must be the one to choose the next Truth."

Knowledge was caught off guard by the traitor's genuine yet serious tone. "Done. I will see to it personally."

Without any more words to exchange between the two men, the keeper approached Gideon. Knowledge laid his hand onto the ex-bounty hunter's shoulder and spoke a phrase of some long lost language. His glove began to glow as a surge of energy pulsated through Gideon's suit. His body began to feel warm.

One by one, the warnings flashing for his attention on his helmet's internal screen disappeared, and his suit began to reach maximum charge. The pain throughout his body began to vanish as the power armor received the charge through Knowledge and rapidly got to work mending and healing its user's injuries.

The light emitting from Knowledge's hand became so intense that it appeared to envelop the room. Within thirty seconds, the aches and pains from Gideon were gone. Even the groggy feeling in his mind disappeared. He hadn't quite felt like this in so long he almost forgot what it was like.

Once the charge was complete, the bright light faded, and Knowledge removed his hand. Gideon tossed away the bounty hunter's pistol. It clanked against the wall.

Spectre flexed his hands then tightened them as hard as he could.

This feels incredible.

The timer in his helmet had also vanished. All his suit's abilities were restored, including being able to create weapons.

Gideon imagined his sword, and it appeared out of a swirl of blue particles. He inspected the elegant weapon for a moment then looked back to Knowledge.

"Thank you."

"Don't thank me just yet. I can't promise what will happen to you after this is over. Peace may want revenge for what you did to him."

Spectre chuckled. "One problem at a time."

Knowledge watched as the traitor strode across the room over to the deceased bounty hunter. Gideon knelt down and stuck his hand into each pocket until he finally located his last stolen belonging. After standing back up, the ex-bounty hunter released his sword and the armor around his left hand and wrist peeled back in a mist. He slid the bracelet over his hand then his armor returned in place.

"I am curious, Gideon, how does that bracelet work? Who gave it to you?" the blue keeper asked.

Spectre shrugged. "I have no idea how it works. It just does. And even if I told you who it came from… you wouldn't believe me."

Knowledge's head cocked to the side. Before he could ask a follow-up question, both armored men's suits detected the arrival of several people exiting the elevator.

"Guess it's time to finish this," the ex-bounty hunter said as he strolled toward the opened door. He gently shut the door to buy them a few more seconds.

"I know where your children are on Antioch."

Spectre stopped in his tracks but didn't turn around.

"Please make the right decision, Gideon. For your children's sake, don't try to run."

A moment of silence fell over the two old friends while the team of thugs began to get into position.

"Once this is over, I'll meet you on the roof," Gideon said assuredly.

Spectre formed a sleek laser rifle in his arms that matched the color of his armor. His helmet displayed the silhouettes through the wall for each of the thugs as they got into position. Saul was near the back, coordinating everyone. Knowledge disappeared out the window as Spectre rolled his neck in preparation. He headed away from the door and went deeper into the apartment.

In the hallway, the fourteen thugs were all set. One large man got in front of the door and held a dense metal door breacher. Saul kept his hand up and began to count down with his fingers. The front thug bashed the door, and it swung open. In a smooth motion, he dodged to the left while two others burst in with weapons drawn, followed by four more men.

Saul waited for the all-clear signal, but he didn't hear one. Bruce glanced over at his boss, his face was already beginning to show his concern.

Just before the crime lord stood up and entered the unit, the door from the adjacent apartment burst apart and out stepped Spectre in his power armor. Saul, and the other thugs still in the hallway, turned their attention to the ex-bounty hunter. Fear began to grip them as they realized the danger they were now in.

Gideon brought his laser rifle up and opened fire on the group as he began to walk toward them. Four of the criminals were dropped right away. Bruce lost it and broke off into a sprint down the hall. Saul fired madly, but the bullets just weren't enough to stop his target.

Another two thugs were killed by Spectre's blue laser bolts. One man dove into the open doorway trying to escape the onslaught, while those in the apartment were now heading back for the hallway.

Gideon aimed at Saul when he was hit in the chest by a scattergun. The force of the impact knocked his aim, and the bolt meant for the brutal killer of his wife went high.

Realizing the precarious situation unfolding before him, Saul took the moment to sprint back for the elevator. Lester and the other surviving members of the criminals and lowlifes fired on the ex-bounty hunter, but only managed to piss him off even more.

Gideon sidestepped, then released his rifle, and his sword formed. In a blur, Spectre phased back and forth until he slashed each and everyone that was left in the apartment and hallway.

Now in the foyer, Bruce rapidly pressed the button to summon the elevator back up to their floor. Saul rushed up to him, terror all over his face. The sound of gunfire back where they had come from had ceased.

"Poosh!" the driver exclaimed as he continued hitting the button furiously.

The crime lord was too afraid to poke his head around the corner and just paced back and forth. He ran his left hand through his hair while he hefted his pistol in his right.

A ding came from the elevator, alerting the men that it had finally arrived. Bruce stood prepared to dive in when the doors slid open to reveal the keeper of Life standing boldly inside.

Before the driver could even react appropriately, she raised her pistol and blasted him into eternity. Saul panicked and ran away from the hall to find Spectre was just standing there amongst the corpses of the thugs. He didn't understand that Gideon's suit had spotted the female keeper ascending to their floor.

The white keeper strode into the hall, and she planted her feet. Saul looked back and forth between the two armored warriors, completely unsure of what to do. His entire plan for revenge had fallen totally apart. He could not see a way out of this.

"No... no..." he muttered as he continued to look at them. "You betrayed us!" Saul cried out to the female keeper.

"Life," Gideon said sternly.

"Traitor," Life said, answering back.

The ex-bounty hunter remained motionless. "I've made a deal with Knowledge. Once I'm done here, I'm giving him the amulet."

Life cocked her head. "I'm not aware of such an arrangement. How do I know you're not working together now?"

"What? Don't be stupid, I'm going to hand the suit over. There's no need for us to fight."

"All that matters now is that the amulet is coming back with me. Hand it over, and perhaps I will let you live."

Saul couldn't hear the conversation back and forth between the other two. Instead, he was left to fret while they spoke back and forth over their radio system.

Gideon wasn't about to turn and run now with Saul trapped right here. But he wasn't exactly interested in trusting the white keeper either.

Death crashed through the window at the end of the long hall behind Gideon. He stood up to his full height and shook the rest of the glass off his armored body. Spectre didn't even bother turning around.

"I'm going to kill this viper, then we can all deal with this," the ex-bounty hunter said.

Life chuckled. "Please, don't let me be in the way of ridding the 'verse of this vermin."

Gideon gripped his sword tightly then began to step toward the crime lord. Saul froze in place in fear, then he got a devilish idea.

"I won't let you get the satisfaction, Spectre!"

Arrogantly, the thug leader raised his pistol to the side of his head. Gideon's eyes burned angrily beneath his helmet at his wife's murderer, attempting to kill himself. He phased forward, and before Saul could pull the trigger, he slashed him across the chest. The crime lord at first didn't feel anything wrong, then his body spasmed from the blood loss. In a savage display of ferocity, Gideon again phased forward, this time appearing on the other side of Saul. He stabbed his sword backward, piercing the thug through the heart.

When Spectre yanked his sword free, Saul collapsed to his knees then fell forward.

Death and Life stood still and watched as Gideon relaxed his stance.

"Now, like I said, I am going to go and hand over the suit to Knowledge."

"I'm afraid I can't allow that, traitor. While it may satisfy Knowledge's conscious. I was told to kill you," Life said bitterly.

Gideon looked down at the carpeted hall floor. Debris and bullet casings covered the nearby area. It indeed looked like a fierce battle had broken out in the apartment complex. Local authorities were unlikely to respond to gang violence on this scale, or at least would give the criminals enough time to finish the job and leave.

"Is Peace still upset for stabbing him? It was so long ago," the ex-bounty hunter said jokingly.

Death remained ready to react, but Life was getting irritated at the traitor's coy behavior.

"I'd say he's pretty pissed for what you did to him. He's been locked in that chamber Knowledge built for him since you betrayed the order."

Spectre shook his head. "Listen, child, you have no idea what you are talking about. I was there when the order was formed."

"And it's time for you to retire, old man."

He wouldn't ever admit it, but Gideon grinned at the nickname the female keeper gave him. "Alright, let's do this then."

The three armored warriors stood still, each waiting for the other to make a move. Gideon saw a pistol form in Life's hand, and he did the same. Death chose a rifle and opened fire. Dark red bolts zipped down the hall and sprayed Gideon's shoulder while he shot at Life.

Spectre dove forward, smashing right through the wall of one of the apartment units. The elderly woman that lived there freaked out at the sight of the intimidating figure that barreled into her home. She ducked behind her sofa while Gideon rolled to safety. He got to his feet, and his rifle formed in his hands.

Knowing he had an advantage to not be visible to the two keeper's sensors, the ex-bounty hunter moved left. Life, however, wasn't going to wait for the traitor to make a move. An explosion blasted the right side of the apartment apart.

Gideon spun and fired into the void, hoping to hit the female keeper. The elderly woman held her head down and screamed. Electric energy coursed through the opening in the wall and began to spread throughout the apartment. Spectre dove for cover while the woman got hit by one of the streams of neon blue lightning and was scorched. Much of her flesh disintegrated, and she collapsed in a smoldering heap.

"Give me the amulet!" Life bellowed angrily.

"Come and take it!" Gideon taunted back.

He rose to a knee and aimed his rifle, just then the wall behind him crashed open, and Death stepped through. Just before the black keeper brought down a hefty looking clawed weapon into the traitor's helmet, Spectre phased several steps away.

He tossed the rifle, and his sword appeared in his right hand. Gideon sliced like mad, but Death was able to deflect each strike with his large two-handed weapon.

Life's hands glowed red and orange. Spotting his comrade's coming attack, the black keeper kicked out and hit Gideon in the chest to give him some distance. Death then darted to the side as Life unleashed a wave of fire.

The ex-bounty hunter's eyes widened as the glow from the fire intensely illuminated the entire room. He barely had time to move his left arm in front of him and for a large shield to form. The wave of fire blew past the traitor and ignited a great deal of the apartment around them. Smoke began to fill the air, and the area grew increasing hotter.

Death jumped back into the fray and swung his clawed weapon as hard as he could, shattering Gideon's shield into disintegrating particles.

The impact also sent the ex-bounty hunter careening through the air and smacking into what remained of the wall behind him. His helmet hit the barrier so hard that his vision temporarily blurred.

By now, the fire had spread further and had totally consumed the living room they battled in.

Gideon pulled himself from the wall and prepared for another go. Life formed a large brutal-looking sword into her hands while Death broke into a ready stance. Each of the heated melee weapons from the armored warriors could easily cut through their suits.

I didn't come this far to die now!

Both keepers rushed forward, and Spectre dove in. Each of them exchanged multiple strikes at one another and were able to successfully defend themselves from any of the attacks.

Gideon used his shoulder to bash Life to the side. She lost her balance and tripped, landing in a burning pile of debris. Death swung wide, hoping to catch the traitor in the ribcage. Phasing backward then forward, Spectre was able to entirely be missed by the potentially crippling attack.

The black-armored keeper realized his mistake when Gideon sliced his left arm off. Using his free hand, the ex-bounty hunter smashed upward, connecting with Death's chin. The clawed weapon vanished when the injured keeper lost his footing and slammed onto his back.

Life stood back up and pointed her sword at Gideon. Being coy, Spectre used his own sword to smack her weapon aside.

"Raaah!" she snarled furiously.

Bringing her weapon up over her head, she sliced the ceiling above her as she brought the sword down. Gideon phased to the side, easily dodging the attack. He formed a laser pistol and repeatedly fired into the female keeper. Her suit did its best to compensate with the attacks and to try to repair itself, but the rapid succession of bolts in such a tight area failed. One bolt got through and burned into her chest, ripping her left lung apart.

She fell to one knee and lifted her head to stare at Gideon. Fighting for breath, the female keeper was unable to speak. The fire engulfed the entire apartment by now, and the sound of approaching sirens wailed down below.

The traitor was about to gloat when he spotted something moving in the corner of his eye. Death's arm moved up beside him as if it was being pulled by some invisible string. It connected back to where it should have been, and the area where it was cut glowed red then dimmed.

"Well... that's new," Spectre said aloud.

Death sprang back up to his feet, and a laser repeater appeared in his grip. Gideon activated his jumper pack and burst up through the ceiling, followed by a stream of red bolts that sprayed all around him. The traitor landed safely and somersaulted away as smoke poured up through the hole in the floor.

Alright, I'm done here... I need to get to the roof.

Gideon broke into a sprint and used his shoulder to bash through the front door.

Death jogged over to Life. Her suit worked feverishly to repair her internal organ.

She looked up to the black keeper. "Sto... stop him..."

While Spectre could have certainly bashed through each ceiling until he reached the top where Knowledge was meant to be waiting for him, it would only take too much time. Death boosted up through the ravaged apartment's hole in the ceiling and nearly fell back through from all of the damage from his lasers. However, before a chunk of it collapsed, he managed to leap to safety and chased after his target.

Gideon ran for the staircase at the end of the hall. He reached out his left hand to pull open the door when several bolts hit him in the back. An alert appeared on his HUD, and he knelt down for cover. He returned fire with his own rifle, which hit Death in the chest and face.

The keeper growled in frustration and bolted straight for the traitor. Suddenly he vanished.

That's not good.

Spectre fired a wide spray of shots hoping one would hit his opponent, which one luckily did. Before he could focus his aim, Death reappeared right in front of him and rammed Gideon through the door so hard that he dropped his rifle.

The two armored men rolled into the staircase, chunks of the door bouncing all around them. Both quickly got to their feet and exchanged several punches and blocks. Death used his knee to kick Gideon in the abdomen. Spectre bent over from the blow to his stomach and lost his breath. The keeper followed up the attack by smashing down onto the traitor with his fists.

Gideon again dropped to the floor but managed to roll onto his back. In one smooth motion, he formed his sword and stabbed the angered keeper in the waist. Death used his gloved hands to grip the sword and hold it in place.

To his surprise, and despite his own enhanced strength, Spectre was unable to yank his weapon free from the other man's grasp. He instead released the sword, and before it entirely broke down into a mist, he swept his legs and caught the keeper behind the knee. Death crashed to the floor, leaving a dent in the stonecrete staircase they fought on.

Gideon got to one knee and pulled his right fist back. A blue glow of particles shaped around his fist and hardened into a thick shape that resembled the head of a massive hammer. He punched with all of his might down onto Death's knee. A brutal grinding and snapping sound filled the area and echoed throughout the stairwell.

The keeper let out a mixed roar of bitter rage and pain. Again, Gideon punched down once more, but this time into Death's chest, crushing several of his ribs. The hammerfist vanished, and the ex-bounty hunter got a new idea.

Using the brief time of respite in the fighting, the traitor grabbed hold of Death by the torso and hefted him up over his head. Before the keeper could react fast enough, he was thrown over the edge of the stairwell and fell deep into the void between the winding staircase.

A very throaty *thud* sound echoed back up once the keeper hit the first floor. Gideon wasted no time and hopped up onto the ledge. Using his jumper pack, he flew up the rest of the way to the top floor stairs. He hopped up the last few remaining steps to the door that led to the roof of the apartment. The door was electronically locked, but that wasn't about to stop the ex-bounty hunter.

Using a laser scattergun, Gideon blasted the door's panel to a shredded metal flower. The secured entrance popped open automatically, and Spectre ran through.

Out ahead of him was Knowledge standing on the ramp of his hovering *Sparrow* spacecraft. The keeper had his hands placed behind his back, and he stood as though he were a statue.

"It's not over yet, traitor!" the female keeper shouted.

Gideon turned to his left to find the white keeper standing there with a sniper rifle. Time seemed to slow down dramatically as the barrel of the long firearm flashed, and a blue bolt flew at him. Spectre phased to the side, but Life quickly aimed and fired again. This time hitting her target in the shoulder.

The suit took considerable damage and was incredibly scorched from the devastating impact. Gideon flinched in pain from his seared flesh beneath his suit, but he knew he couldn't stand still. He formed a pistol in his right hand, and he fired repeatedly.

Life dodged left then exchanged the elegant sniper for a huge cannon weapon. A charging sound vibrated in the air.

Gideon tried to move horizontally from the keeper, but his boot slipped on the slick roof. He lost his footing and tumbled down.

The keeper aimed her large weapon and fired. A super energized blue ball shot out and zipped forward. Gideon pushed himself up just enough then fired a burst from his jumper pack, causing him to hop just up in time to avoid the attack. The sphere flew on by and burned through a portion of the waist-high wall that bordered the roof and kept on going. It finally slammed into some other apartment building then exploded, blasting out many nearby windows. The glass shards fell on top of the emergency crews setting up on the streets below.

"No!" Life screamed.

Knowledge did not budge his movements, nor did he attempt to intervene. He observed the entire battle with great intrigue.

The female keeper stormed forward, discarding her cannon weapon in her fury. Gideon's suit was

371

fighting to heal its user's wound, but he needed to act. Both warriors formed their swords, and they fought.

"Why... won't... you... die?!" the female keeper shouted bitterly in between swings of her weapon.

Spectre deflected each attack and feigned that he was hurt. Life bought into the ploy and she attempted to stab the traitor through the chest. Instead of getting hit, Gideon phased through the woman and spun on his heel. He sliced across her lower back, severing her spine.

The keeper shrieked in pain and again fell to her knees, before landing on her face. A blue glow filled the void of her suit and instantly started to repair her otherwise brutal injury.

Gideon stood over the female keeper. He breathed heavily and gripped his sword's handle tightly.

I could just kill her here and now.

Life knew there was nothing she could do until her spine was healed. "Do it!" she shouted in her helplessness.

The keeper of Knowledge continued to observe the situation. He had no idea what Gideon would do at that moment. There had been plenty of times that he had slain downed enemies to ensure that they were no longer a threat to the Republic. But now he wasn't a keeper, he was a fugitive fighting for his own survival.

Life weakly managed to turn her helmet to the left, toward both Gideon and where Knowledge was further off. "What are you waiting for?!"

Spectre knelt. "I want you to remember this moment... when I spared your life. Do not come looking for me or my family. Know that even without this suit, I can and will kill you next time."

The keeper's eyes burned beneath her helmet. She was enraged further as she watched the traitor who had defeated her stroll off toward her fellow keeper, who did nothing.

Gideon's suit vanished in a puff of blue specks. His clothes and hair were blown around from the *Sparrow's* engine.

The ex-bounty hunter walked the rest of the way up to Knowledge and extended his hand. He held the amulet and its necklace in his grip, but he had a moment of reconsidering the agreement.

I should hang onto this. I know I can't trust Peace.

Knowledge remained like a stone. He anticipated that the fugitive would have some inner turmoil when the moment to hand the suit over arrived.

Gideon's eyes moved from the necklace and up to the blue keeper's pitch-black faceplate. "I just want to know one thing, Kay... did you know about that facility?"

"I honestly did not," Knowledge replied with his arms still tucked behind his back.

"No doubt you went back and discovered what was really going on there? What they were experimenting with?"

Knowledge did not respond.

Gideon half-smiled and averted his eyes. "Seeing as how you are a part of the order means you either support it or are at least turning a blind eye to it."

The keeper smoothly reached out his right hand and opened it. "If we ever meet again, I will explain everything in detail. Until then, you will have to trust me."

Looking back up to the keeper, the ex-bounty hunter took a breath then set the amulet in Knowledge's hand. Life's suit continued repairing her spine, and she could again feel her fingers. She winced from the vanishing pain but was able to raise herself up, and she formed a pistol.

Knowledge spotted the move and held up his hand. A strange sound emanated through the air, but Life found that she couldn't move at all. Her finger was on the trigger of her weapon, but she couldn't fire it.

Gideon spun around to discover the female keeper had nearly killed him.

"She can't move?" the traitor twisted back to face Knowledge, his mouth agape. "Ho... how?"

The blue keeper looked down at his old friend. "I've had this power for quite some time."

"But... then why didn't you stop me before I stabbed Peace?!" the traitor asked confusedly.

"At that moment... I was afraid of making the wrong decision."

Life tried with all her might to budge, but her suit simply would not respond. She wrestled within her armor angrily but could do nothing but watch.

"Before we knew each other, Gideon, I worked on a team to develop new technology."

"What do you mean?" the ex-bounty hunter asked nervously. "What did you create?"

"I helped construct the prototype technology that could create a truly unique connection of algorithms that could emulate the brain of a human but combined with that of a synthetic mind. Unfortunately, in order to make such a creation, the human mind had to be eviscerated in the process, thus killing them. Due to the breakout of the war against the machines, and the potentially dangerous application, I hid away the research."

Gideon's eyes widened then became like cruel slits. "You knew what they were doing on Ash after all?"

Knowledge shook his head but kept his hand in place. "Again, at the time I honestly did not. However, what startled me was that I feared someone had discovered my research without my knowing."

"And you did nothing to prevent this?! The Republic is harvesting its own citizens to become the mind of its mechs!"

The keeper remained patient. "What is more troubling is that the only one who could have accessed my research is another keeper."

Instantly Gideon suspected precisely who was behind the plot. "Peace…"

To his surprise, Knowledge shook his head. 'I do not truthfully know who it was. Only that it was not you. I am still looking into it."

Spectre's stomach dropped.

That would mean that someone is coordinating a massive secret effort. What have I done?! I gave him my suit!

Gideon carefully glanced at the amulet gripped in Kay's hand. He knew that there was little chance he could take it from him.

"Think of your children, Gideon," Knowledge warned.

"How? How can you willfully be a part of this?"

"It's simple, I swore an oath to protect my country. Even if a portion of it is evil, I cannot ignore the rest."

The keeper took a few steps back onto his ramp. "Your part in this is over. I will honor my agreement with you, just as you have done to me. Peace will not get his hands on the amulet. I will choose the next Truth. Goodbye, my friend."

Despite the whirlwind of questions and anger swirling within him, the ex-bounty hunter knew that it was over. Without another word, he strode away from the hovering ship and headed for the ledge. He stopped to turn back to Knowledge, who watched him and maintained Life's suit being frozen in place.

The two men stared for several heartbeats then Gideon leaped down to the roof of a nearby building. Without being able to use cameras to track his movement, it would be incredibly difficult for either of the two healing keepers to pursue him.

Chapter 32

Cycle: 412 Month: 9 Rotation: 24
Corre Republic Space
Prefecture: Unknown
Planet: Unknown
Location: Keepers of the Republic Secret Base

Each of the keepers that had pursued the traitor and his suit made the venture back to their joint secret facility. Knowledge's *Sparrow* rocked from re-entry into the atmosphere. The nose of the spacecraft began to glow red as the metal warmed.

The keeper replayed the last conversation between him and Gideon in his mind. A piece of him still longed to have his old friend rejoin the order, but he knew it would be impossible.

"We should arrive within thirteen minutes," Catherine said kindly.

Knowledge readjusted himself in the pilot's chair. "Thank you."

The artificial intelligence had handled the trip back all on her own. Knowledge needed time to think. He planned on honoring his commitment to Gideon about selecting the next keeper of Truth, but Life, or more so, Peace, would not be thrilled with that decision.

How did we get here? The order used to be so united. I now feel like we are on the brink of being fractured.

Knowledge nodded to himself while he analyzed every possible angle he could surmise.

Gideon's right, I need to be the one to choose the next Truth.

The remaining distance to the base seemed to move by quickly. After the war against the Synthetics had ended, prefect major Magnus II had chosen to place the keepers' base on one of the worlds that had been wiped of human life. Knowledge never understood why the planet was selected, but one of his first tasks as the keeper of information and data was to expunge any and all records of this planet from all systems.

He peered out the cockpit canopy to see the dry and arid landscape that stretched as far as he could see. There were no ruins, no distinguishable signs of humanity ever living on this rock. While it once was compared to a beautiful garden, it now was devoid of any life above bacteria. The Synthetic commander, Delta, had personally seen to the extermination of the human colonies here all those cycles ago.

The *Sparrow* slowed as it came upon a rugged mountainous area. Catherine angled the ship through a narrow crevice. Two thick metal doors began to open ahead of the approaching vessel. Dust streamed down as they opened, giving the keeper clearance.

Due to the extreme situations and issues throughout the sixty-five worlds of the Corre Republic, the keepers did not visit the base often. Typically, it would only be due to a need to organize a meeting of every member, such as the confirmation of a new candidate into their order if a keeper died. Thankfully that ritual was not often.

Knowledge recalled the last time the keepers convened together to confirm the current keeper of Liberty. He had personally overseen the young woman's selection and ran into no opposition in her candidacy. However, the position of Truth was still vacant due to Gideon possessing the amulet, and Peace was still locked away in his chamber.

It has been so long since there have been all seven keepers working together. Much too long. At least that could all change soon.

The *Sparrow* flew through the opening in the mountain wall and slowed to a hover. It lowered down and landed smoothly in the large cargo space that was used as the keepers' hangar.

Knowledge stood up from his seat in the cockpit. Despite being in the same location since he had left Benedictus, he felt no aches, pains, nor soreness. That was something that he did his best to ignore thinking about.

The ramp was already lowering by the time he reached the back of his spacecraft. Several ships of varying sizes lined the hangar. However, no one else was present. The sound of each of the keeper's steps echoed off the walls.

His HUD displayed icons for the other keepers' deeper within the facility. He had been in no rush to arrive since he needed time to think everything through, and it seemed that everyone was gathered.

"What are you going to tell them?" the AI asked cheerfully in Knowledge's ear.

"I am going to inform them of my decision that I will oversee the selection of the next Truth."

"Do you think Peace will approve?"

Knowledge stepped up to a thick blast door. A scanner beam traced up and down his body then confirmed who he was. The entrance opened with a *swoosh*.

"Peace's approval is not my concern."

The keeper walked through the rest of the base until he reached the Sanctum, an inner room where much of the planning and meetings of the keepers were held. There was a multitude of rooms and other spaces throughout the compound, including private areas for each keeper to store belongings and to work on their own projects when on site.

Knowledge entered the room, and all eyes fell to him.

"Took your time getting here," Life quipped.

Liberty half waved to the newcomer. "Hey, Kay."

The door slid shut behind the blue keeper, and he made his way over to the center of the room. A circular table began to rise out of the floor, and the holotable built into it warmed up. A two-dimensional silhouette image of Peace in his life chamber, deeper within the base, appeared over the table. His head was canted to the side, and his face was shrouded in the darkness of his sealed room.

War leaned up against the wall with his arms crossed, his bronze-colored armor was just as imposing as ever. His massive physical size made the keeper of Liberty, who stood just an arms reach away, seem incredibly petite. Granted, she wasn't the tallest woman in the known 'verse, but she wasn't a small woman either. No less dangerous in combat, though. She was the only keeper to have removed her helmet, which made her stand out in a way from the rest of the group. Her shoulder-length blonde hair glowed purple from the lights illuminating from her armor.

Knowledge nodded to the copper-colored keeper. Instead of greeting everyone in the room, he got straight to business. The keeper raised his arm and opened his hand outward. The red-colored amulet Gideon had given him digitized back into reality.

All of the other keepers got to their feet and stepped over to the table.

"With possession of the amulet back in our hands, we can move forward with selecting a new Truth and subsequently getting Peace out of the chamber."

War nodded confidently, while the others remained quiet. Knowledge glanced up at the display of Peace, but the silhouette of the keeper remained still.

"Thank you, Knowledge, for securing the amulet," Peace said neutrally.

Life lowered her head, and the motion caught Knowledge's eye.

Is she still pouting?

The blue keeper looked up to the screen, his arm still extended. "I am only glad that we finally were able to track it down, successfully this time."

"Life and Death brought back a report of what occurred on Benedictus. I'm curious, why did you allow the traitor to survive?" Peace asked, a hint of subtle anger in his voice.

The tension in the room went up several notches, and Knowledge could sense it.

"My mission was to bring back the amulet, which I did."

"Your "mission" has been to hunt down the bastard that has left me trapped in this prison for all of these cycles!" Peace growled.

Liberty stood up to full attention, and Life felt anxious.

Unbothered by the outburst, Knowledge digitized the amulet back into his suit, and the necklace became particles that were absorbed into his hand.

"What are you doing?!" the white keeper exclaimed.

Knowledge tilted his head to the female keeper. "I am going to maintain possession of the amulet until I locate a suitable candidate to accept the mantle of Truth."

War and Life were a bit surprised by the situation. Both looked to Peace while Liberty and Death glanced at one another.

The silhouette man rolled his shoulder, then leaned back. "Why?"

Knowledge turned his helmet back to the hovering projection. "The position of Truth is vital for the success of our order. I feel I am the most capable person to select such an individual."

A momentary pause set in over the room. Despite being trapped in the chamber that kept his frail body alive, Peace had been the de facto leader of the order for longer than some of the current keepers even held their positions. If he was against Knowledge's decision, then there was no telling what could happen. However, Peace wasn't really in a place to stop him.

"So be it," Peace said reluctantly. "You are the one who built this room to keep me from dying. I trust you."

Knowledge remained still, not wanting to give away any emotion one way or the other. Life clenched her fists while War audibly scoffed.

Peace's voice became more solemn. "Whoever you select will undoubtedly be a worthy candidate."

"I will not let our order down," the blue keeper said plainly.

"For the greatest good," Peace said calmly.

The rest of the keepers in the room all replied in unison, "For the greatest good."

Knowledge turned and strode confidently out of the room. Life glared at the back of the blue keeper's helmet while Liberty slowly followed after him.

Once the two others had exited the Sanctum, the rest of the keepers looked to Peace's projection.

"Can we trust him?" Life asked with a point-blank tone.

"There isn't much choice," Peace said calmly.

The white keeper was still not satisfied with how all the recent events played out. "What of the traitor? He shouldn't be allowed to get away with stealing the amulet."

War again crossed his arms while Death stood still.

"I have a lengthy list of priorities I wish to deal with once I am free of this chamber," Peace said before leaning slightly toward the camera in front of him. His head remained tilted to the side. The dim light from the screen the keeper had to use to see the others gathered together in the Sanctum, lit up his dry lips and warped teeth while his eyes remained in the darkness. "But if I ever find him, I will make him suffer. He will scream for mercy, and I will be the one to end his pathetic life!"

Chapter 33

Cycle: 412 Month: 10 Rotation: 8
Turon Commonwealth
Planet: Antioch
Location: Braeville

The cooler season was beginning to take shape on Antioch's main continent. Various tree leaves had already started to change color, and a chill was in the air. Two bright green birds landed in front of the window of Mrs. Landry's home. Little Aiyla watched as the birds played back and forth.

"Oooo, birdies!" the young child said with glee.

It had been weeks since the Adama's children had heard anything from their parents. Last they knew, their mother was recovering and would be released from the hospital soon.

Between the trees, Aiyla spotted a loan truck driving along the winding road. Immediately she recognized it and her face lit up cheerfully.

"Daddy!"

Mrs. Landry and the other children were all sitting around the kitchen table, playing a board game. They each looked over to the little girl as she hopped up and down with excitement.

"Daddy! Mommy! Mommy!"

The old woman slid her chair out, then stood up. "What is it, Aiyla?"

She then confirmed the sighting of her neighbor's vehicle. "Well, would you look at that…"

Kev and Izzie both got equally excited and rushed for the window.

The truck slowed down, then turned up Mrs. Landry's driveway. Each of the children was beyond thrilled to see their parents' home and clamored to run out the door.

Gideon had spent a great deal of time thinking about what he was going to tell his children. He had finally come up with something to say, but it completely escaped his mind at the sight of their joyful little faces. Aiyla and Kev went right and came up to Gideon's window, while Izzie walked over to the passenger side.

"Mom?" the oldest daughter asked aloud when she realized the other side of the truck was empty.

Powerful emotions tugged at Gideon's mind, but he did his best to suppress them. Everything since Joan's murder had been a whirlwind. He barely had time to process her death, let alone come to grips with it. Now here he was to deliver the terrible news.

I have to be strong for them... No crying...

The father slowly opened his door and got out. Both of the other two children didn't notice their mother was absent, so they were still just as happy as ever. Mrs. Landry could see by Gideon's expression that something was dreadfully wrong.

"Daddy!" Izzie and Kev shouted in unison.

Gideon's hands trembled, but he forced himself to reach out and pull them in close.

"I missed you all so much," he said, fighting back his tears.

The young girl squeezed her father as hard as she could, then she saw past him. She then realized that their mother was absent.

"Where's Mommy?" she asked with her sweet tiny voice.

Gideon wiped his mouth and accidentally made eye contact with his neighbor. Her eyes were already beginning to swell up, but she too was trying to remain strong for the children.

Izzie walked back around the front of the truck to join her siblings. "Yeah, Dad, where's Mom?"

The father got down on one knee and looked into his children's eyes. They were beginning to piece together that something was really wrong, but it was the sight of their father beginning to cry that scared them more.

Dammit… I couldn't even keep myself from crying..

Sierra WarMech:

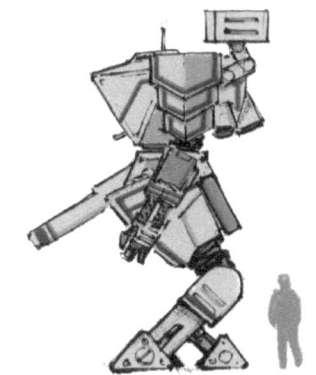

Enforcer WarMech:

ENFORCER WarMech

FRONT

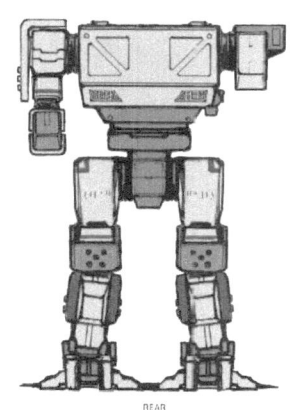

REAR

ENFORCER WarMech

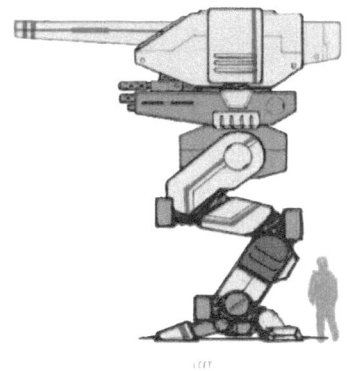

LEFT

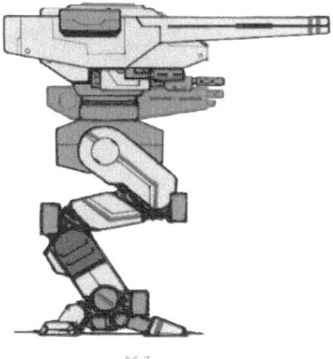

RIGHT

R. E. Graham

Keeper of Knowledge

Keeper of Life

Keeper of Death

Keeper of War

Keeper of Peace

Keeper of Liberty

Excerpt from
"Judgment Day"
Available now on amazon.com

Cycle: 434 Month: 2 Rotation: 14
Corre Republic Space
Prefecture: Siimon
Planet: Noire
Location: High Tower, downtown

The pirates hovertruck had followed the navigation system that led them straight to the teal building. They turned off the road and pulled up into the parking lot. Mikhail looked around but only spotted one other old vehicle parked in the area. The building itself appeared to be very old and desperately in need of a coat of paint.

To their right was a large loading door to the facility, but there were no markings that said what the building was used for.

"You think this is the place?" Rhonda asked from the backseat.

The Captain noticed the metal door slowly raise up.

"Yeah, seems like it," Mikhail said as Hern drove the truck up to the door and slowly guided it in.

Inside the building, it seemed very dark, but from what they could see from the headlights of the truck was stacks of crates and old manufacturing equipment.

Hern steered the truck forward. He put it in "park," and the hover vehicle lowered itself to the ground and then the engine was cut.

The door behind them dropped carefully, but the lights were still off.

"Okay Hern, remember what I said, no shootin' unless I give you the signal. These guys are real touchy."

Hern looked emasculated. "I got it, Cap, you don't gotta worry. I'll play nice."

Suddenly the lights turned on, and they realized that they were surrounded by a sizeable number of armed members from Onyx. Each of the men had tattoos covering their arms with many also having some on their faces. Most of the other pirates were carrying military grade rifles.

"Holy…" the gunner started to say under his breath before the Captain cut him off.

"Easy Hern…" Mikhail whispered back.

The Captain slowly reached over to the door handle and opened his passenger side door. He took one step out and poked his head up. "Hi there."

Rhonda and Hernando followed suit and exited the vehicle slowly and kept their hands clearly by their side.

None of the Onyx pirates made a move. They just stared at them with blank faces.

"Uh…my name is Captain Mikhail Tarvus, who am I supposed to speak with?" Mikhail asked trying to move quickly beyond this strange awkwardness.

"That would be me," came a gruff voice from the behind the crew.

Mikhail spun around and saw a rather short man with long bright yellow hair formed into a mohawk. The other man was also covered with tattoos but had decided to amplify his appearance by having a small animal bone pierced through the bridge of his nose.

"I am Otto," he said. "Do you have the goods?"

It was strange to the visitors that the group leader seemed so tired in the way he spoke.

His brain was probably fried from drug use…

"Uh yes, yes we do," Mikhail said as he slowly walked around Rhonda and went to the back of the truck. He reached in to push aside a box on top of the heap when several of the Onyx pirates raised their weapons.

The Captain froze in place while Rhonda raised her hands. Hernando stood absolutely still but was ready to spring into action if anyone even so much as twitched wrong.

"I was just going to show you the gold."

Otto's eyes appeared heavy as he raised his right hand signaling his people to lower their weapons. As the guns aimed downwards, Mikhail also lowered his hands.

He again reached down into the bed of the truck, but this time was able to move aside the box and lift the sheet covering the gold beneath.

The other pirate leader seemed entirely indifferent to the glimmering dragon sculpture.

"Where did you find all this?" he asked looking up to Mikhail.

"We appropriated it from some fancy mansion on Marie," Mikhail said hoping that Otto would buy his lie.

"Hmm," the Onyx pirate said as he walked up to the truck. His men kept their focus on the three rogue pirates.

"Seriously, where did you get all of this?" Otto asked as he rummaged through some of the different boxes.

"Like I said, from some house on Marie," Mikhail said calmly.

Otto looked up from the loot and looked at the Captain with a tired face. "You mean to tell me that you flew all the way from Marie and came to Noire to offload all this?"

Mikhail licked his lips as he thought. "Well yeah. You're right, it probably does sound suspicious. It would have been a much shorter trip to deal with the Rubies, but those guys are stupid inbred bastards."

The Onyx pirate got close to the Captain's face and stared intently into his eyes.

Mikhail was just about to change his story when Otto busted out laughing. His men joined in, and all enjoyed the joke at the expense of the other branch of the Five Skulls.

"You're alright Mik," Otto said as he sat down on a crate that was behind him. "I'll give you fifty-kay for everything."

"Poosh!" Hern exclaimed. "All that is at least worth double."

Mikhail's eyes grew very wide, and he gave his gunner a stern look.

"Your friend may be right, but I figure you are here offloading this on me because it is too hot for you to go someplace else."

"Fifty will be just fine," Mikhail said with a tight smile.

"But Cap we..." Hern started before the Captain gave him a nasty stare again.

Mikhail turned back to Otto and grinned. "Like I said, we'll take fifty."

Several of the pirates set their rifles down on a table behind them and started to offload the content of the truck bed.

The *Only Hope's* crew stepped aside and let them go about their job freely. Mikhail kept a close eye on everyone while Hern hadn't quite let his guard down just yet. Rhonda, on the other hand, had backed up near a stack of random crates. She hadn't noticed the greasy looking pirate who slowly approached her from behind. Without a doubt, it was clear that the man had not bathed in rotations.

He licked his lips as he extended a trembling hand. Before Rhonda knew it, she felt a strong hand grasp her bottom. She spun around immediately and drew a sidearm she had concealed and aimed it square at the pervert's forehead.

Seeing Rhonda draw her weapon caused both Hern and the Captain to do the same. This of course caused all of the other Onyx to do the follow suit.

Otto remained relatively still and blinked his weary eyes at the three troublemakers.

"Whoa now!" Mikhail shouted as he used his free hand to gesture everyone to stop.

"Mik put down the gun."

The Captain ignored the order but kept his focus on the men aiming their rifles at him. "Rhonda, what happened?"

"Sorry Cap, this guy here got a little too frisky for my liking," she replied as the pervert looked squeamish.

Otto's face turned angry when he slowly looked over to the man causing all the ruckus.

"I'm sorry Otto, I don't know what came over me," the man said pleading for his life as he stayed still so that Rhonda didn't blast him into eternity.

"Did you molest that woman Teeto?" Otto asked coldly.

"I...I...I..." Teeto stammered as he sought for the right words.

Otto did not wait for a proper response. He drew his own pistol and fired it right into his fellow pirate's stomach. The dirty man fell to his knees and gripped his bleeding torso. He tried to speak, but the lead Onyx pirate shot him six more times. As the dead man's body slumped to the floor, wisps of smoke trailed upward from Otto's gun.

Rhonda breathed heavily as the bullets weren't that far away from her. She had felt the gush of wind blow past her in the shooting.

Otto was the first to speak, breaking the awkward silence that had fallen on the room. He holstered his pistol, and everyone else in the room slowly lowered their own guns. "I apologize for that miss," he said before he turned back towards Mikhail. "I don't tolerate that sort of behavior within my house."

"Understood," the Captain said as he holstered his own sidearm. "I feel the same."

The Onyx pirates got back to work while Otto whistled loudly. A small boy carried a heavy black box from some other room. He handed the case to the pirate leader and stepped back. Otto opened the container and pulled out two bundles of cuso bills. He tossed both to Mikhail and then closed the case before handing it back to the child.

"Pleasure doin' business with you," the Captain said happily.

Glossary

Revelations is set in a universe where humanity does not originate from Earth. As such, some of the terms we use in our daily lives is not quite the same that they use. I have included this section to help you better understand the words and their definitions without it slowing down the pace of the story.

Stonecrete: [stone-creet] Very similar to our modern-day concrete but much stronger and doesn't break down as poorly with time.

Rotation: Equivalent to our 24-hour day. The length of a rotation is how long it takes any planet to orbit around its star.

Cycle: Equivalent to one sequence of rotations around a star.

Communicator: Similar to a cellphone with even more robust features and capabilities.

Synthetic: A Synthetic is an Artificial Intelligence (or AI) that was created out of a human mind. The sophisticated program operates a humanoid like body and was used as the soldiers of the Synthetic Armada against the remnants of humanity in the war.

ANE: After Near Extinction (or more commonly known as ANE) was a new epoch that began to signify humanity's survival against the Synthetic Armada.

Cuso: [coo-soe] The currency used in the Corre Republic.

Plasti-Crate: Very common storage case made of plastic. They come in a variety of sizes and are extremely durable.

Prefect Major: The Prefect Major is the leader of the entire Corre Republic. There are many other positions under this rank that assist in ruling, but whatever the Prefect Major says goes. The Senate plays the role of the legislative branch of the Republic's government and can affect policy. While the Senate is elected from the planets' citizens, the Prefect Major is chosen from the other Prefects that rule the 10 prefectures.

Prefect: There are 10 prefectures within the Corre Republic, and one Prefect rules over the worlds within that prefecture.

Governor: A governor is a ruler over a world. There is one governor per planet in the Corre Republic.

The Creator: With His voice, He created all of existence. The Creator is the godhead of the Light

Bringer faith and has been hated for a long time in the Corre Republic as it is seen as archaic.

Stream: This is the Corre Republic's version of our own internet.

If you enjoyed this novel, please leave me a review on Amazon.com:
https://www.amazon.com/-/e/B07GY2DNM8

Every honest review helps my stories become more and more visible for other readers to possibly discover Revelations. Which, in turn, helps me to be able to provide new installments. See, it's a win-win :D

Thank You

To all my patrons who support the growth and development of the Revelations Universe through patreon.com, I want to take a special moment to thank you specifically by name…

Adam Thomas
Austin Patten
Harry Chapman

If you would like to add your own name to this list, then please visit us on patreon at: www.patreon.com/revelationsuniverse

Note from the author: R. E. Graham

I want to take a quick moment to thank you for taking time to read this novel. For years I have wanted to explore the Revelations universe but was unsure of how to go about it. In 2017 I figured that if I didn't just go for it, then I never would. I didn't want to find myself on my deathbed and feel regret for never going for my dream. But I cannot create this universe without thanking those who support it and to also extend a welcome to you if you are new to the stories of Revelations.

If you would like to learn more about other novels, products or just join an awesome growing community of fellow fans, then consider checking out any of the links below.

Email List: https://dl.bookfunnel.com/4o817ero7w
Facebook: www.facebook.com/revelationsuniverse/
Website: www.whitelightmedia.org

Thank you again, and I look forward to us creating Revelations into something we can all enjoy together!
Rick

www.ingramcontent.com/pod-product-compliance
Lightning Source LLC
Chambersburg PA
CBHW050901250626
47155CB00001B/61